TIN MEN

LINDA COLES

Blue Banana

Chapter One

One year earlier

He ate his cereal, his two young boys in their high chairs by his side at the table. Part of him wished he'd had them earlier in life, perhaps when he'd been in his late twenties or early thirties like his friends had. The noisy part of the young boys' lives would then have been at a time when he'd been able to cope better, was less distracted with work. And other issues. But right now, he was conscious of how draining their exuberance could be, particularly when his head was someplace else. He craved peace. And escapism.

He watched Jo, all the time chattering to the youngsters, encouraging them both to eat up and become strong boys as she fed them simultaneously. Through the window of the spacious kitchen, the morning sun streamed in and he noticed the miniscule particles of dust floating lazily in the air around her and the boys' heads, the light catching his wife's highlights and the ever-present twinkle of her eyes.

He'd struck lucky when he'd met Jo. After being married for nearly ten years, they'd decided it was time to start the family they'd both been putting off. Mainly because of work. As a lawyer, Stuart had had no choice but to put the hours in. It came with the territory, and since Jo had worked at the same firm as a legal secretary, they'd more or less made it their way of life together. Each understood the demands of the other's role, and that made their relationship work despite the gruelling workload they each undertook. And that understanding carried itself to their home life too. With Jo about to resume her position after an extended maternity leave, Stuart would find himself in front of the cooker of an evening just as much as Jo would.

The thought depressed him a little. He was getting too old for the constant demands on his time and had enjoyed the little extra solitude he'd stolen here and there while she'd been off. But Jo wasn't one to sit at home all day with nothing to occupy her acute legal mind. Endless coffee mornings and lunches with the girls were as far away from her ideal as a wet weekend in Bognor Regis.

Stuart often wished it were otherwise. It would take the pressure off.

He was aware she had spoken and he hadn't answered.

"Sorry, did you say something?"

Her smile was always a bright one; rarely was Jo ever cross or grumpy. "I said you look miles away, and you obviously were. Anyplace nice?"

Soon he would be. So soon.

"Oh, idle thoughts. Nothing to write home about," he said casually, though the comment had pricked at him. Anxious to change the topic, he enquired about her day ahead. "What time are you all leaving? Need a lift to the station?"

"All organised, thanks. Train leaves at eight forty-five, so you'll be long gone." She smiled across at him and it nearly broke his heart. The irony of what she'd said hit him full in the chest and he struggled not to gasp out loud. When he was confident he could speak without his voice wobbling, he said, "Well, enjoy your day out. Bring me a stick of rock back."

"Do people still buy rock at the seaside, do you think?"

"I doubt it. I'll Google it," he said.

She wiped the two youngsters' hands with a cloth as she spoke, adding, "Let me know what you find out." She then removed each child from its high chair and allowed them to wobble off on socked feet as she followed close behind. She glanced up at the replica old station clock on the wall and turned to her husband.

"You'd better get a move on, dreamboat. Have you seen the time?"

Time doesn't matter today. There's plenty where I'm going.

"I have an errand out of the office," he said. "A bit more time spare this morning." It wasn't exactly a lie but it felt like one.

It was like watching his life roll out in front of him, like a play being performed and he wasn't in it. He played along anyway and silently placed his bowl and spoon in the dishwasher along with the other breakfast crockery. He added powder to the dispenser and pressed start, and the machine hummed into action. The digital counter on the front told him it would take sixty minutes. He watched it for a while.

Fifty-nine.

Would it be finished in time, he idly wondered? So he could put the contents away beforehand?

"Right. Okay. I'll finish getting me and the team ready, then we'll be off," she said chirpily. He could only smile in return. He sat back down at the table and picked the morning newspaper up, though he wasn't really reading it; he was distracted. It was more to pass the time, pretend everything was normal.

About as far from normal as it could be.

Upstairs, little giggling sounds were barely audible as the three of them dressed and teeth were cleaned, a day bag packed with the necessary equipment two little boys would need for their outing at Grandma's. When the small gang were finally ready, Stuart helped them outside to Jo's car and loaded everyone safely inside. The boys blew bubbles as Stuart bent to kiss them both on their tiny flushed cheeks, hiding his emotions at the pain that was about to fall down on them. He looked across at Jo, already strapped in and ready to rumble.

Damn, she was a lovely-looking woman.

"Have the best time. Stay safe."

It didn't feel enough. What would be enough?

"We will," she chirped back, and flashed him a dazzling smile.

The words caught in his throat as he added, "I love you all," and coughed lightly to cover over the unsteadiness.

"Love you too!" she said and waved brightly as she reversed out on to the road. Stuart waited for her to pull away, his hand raised ready to wave them off.

Forever.

The car disappeared around the corner, leaving Stuart alone on the front step. Satisfied they had gone, he sauntered back inside. The house was silent. It was deathly quiet inside his head. He noted the dishwasher still had fifteen minutes to go.

I can't wait.

He retrieved the old sports bag from its hiding place in the under-stairs cupboard and pulled out two pieces of card. Each was about the size of a novel, and he re-read the words printed on them, though he knew every single one.

He'd written them.

With sticky tape, he attached one first to the back door and then one to the front, message side visible to anyone who called. He was only expecting one visitor, but as a lawyer, he'd always planned for the unknown, other eventualities. This couldn't go wrong; it was too important. When he was satisfied all was in order, he took the old sports bag and its remaining contents upstairs to their bedroom and carried out the rest of his plan.

By the time Jo's train pulled away from the station, Stuart's life had already left his body.

Chapter Two

Once a spook, always a spook. Even though she'd been retired, if that was the right word, for more than five years, the threads of a previous life as a government agent still dangled and teased in her veins. At the ripe old age of 41, she was hardly the normal retirement age—but then you'd never describe Chrissy as normal. Ever. And she definitely hadn't retired in the conventional bored-out-of-her-brains manner that so many folks hurtled towards when the big R word loomed in the distance. No, not Chrissy. She hadn't time to retire. Not yet. And certainly not today.

A horn beeped outside—her Uber, ready to pick her up. She was more than capable of driving herself to her sister's place, of course, but Adam would be meeting her there later and they could ride back in his car together. She grabbed her bag and keys and pulled the front door of the brick house closed behind her. Cornflowers were showing off their blue heads in the garden bed adjacent to the garage on her left. The loose shingle of the drive crunched noisily as she stepped carefully so as not to scuff her patent boots before she climbed into the back seat of the car. Since the driver already knew where they were headed, he simply greeted her and offered her a mint.

"No, thanks," she said politely, her tone sending the message she wasn't up for conversation. He really didn't need to work at it. Should she tell him he'd get a better tip if he kept himself to himself, kept quiet? It seemed a bit harsh, really, to say such a thing, so she kept the thought to herself. For the duration of the journey from Englefield Green to her sister's place, which was all of ten miles away, she gazed out of her side window up at the summer sky.

It was Wednesday July 11th, 2018, and Chrissy Livingstone was on her way to discuss their father's funeral arrangements over tiny sandwiches and afternoon gin.

Deep in thought and enjoying the feel of the warm sunshine on her neck, where her jacket collar was opened casually, she startled when the phone in her bag vibrated and rang loudly with an incoming text. The loud bike horn indicated it was Adam; the tone suited him, and instinctively she smiled at his presence in her bag on her lap. The message was simple, as they always were.

'Be nice to Julie. I'll see you later.'

He ended it with an emoji with a halo on top of its head—*Good girl*. She felt like patting the top of her own head for good measure, like a parent might pat their 'good girl.'

But Julie riled her up terribly, particularly when the gin was flowing, although Chrissy always did her best to let it wash over her. Why she did so, she had no idea, since Julie had the perfect suburban life on the surface, though that was maybe the problem. With 2.2 beautiful children, a purebred moggie, and a nice though dull husband, Julie wanted for nothing. Although maybe something a bit less dull in the husband department. To Chrissy, a woman who'd worked hard all her life and held down a career while raising her own family with Adam, it seemed her sister whined about and focused on the trivial things in life way too much. The best place for a facial, the newest eatery, the this, the that and not much of the other. Julie, for her part, thought that Chrissy needed to get out more, make more of herself, get her hair coiffed regularly, but those things didn't interest her. A social butterfly she didn't need to be; she was fine as she was. If only Julie knew the half of what she did. Had done.

The thought amused her again as the car pulled up to the front gate and Chrissy pressed the buzzer to notify her sister she had arrived. Knowing full well a camera was focusing on her right then and there, she smiled, Garfield-like, into the lens and heard the familiar click of the lock. The gates opened at a snail's pace. Pulling her head back in through the open side window, she caught the eye of the driver, who'd seen her grin through the rear-view mirror.

"I know. I do it because it bugs her. Too straight-laced, that sister of mine. She needs to let her hair down sometimes."

He nodded his approval. She smiled in return.

Grinning like Garfield was hardly letting her hair down, but it amused Chrissy anyway.

A moment later, Julie could be seen gracing the open front door, looking like she'd stepped straight out of *Hello! Magazine*'s celebrity pages. Clad head to foot in a cream linen trouser suit, she looked stunningly beautiful, though Chrissy thought her head of stiff blonde waves were in desperate need of liberating. One day she'd tempt her sister to let them hang loose. Or perhaps Chrissy could push her hands inside the lacquered fortress and force them loose herself, though she doubted they'd gain entry through the half pint of hair spray.

If two sisters could be polar opposites, the two women at the front entrance were a prime example of chalk and cheese, yin or yang, and if you didn't know their origin, you'd have said they couldn't possibly be related. Indeed, Chrissy had wondered if she herself had been adopted early on, or swapped at birth even, but blood tests when she'd needed surgery a while back had confirmed she was indeed the product of a diverse-looking family. She was her parents' offspring through and through. And so was the woman in cream.

"Darling!" Julie cooed. She not only looked the part but acted it full time.

"Hey, sis," Chrissy said as she gave her sister a bear hug. She could feel Julie's ribs through her clothing. "You could do with a hot meal or something, put some meat on your bones. You're feeling a bit thin."

"And you sound like Mum," Julie said, smiling at their regular dig at each other. Chrissy herself was on the lean side, but a sporty lean as opposed to an 'I-don't-eat-much' kind of lean, celebrity lean. Julie went to the gym to walk on the treadmill and read her book at the same time, somehow managing to stay on the dry side of a sweat in an effort to burn a few extra calories. She'd rather do that than get a full healthy workout and have to re-fix her waves. Chalk and cheese, yin and yang.

"Is Mum inside?"

"She is. Hardly said a word, though. I expect talking about Dad's funeral won't be easy. Be gentle, eh?"

Chrissy noticed the pink rings under her sister's eyes, though Julie had evidently tried to conceal them with foundation. So her sister did cry after all. Chrissy headed inside and on to the lounge where their mother was sitting alone. A glass of clear liquid had been set down in front of her; the gin had already started to flow. She bent and pecked her mother's thin cheek before sitting on the rather formal and extraordinarily uncomfortable sofa, wriggling a little to find a soft spot. Julie joined them in a chair opposite. Their mother kept her head down low; she looked more frail than usual and hadn't yet said a word.

Julie prodded a little. "Mother, would you like to start? I expect Daddy had his own wishes for his funeral."

Sandra Baker raised her head for the first time since their arrival and spoke so low Chrissy had to ask her to repeat what she'd said.

With unexpected ferocity the older woman repeated her words, her voice a sudden angry shout in the stillness.

"I said, I really don't care what you girls organise. Do what you wish. I'll have no part in organising it, not after what he's done."

Chapter Three

"What has he done?" enquired Chrissy, dumbfounded. Whatever it was, was news to her. But then her mother had never confided in Chrissy, preferring the perfectly formed model ears of Julie. They shared the same surgeon.

Nobody spoke. She tried again. "Is either of you going to enlighten me or do I have to guess?" Chrissy's voice rose an octave as she finished the sentence so 'guess' came out a tad higher than normal.

Julie voted herself in as spokesperson. "It seems Daddy had a secret or two. Mummy found a letter, from a man."

"Dad was seeing a man?" Chrissy asked, incredulous.

"No, silly! It wasn't that kind of letter."

"Well, you said it was from a man, and Dad had secrets. What did you think I'd think?" Chrissy leaned forward and helped herself to a gin since everyone else had one. She took a mouthful and winced. She preferred a glass of wine. White.

"It was a threatening letter, actually. Dad owed the man some money, though I've no idea how much. And the man was pretty upset about it. The letter was rather nasty."

"Oh. That's a bit odd, isn't it? I mean, Dad wasn't in debt—was he, Mum?" Chrissy looked across at the woman who seemed to have gotten frailer since she'd arrived. Her head hung low again, and Chrissy noted the thin line of her mother's hair, pink scalp showing through the white silky threads.

"Mum?"

"No, Well, not that I know of." It wasn't much more than a whisper, and both sisters strained to hear her reply.

Chrissy turned her attention to Julie. "Then what did it say? What made it threatening?"

"It merely said his time was up to repay and if he didn't ..." She trailed off.

"Go on. What would happen?" Chrissy prodded, but Julie clearly didn't want to have to say the words. Maybe it would be easier without their mother present. Chrissy made a sideways nodding motion with her head towards the conservatory door. Julie picked up the hint and they both stood. They doubted their mother would even notice them leaving the room for a moment; her head was still bowed to her knees.

When they were both out of earshot, Julie closed the conservatory and resumed speaking.

"Daddy apparently owed the man a considerable sum, though he doesn't say how much exactly. Reading how it was phrased, the words he'd used, I'd say we're talking hundreds of thousands." Julie's face wore a disapproving, worried look, her designer lips twisting awkwardly.

"Holy shit, Jules. Does Mum know you think it's such a vast sum?"

"Afraid so. That's why she's so upset, and quiet. She's barely said a word since I mentioned it. She's angry at him, understandably."

"What the hell did he owe money for? It's not like he wasn't well off." Chrissy fell silent again, processing what Julie had told her a minute or two ago.

Threatening.

"Have you still got it, the letter?"

"No. Mum took it back, shredded it and threw it in the rubbish. It's in the kitchen bin if you want it, in tiny pieces."

"Great," Chrissy said sarcastically. "I'd have liked to see it with my own eyes before she ripped it up."

"Why the interest? He's dead now, so whatever it was, he can't pay it back anyway." The sunshine peeked out from behind a cloud and the furniture in the conservatory gleamed a brilliant white. It was almost too dazzling, and provided a break in their conversation; both stood with their own thoughts. When the sun disappeared behind another cloud, Chrissy spoke first.

"Still. It's a puzzle, isn't it? And Mum's upset and that's not right. She should be grieving her loss, not being angry at the man for having a secret."

"Do you think she's safe? We're safe?"

"Eh?"

"That they'll come after Mummy or us for the money? You hear of these things."

"Drama Queen Julie," said Chrissy, rolling her eyes. "The man's dead. End of story. Surely." Despite herself, there was a slight question in her voice. *Surely?*

"You don't sound convinced yourself," said Julie. "And I've been thinking since I found out. . ." She sounded a little cagey, almost embarrassed to say what she had been thinking about.

"What about?" A beat passed. "Spit it out, then."

Julie turned towards the manicured back garden so her back was towards her sister. Maybe she was embarrassed after all. Chrissy waited and watched a sparrow land on the lawn, its tiny beak pecking the ground, looking for food. With a couple of hard tugs, a couple of inches of worm dangled from its beak as it prepared to devour it. It swallowed its meal and then pecked for more.

"Do you think he could have been killed over it?" Julie said at last. "He is dead, after all. And it's a lot of money, remember." Julie turned back to face Chrissy. Her brow was wrinkled slightly, Chrissy noticed. That in itself was unusual. Botox was hard to wrinkle. Chrissy wore the wrinkles for them both.

"Dad had a bad heart, Julie. He died of cardiac arrest. He had an electrical malfunction and nature took its course. Nobody knocked Dad off. You've been reading too many crappy books."

"Well, I think we should have a post mortem," Julie said haughtily. "He could have been drugged and it caused the heart to stop. I've heard of it before—minute traces of a substance that go undetected. Spies use it. Bond used it."

Chrissy couldn't help smiling. "Well, if James Bond uses it, it must be real. You'll be telling me you've seen it on Facebook next. Because everything on Facebook is true."

"Spies *do* use it. And double agents," Julie said petulantly, putting out a perfectly collagen-filled lower lip.

Spies, eh?

"Look, if you're worried, we can talk to the doctor and see what he says," Chrissy said, relenting. She walked over to her sister, arms outstretched for a hug. Even chalk and cheese could be pals, after all, and she had no wish to fight with her sister right now. As the two women connected, Chrissy squeezed tighter than usual, sensing her sister could really use the support she was offering. Citrus fragrance filled her nostrils and she tried not to sneeze. At least it was fresh smelling and not cloying, like her mother's would be.

"Let's go back to Mum, eh? There's plenty to sort out for Dad's day, and we need to get her involved somehow. It's not good for her to send him off angry, so no more mention of the letter. Agreed?"

Her sister's stiff blonde waves bobbed up and down. They opened the conservatory door and, arm in arm, walked back to their mother.

Chapter Four

In reality, their mother had little to do with their father's arrangements and stayed speechless for most of the afternoon, quietly sipping gin and tonic and staring at nothing in particular. It hadn't gone unnoticed. The two sisters carried on regardless; someone had to organise his funeral. At just after 4 PM, they had done all they could and were now chatting about things other than fillings for the sandwiches and what type of sherry would be available. The local pub would be the venue, it was decided; it had a large bar area and back room to accommodate those who wished to mingle. Gerald Baker had been a popular man.

Though it seemed at least one person would disagree.

Chrissy checked her watch. Adam would be arriving shortly.

"I think we've covered the most of it. Are you happy with everything, Mum?" she asked. She got barely a nod back, but at least their mother was communicating.

"Don't worry," Julie said. "She's stopping with us again tonight; probably until the funeral is over, I expect. Which reminds me, there's probably flowers backing up at her front door. I should get a notice organised to bring them here."

"Good idea. I'll drop by on the way home. Find me some card, will you? I'll make it up."

"It's in the desk drawer. You'll find all you need in there," Julie said, pointing to the nook at the back of the room. On the desk sat a Mac, which Chrissy knew was more for the children. It had been placed out in the open so that Julie could keep a close eye on what they were researching rather than them being closeted away in their rooms surfing goodness knows what. Chrissy sniggered under her breath. Both children had their own smartphones. Any dubious sites they surfed would be viewed in the privacy of their own palms, and they certainly wouldn't be sitting in the lounge while they gawped. Julie was going to have a shock one day at just how much her young teenagers knew about life. And how life itself was made, no doubt.

Chrissy strode over to the desk and found the card in the top drawer of the desk; she grabbed a roll of sticky tape while she was at it.

"We don't want prospective burglars to think there's no one home," she said to her sister as she began to write. "I'll simply put 'Flowers to be redirected to. . .' and this address."

"Perhaps add in 'Other deliveries please knock'? That way it won't look so much like no one's home."

"Fair point." Chrissy added the extra text. She heard the gate buzzer ring. Adam had arrived.

"Will he stay for a drink, perhaps?" said Julie hopefully.

"No, I doubt it, thanks. We'll get straight off. I'll get this done," she said, indicating the card sign, "and I'll collect what flowers are already there." Chrissy rose and went to the door to let Adam in.

"Who's that?" said a faint voice from the sofa. Mrs. Baker was finally taking notice.

"It's Adam, Mummy. He's come to take Chrissy home."

"Oh. Good. No more funeral talk, then."

Chrissy saw Julie refrain from rolling her eyes as Adam entered the lounge. She never ceased to marvel at how Adam filled a room with his presence. As usual, he wore a well-cut suit and a grin that would make any *GQ* model envious. Six feet tall, with strength and width in his shoulders from his early rugby days, he was many women's hot dream.

Julie had had a couple herself, Chrissy suspected. His entry was always a good excuse for her to get close to him for a moment and, right on cue, Julie stepped forward, arms outstretched.

"Hello, darling Adam. How are you?" she enquired formally, perfect teeth peeking out from perfect lips. Chrissy watched in bemusement as her husband went to her sister and pecked her lightly on the cheek. She caught Adam's quick wink back at her. They'd giggled about Julie's crush on him, but they both gamely played along.

"I'm good, thanks, Julie. You look lovely as always."

Chrissy rolled her eyes.

"Oh, thank you, Adam. Under the circumstances, I'm holding up."

Heavens above, give me a break.

"Well, you're doing well."

Chrissy stepped in. "I'm ready to leave when you are, Adam. I need to make a slight detour on the way back to Mum's place, though," she announced brightly. "We'll collect the flowers from the house. Mum's stopping here with Julie tonight."

Adam turned to his mother-in-law, who was still sitting on the sofa. He placed himself gently down beside her, reached out for her hand, and squeezed it gently. She turned to him, her eyes moist, and said 'Hello.' As it had been all afternoon, there was no power in her voice; it was a defeated sound, full of lethargy.

"You'll feel much better when the funeral is over, I expect. And we're all here to support you, remember that." Her eyes were still locked onto his, though they were vacant, like she had left somehow. Adam squeezed her hand lightly again and held it to his mouth to kiss goodbye. "It's good you're staying here with Julie. It wouldn't do you any good being at home all alone." He stood and caught Chrissy's eye. Time to leave.

As the two of them headed towards the front door, Chrissy

called over her shoulder, "I'll call you tomorrow, sis. Watch out for flower deliveries."

"Thank you for coming. See you soon," Julie called back as they started down the front walk. They climbed into the car and Adam started the engine as Chrissy opened the passenger window. Julie was standing on the front step waving like the Queen Mother.

Lady of the Manor.

"Bye!" she called brightly.

When they were safely on the road and heading towards her mother's place, Chrissy told her husband all about the letter. "What do you make of that, then?" she asked him.

Adam was silent for a moment. "Well, let me put it this way. As an investment banker, and knowing Gerald, I'm not at all surprised."

Chrissy turned and stared at him in surprise. That was not the reaction she had been expecting.

"Oh?" she enquired, her interest piqued.

"He wouldn't be the first, and he certainly wouldn't be the last."

But still, it seemed a little too close to home to Chrissy.

Chapter Five

Half an hour later, Chrissy and Adam pulled up in front of her mother's house. Judging from the heaps of flower arrangements around the front door, it looked like the florists' delivery vans had already been busy. And probably sold out of chrysanthemums. Chrissy wrinkled her nose at the sight of them; they were her least favourite flower. Cheap, nasty petrol station bouquets usually bought as an afterthought, but in this case, organised and delivered nicely.

"Looks like it's started," said Adam. "What shall we do with them all?"

"Load them up, I guess. Take them home. There'll be more to come as the week wears on and people hear the news."

They both got out of the car and made their way up the front path. Chrissy took the makeshift sign out of her bag and taped it to the door.

"There," she said, standing back to look at it. "That should redirect any more bouquets."

Adam picked up a wrapped arrangement and poked at a chrysanthemum nestled amongst the irises and freesia. "Are you sure you want these at home? You hate them."

"I know," she said, sighing. "I'll take them out and put the rest into vases. The compost heap will enjoy them."

Adam raised his eyebrows at her; he hated waste. "Seems a shame."

"But why display something you can't stand? It's hypocritical. Cut flowers die soon enough anyway, so they may as well go and die now."

Adam raised his eyebrows again. He couldn't argue with that. Between them, they carried the rest of the flowers over to his Audi and loaded them into the boot. When it came time to close the lid, Chrissy pushed straggling flower heads out of the way so they wouldn't get chopped off. Chrysanthemums or not. She'd sort them out when they got home. When they were done, they climbed in and set off towards home.

"He was a popular man, judging by that lot already," Adam stated.

Chrissy stared at the road ahead. "I'll read the cards later, see who they are all from. The obituary notice is in the paper now. I expect there'll be a big attendance at the service."

Traffic was building up as rush hour spewed more and more vehicles on to the road making the journey home slow. And warm. In July, and inside the car with the late afternoon sun streaming through the windows, she was starting to bake. Chrissy reached for the air conditioning, leaving it on low. It would be just enough. The bus directly in front of them chugged out diesel fumes, the dark grey emissions rising in a thick cloud and eventually disappearing. Chrissy watched them rise and drift away, transfixed. Idly, she wondered if the smoke from her father's cremation would look the same. Dark grey. Would the crematorium wait until everyone had left to burn her father's body? And what if another service was due directly after theirs? Did they wait and light the fire at the end of the day, perhaps? Did they then all go in together, to save on the gas bill? Could she even be certain they would receive only her father's ashes? Maybe the funeral home mixed all the day's ashes together and then doled them out to the families, she thought grimly. The family of a big man would get more ashes back; the family of a skinny woman only a few. It was a sobering thought. She hoped not.

The traffic ahead freed up slightly and it wasn't long before they were turning down their leafy lane on the outskirts of Englefield Green. Elton John had a place not far away. More like a small park and mansion, actually. And Chrissy and Adam's two boys attended the prestigious Bishopsgate School nearby, though the education fees made them both wince. Still, the boys enjoyed it, particularly the sport programme. Like their father, they preferred rugby to cricket.

At fourteen and fifteen, the boys, Thomas and Harry ate them out of house and home and were each other's best mate—unusual for many boys, indeed many families. Chrissy and Adam had raised them fairly, teaching them manners, responsibility, and accountability and showering each of them with quality time doing the things they loved individually. All in all, the Livingstones were a wonderful, happy family.

Chrissy needed her own individual time too, but like most mums, she rarely got it. Yes, she couldn't complain about her life at all, not the life she led with Adam. She hadn't been entirely truthful with him since ... Well, since they'd first met about twenty-five years ago. And that's how it had always been. She'd never seen a reason to upset the way they worked and lived; there was nothing to gain by filling him in on her past now.

But there was a whole lot to wreck.

Adam believed she worked as a freelance HR contractor, a job she ran from her home office. And since she'd always been vague on the details and refused to gossip about her colleagues, particularly as they were nonexistent, the subject of her work rarely came up. And that was a good thing, because Chrissy didn't work in HR, never had. No, Chrissy had only ever worked for one employer since leaving university and that was the government.

As a spook. An agent.

But she'd retired a handful of years ago, and continued with the pretence.

Why?

Because she loved her own time. Her time away. Her time abroad. On her own. And it continued to work for her, and no one was any the wiser. It was too late to come clean now. She didn't like it, but the alternative could be far worse.

"Looks like the boys are back," Adam said, pointing to the two bicycles laid on the pebbles near the front door. The door itself stood wide open, and two school bags had been tossed onto the lawn. Manners and respect or not, the boys were always in too much of a rush to stand their cycles up properly. At the sound of the car tyres on the pebbles, the two boys appeared in the doorway, both with a peanut butter sandwich in hand. Their mouths worked hungrily, the boys' mousy brown curls bobbing slightly with the ferocity of their chomping.

"Some things never change, eh? Good job they're eating now because I've no idea what's for dinner," Chrissy said wearily. She climbed out of the car and strode to the front door, kissing each boy in turn before going inside herself.

Adam sat behind the wheel for a moment, watching his wife and sons from a distance. He had something rather more pressing on his mind: he'd found an envelope while collecting the flowers and had slipped it into his pocket without showing Chrissy. He pulled it out now. On the front, in flowing handwriting, was one word —*Thief*.

What had Gerald Baker been up to?

Chapter Six

Adam waited until after dinner and Chrissy was upstairs reading on the sofa in her den. He pulled out the envelope again

Thief.

He ran his fingers over the back of the envelope and, listening to make sure he was undisturbed, carefully opened the flap. There was a piece of paper folded up inside, and he opened it. The writing was just the same as the handwriting on the front of the envelope. And of course, it would be. Why wouldn't it? It would have been odd had it been different.

He read it to himself. There were only a few sentences, and he quickly scanned to the bottom. It wasn't signed.

I'll not let you rest until I have back what is rightfully mine.

And I know I'm not alone.

Others are waiting behind me, ready to stake their claim.

You're a common thief and nothing more.

It wasn't a surprise really. He'd heard the rumours about Gerald —that he had been involved in a scheme or two. He'd heard that some folks weren't exactly happy with their arrangement, their returns, but then Adam worked in finance himself. It happened all the time: gossip, and vocal clients. Gerald's activities didn't sound any different from what other financiers he worked with were doing, how they handled their business, and so he'd never given it any further thought. But this letter put a new spin on things. The word *Thief* felt threatening.

He slipped the letter back into his pocket, for safekeeping more than anything. Would he tell Chrissy? Not yet. Better to wait until after the funeral, he reasoned. No point upsetting her beforehand.

The leather crunched underneath him as he got up off the sofa and stood and stretched. He was a big man, though not overweight; just chunky. Chunky in a way that he liked, chunky in a way that Chrissy liked. Solid, she'd told him.

He opened the den door and headed upstairs to Chrissy's den. He stood for a moment before rapping on the solid wood door, as was their custom. Since their dens were each other's private territory, they respected the self-imposed rule and didn't go barging in like other rooms of the house. Apart from the toilet, of course. In all the years they'd been together, he'd never once seen her on the loo, and vice versa. They were a close couple, but there was simply no need to see each other doing their ablutions.

"Come in," Chrissy shouted through the door. Tentatively, even though he knew he wasn't going to say anything about the letter, he opened the door and smiled at the back of the head of his beautiful wife. She was at her laptop typing. She finished off a sentence before turning to give him a dazzling smile as she always did. Chrissy was one beautiful lady, he thought again.

"Hey," Adam said. "What're you up to?"

"Just finishing some paperwork. I have that conference soon and I need to be up to date before I go."

"Where is it this time?" Adam asked. He was used to Chrissy going away occasionally, often abroad.

"West coast of the US of A," she said in a mock American accent, sounding like one of the cast from *Gone with the Wind*. Her southern drawl amused him and he smiled at her effort, raising his eyebrows comically. Georgia was nowhere near the west coast.

"Again," she added. "Most of these things seem to be. I don't mind, though; the sun is always out on the west coast. What do you need, hun?" she enquired.

"Oh, you know, just seeing how my favourite woman is after an emotionally stressful day. It can't be easy losing your father, but I must say you're handling it remarkably well."

"You know me—emotionally detached from my family where possible." She smiled wryly.

Adam was aware of family feuds in the past, some more bitter than others. Chrissy had only recently begun speaking with either of her parents again after a disagreement about Adam a couple of years ago. They had, however, started to heal the old wounds.

"How is Julie? She seemed a little dazed. As did your mum."

"She's just Julie; nothing changes there. Everything is a drama, hanky at the ready. But her looking after Mum is probably doing her good, giving her something to focus on. Two people in the house can't both be in the same down place. When one is up, the other one is down, then the other way around. That's how it works; they'll bounce off each other for a couple of days, no doubt. Being together could do them good."

"Well, like I said, I think you're being remarkable," said Adam, "but you're always remarkable at everything, so why am I surprised?" He ran his fingers through the back of her hair and she looked up into his eyes. They were still the lovebirds they had been when they'd first got married.

"I'm only remarkable because you support me the way you do, and I thank you for that," she said. "Anyway, enough of the mushy stuff. Fancy a cup of hot chocolate? I just have a yearning for one."

Adam checked his watch. It was nearly 8 PM. It would mean a trip to the loo during the night. Oh well. "Why not?" he said. "I've not had one in ages."

Christie closed the laptop lid and stood quickly, pecking him on the nose. She took hold of one hand and led him out of her den towards the stairs. As they walked, the low bass of both boys' music could be heard from behind their closed doors, the deep throbbing of a dance beat. Since Chrissy and Adam were now some way past their teens it wasn't their kind of thing. Still, the boys needed their own space, and giving them theirs was part of raising two intelligent, well-mannered young men. Downstairs, Chrissy closed the kitchen door behind herself and Adam, and the *boom boom boom* could hardly be heard.

"I don't know how they can listen to that all the time," Adam said wearily. "Perhaps I'm getting old."

"No, you only *sound* old. We were no different when we were their age. We just weren't allowed to play our music so loud. Well, not in my house anyway." Chrissy busied herself filling mugs with milk and placing them both in the microwave. Adam grabbed the drinking chocolate from the cupboard along with a half packet of Hobnobs. Taking one from the pack and offering Chrissy one, he changed the subject back to the funeral.

"So, what have you still got left to organise?" Adam asked, crumbs falling to the floor as he bit into a biscuit and it broke awkwardly. The microwave whirred in the background.

"Not much on my side, to be honest. Julie is taking most of it on. I've got work and she's only got spa. Give her something meaningful to do for a change." There was no malice in her voice, and it was the truth. Julie really did not have anything important to fill her day with, and every day was the same. It would drive Chrissy nutty.

"Well, I think, when the funeral is over, we should head away for a weekend somewhere, just two of us. What do you reckon?"

"Sounds good. Anywhere in mind?"

"Oh, I thought there might be a music festival on somewhere. We could go and hang out by the beach for the weekend."

The microwave pinged; their milk was hot. Chrissy smiled at his suggestion, knowing full well he was only joking about the music aspect. Shame; she enjoyed music, even dance music, and a festival would be fun.

Adam would have hated it, though.

Chapter Seven

The next five days went by in a flash. On the morning of the funeral, Chrissy looked stunning in her simple black dress, her hair tied into a loose knot behind her head. She wore simple stud pearl earrings, just like her mother undoubtedly would. She sat in front of her dressing table mirror and applied the last of her tinted lip gloss, rubbing her lips together.

Adam watched from the doorway. The day would probably be hard on Chrissy and the rest of the family, he knew, as funerals inevitably were. He looked as handsome as ever in a dark fitted suit. In a low voice he said, "Everyone's here. We're ready."

"I'll be right there," Chrissy said and stood gracefully, glancing back at the mirror one more time before approaching Adam. She slipped her arm through his and he slowly led her back through the doorway and downstairs. From the bottom of the stairs, Chrissy could see a gathering of people, or, really, the hats of the gathering of people. And the sea of hats was all black. She wondered why people felt the need to wear a hat at weddings or funerals. Perhaps she'd missed a tradition along the way; she wasn't wearing one herself.

It's a funeral, remember?

Yes, but does it matter?

They went through to the lounge; through the tall bay window, she could see a group of black cars waiting outside. The hearse was parked out front and four sombre-looking gentlemen stood nearby. They belonged to the funeral parlour and were ready to look substantially more sombre and mournful when the family were ready to leave.

"Would you like a quick drink before we go?" Adam asked.

"Right now, Adam, I would love a wine but I don't think it would be appropriate. And it's a bit early, though I expect it's got to be five PM somewhere in the world." She managed a weak smile, and Adam squeezed her shoulder affectionately. Someone came up behind them, and given the cloying smell of the perfume, Chrissy figured it would be an older relative. She was right.

"Chrissy, darling," the woman said, as Chrissy turned and fixed her weak smile back on her face.

"Hello, Clara. Good to see you!" Chrissy said almost too cheerily for the occasion, and she meant it. Clara had been a friend of the family since Chrissy had worn nappies, and used to push Chrissy in her pram when she was a tiny girl. To her mother's annoyance, Clara had inevitably had a biscuit or two for Chrissy in her handbag, meaning the pram had always been covered in crumbs and prints from chocolatey little fingers. Chrissy being Chrissy, she bent in close to the older woman's ear.

"I don't suppose you have a chocolate biscuit in your bag, do you, Clara?"

Clara laughed lightly as Chrissy turned to introduce her to Adam.

"Adam, this is Clara. I don't think you have ever met her. Clara was always a bugger for giving me a biscuit in my pram and pissing Mum off." She smiled warmly, and Clara and Adam both smiled in return.

"In that case, I'm pleased to meet you Clara," said Adam. He reached out and took her hand, giving it a gentle shake.

"And nice to meet you Adam, though on such a sombre occasion. I'm sure there will be time afterwards to chat more over a sherry." She winked at Adam, who, ever the gentleman, bowed slightly and replied, "Then I will look forward to it."

The conversation was interrupted by an announcement from the front doorway that the procession was almost ready to leave, and people began to filter out into the driveway, Chrissy, Adam and Clara included.

Clara bent in to whisper in Chrissy's ear. "Thank goodness it's not raining. I hate rainy funerals. It makes it even more depressing."

Chrissy could only smile. It was true; there wasn't a cloud in the sky. Birds tweeted cheerfully from nearby trees and bushes, adding their own chorus to her father's *other* big day. Shame he wasn't able to see it, to enjoy it, Chrissy thought, though she felt he was with them in spirit.

She thought uneasily of his body in its wooden box that would soon be turned to nothing more than ashes. But that had been her father's wish. He hadn't wanted to rot in the ground; he'd wanted to have a warm sending-off.

It would be warm, all right.

Damn hot, actually, Chrissy.

She'd seen a joke earlier on Facebook saying, *"The only time I'll ever have a smoking-hot body is when they take me to the crematorium."*

It had made her laugh out loud then, and she fought off the urge to giggle again now. Her father would have loved that.

Car doors slammed shut noisily as people filled the waiting cars, and the sound of voices finally ceased. Chrissy felt Adam steer her gently towards their appointed car, and it was only as she approached it that she noticed Julie and her mother were already seated inside, ready to go. Julie's husband, Richard, had made his own excuses not to attend and so the two women were alone. Chrissy bowed her head in thanks to the funeral home staff who was holding the door open for her and climbed in. Adam was sitting in the front seat beside the driver.

The car was now full. Nobody said a word, and Chrissy didn't catch anybody's eye. She turned and gazed out the window; it was the safest place to look, and she had her own thoughts to keep her company. The driver took his seat and the car moved forward, headed towards the tiny church in the centre of the village.

They could have walked, in reality. It wasn't far, but with older relatives and mourning family members to take into account, the short drive was more appropriate. The drive took precisely three minutes. While it wasn't the longest three minutes of Chrissy's life, it felt right up there. Adam reached between the seats, took her hand and squeezed it gently. As their car pulled to a standstill, Chrissy fought to control the tears threatening to spill down her cheeks; it was all so final now.

Out in the front of the church, on the small lawn where the summer garden market took place, there wasn't a blade of grass without a foot on it. There were cars of all descriptions parked on grass verges, in the church car park and as far as the eye could see down side roads. It was fair to say there were people everywhere. She knew her father had been popular, had lived in the village most of his life, but hadn't realised just how many people he had known. From the gathering, you would have thought a local celebrity was in town.

And perhaps there was.

You will always be a celebrity to me, Dad.

She and Adam climbed out of the car and began to walk towards the church, Adam tall and strong by her side. Julie and her mother climbed out the other side of the car; they still hadn't spoken a word to her. Likely, they were struggling with their own thoughts, their own grief, Chrissy thought. She could hear the sound of an organ coming from inside the church, though she had no clue what the tune was, not being a regular churchgoer. Julie and her mother had decided on the hymns to be sung—slaughtered, more likely— by relatives and acquaintances during the service.

The crowd made its way inside the cool stone church that had stood centre stage in the village for more than a hundred and fifty years. Chrissy and Adam took their seats in the pew at the front of the church. She wished Thomas and Harry were with them, but they had asked to be excused from attending, and Chrissy and Adam had decided there was no point in forcing them. What good would it do? They were good kids, and they would pay their respects in their own way; they didn't need to be in church beside their grandad's casket to do it.

She turned towards the front of the room as the vicar took his place. The organ music drew to a close and conversation ceased.

Gerald Baker's funeral service was now in progress.

Chapter Eight

Julie and Mum had done well. Chrissy guessed, rightly so, that Gerald had left a detailed will of what he wanted to happen at his funeral, and they had done him proud. "A warm send-off," it had said and that's what he'd gotten.

The hymn he'd chosen to be played at the end of the service was *All Things Bright and Beautiful*. It was not a common choice for a funeral, more a wedding or christening, but her father had never wanted people to limp along singing songs they didn't know. Chrissy made a mental note she'd quite like the same hymn at her own funeral. She must mention it to Adam—and they must update their own wills.

When the service was over, the sea of black hats made their way to the front door and back out into the sunshine. Preferring to keep herself to herself, Chrissy guided Adam away to the side and under a shady tree. She didn't feel much like socialising. It was an odd place to be social, a funeral, though there would be plenty of time for small talk over more gin and tiny sandwiches later.

Adam spoke first. "That was nice, Chrissy, wasn't it?" he said gently. "Great last hymn."

"Yes, it was," she conceded. "Mum and Julie did a good job; I knew they would. I wish the boys had been here, though, don't you?"

"I know what you mean, but there was no point in making them come. They will remember him in their own way."

While they stood, Chrissy people watched for something to do other than interact with a bunch of strangers. There were many people she didn't know, of course. But someone took her interest. Through the canopy of black hats, she noticed a single man on his own, leaning by a car. Why she'd noticed him she'd no idea, and as she watched him, she couldn't think why he stuck out to her other than that he, too, was alone. He looked like any other man there— dark suit, sombre expression—but somehow, he stood out. She nudged Adam and nodded towards him.

"Any idea who that is?" she asked. Adam looked but didn't recognise the man either.

"No idea. I guess he knew your father, like most people here. You don't get many funeral crashers."

That made Chrissy smile. "You're as bad as me," she said, stifling a giggle.

Adam squeezed her affectionately and glanced towards the man again. "But seriously, why do you pick him out? There's plenty of people here you don't know."

"I know. But there's just something about him. It's almost as if he's..." She searched for the word. "...browsing. Watching people. Seems odd."

"Aren't *you* doing that?"

"Yes. But I'm family, I'm his daughter. I'm allowed to watch people and be on my own."

They fell into a comfortable silence together and watched the crowd some more; Chrissy kept one eye on the man by the car. A moment later, he turned in their direction and looked straight at Chrissy. Their eyes locked for a moment, but the man's face remained unchanged; not a muscle moved. It was unnerving. Surely he'd give a tiny smile, a nod of recognition, something?

The man looked away again, then dropped the cigarette he'd

been smoking and stubbed it out in the dirt. He opened the driver's side of the car he'd been leaning against, climbed in and started the engine. Without a backwards glance, he drove slowly away down the lane, which was packed with parked cars.

"See? I told you," Chrissy said. "As soon as he saw me watching him, he took off and I bet he's not going to the crematorium."

"I wouldn't pay any attention to him," Adam said. "Your dad knew so many people there are bound be some here that you don't know."

From the corner of her eye Chrissy could see Julie approaching them both. Her black hat was somewhat bigger than everybody else's and it was hard not to miss the stiff blonde waves peeping out from underneath. As she got closer Chrissy could see that she had been crying. She extended her arms to greet her and Julie slipped between them. The two women hugged as more black hats milled about nearby.

Finally, Julie pulled away and dabbed her eyes. "Who was that?" she said, inclining her head in the direction the car had gone.

"That's just what Adam and I were discussing. He stuck out to you as well, did he?"

"He did, actually, yes. Don't know why. He was quite good looking, though."

"I don't know about that part. Anyway, he's gone now. I doubt we'll see him again."

Changing the topic, Julie said, "It's time to go anyway. Are you coming in our car? We're setting off now if you want to ride with us."

"Of course we are," Chrissy said, smiling slightly. "Our car is back at the house."

The three of them made their way back towards the car they'd arrived in. The black hats were thinning out now, with those who had come just for the church service making their way home or on to the pub to make an early start on refreshments. Chrissy hoped the sandwiches wouldn't be put out until later. She hadn't felt like eating at lunchtime, but her stomach was now starting to grumble for sustenance.

The service at the crematorium was short, almost perfunctory, and they all said their final goodbyes to Gerald Baker.

Chrissy hoped the staff would wait until everybody had left the grounds before they struck the match. She had no desire to see the smoke billowing from the chimney. Shivering, she made her way back to the car, tucking herself under Adam's arm for comfort.

Chapter Nine

It hadn't been his intention to be spotted. The man had stood by his vehicle watching the funeral like any other nosey local attendee. But she'd seen him, and that annoyed him because now it could make things difficult.

The summer sun glared in his eyes as he made his way back towards the motorway and towards his hotel. He'd shown his face, though unintentionally, but he'd needed to go and make sure that the old bastard was dead.

He owed them that much.

There wasn't much else to do, apart from keep his nose clean and stay out of the way. Between them, they had come up with the plan, but it had been he who had actioned it on their behalf. Why? Because three of them were already dead. And why were they dead? Because Gerald Baker had killed them. He might not have meant to kill them, he might not have actually done it with his own hands, but they were dead nonetheless and it was all Gerald Baker's fault. Their deaths were on his hands.

The man retrieved his iPhone from his inside pocket with one hand on the steering wheel, and with his other hand checked the time in LA on the phone app. It was late afternoon, so he pressed the appropriate number on his speed dial and waited for the phone to connect on the other side of the world. It didn't take long before it was picked up. He recognised the male voice instantly and it gave him some comfort.

"How did it go?"

"Nothing remarkable; just as expected. It was a church service."

"Didn't think he'd be much of a churchgoer. Definitely dead, then?"

"Oh, definitely dead. I didn't hang around to go to the crematorium and check it was him in the box, but the whole family—in fact, it seemed like half the village—were in the church. The old man certainly had a decent send-off."

"He doesn't deserve it."

"No, but he won't be doing any more damage."

"Three dead is damage enough, but there will be no more. Not from his actions, anyway."

"My flight home is tomorrow morning, so I'll catch up with you sometime after I get back, eh?"

"Yes. Safe trip. And nice work."

The man in the car rang off, then carried on towards his hotel and a change of clothes. He hadn't packed much for his short visit; he was only in the country for one reason, and that reason was now taken care of. He'd made sure the old man was dead and buried. Now, he figured he might as well enjoy what London had to offer and be a tourist for the day. Tomorrow, he'd fly back to LA and carry on with his life.

As a lawyer.

Chapter Ten

As Chrissy had expected, the staff at the crematorium waited until everybody had gone before striking their match. A handful of family members and close friends had stayed for the brief service before seeing Gerald Baker finally rolled away to be turned into ash and dust. The next time she would see her father would be in an urn on the mantelpiece. They hadn't talked much as a family of what was to happen to his ashes; he'd never stipulated that far ahead in his will. Chrissy suspected Julie would like them stored in some elaborate box on proud display and that her mother, given how annoyed she had been with him of recent, probably couldn't care less. After forty-odd years of marriage, it seemed a sad end to things, but that kind of indifference was not unusual for many older couples, Chrissy knew. She hoped she and Adam wouldn't fall out of love after forty years of marriage. They loved one another now even more than they had on their wedding day.

But everyone was different and different generations did things differently. Her mother and father had wed at a time when the woman stayed at home and cooked and the man went out to work. Chrissy didn't ever remember her mother ever working a paid day in her life. Maybe if she had, Sandra Baker would have had a better understanding of what her husband had felt like at the end of each day. And maybe Gerald could have spent a day in Sandra's shoes experiencing the monotony, the drudgery, the tediousness of running a home, of running a family, and how different it was to his own day. Maybe that way they could have shared each other's lives a little more and deepened their relationship through understanding. It was all too late now.

The small local public house where they were all now stood was a busy hive of activity and conversation. Those who hadn't attended the crematorium service had obviously started early on their gin and tonics and were now rowdily telling jokes and stories about the deceased. In a nearby corner, Chrissy could see three ruddy faces of people she knew from neighbouring properties, though somewhat worse for wear from the afternoon's drinking session. A barmaid was busy pulling a pint as Chrissy made her way over to order herself a glass of wine, though it was a cup of tea she fancied more than alcohol. She caught the eye of the barmaid, who motioned with her chin that she would only be a moment. As Chrissy stood there on her own with lively chatter bouncing all around her, she was aware of Clara's perfume filling her airspace once again. Turning slightly, Clara's smile greeted her.

"What a lovely day it has been Chrissy. Well done to you and your family for organising such a splendid occasion."

"I can't really take credit, Clara," she said. "It was Julie and Mother doing it all. I had nothing to do with it, really. And I believe Dad chose most of the hymns."

"Well, still, it was a lovely service. Gerald would have loved it."

The barmaid sauntered over. "What can I get you two girls?" she said brightly. Chrissy turned to Clara and offered to buy her a drink.

"Thank you, Chrissy. I'll have a dry sherry, please." Chrissy turned back to the barmaid and said, "I don't suppose you can make a cup of tea, could you?"

"Of course I can, my love. I'll get the sherry and bring your tea over shortly." Chrissy smiled her appreciation and turned back to Clara. "I bet you know everybody here, don't you?" she enquired.

"Yes, pretty much. I've been around the family long enough, though I don't know all of Gerald's work colleagues and business associates. A few strange faces. Why do you ask?"

"I noticed a chap earlier at the church, standing by his car. Did you see a him at all?"

Clara stood thoughtful for a moment before responding. "No," she said, "can't say that I do remember anyone like that. What did he look like?"

"He was smartly dressed in a nice suit. Probably mid-forties, and he was smoking a cigarette. Julie thought he looked quite handsome, but I didn't notice that aspect. As soon as he saw me looking, he got in his car and drove off. I just thought it was a bit odd, really. Anyway, it was probably nothing. Just someone paying their respects."

"Gerald knew an awful lot of people."

"Yes, but for some reason I was curious who this one was." Chrissy felt Adam approach her from behind. She always knew when Adam was close by; it was as if she picked up his scent or his vibe.

"What are you two lovely ladies chatting about?" he said now.

"Chrissy was just telling me about a man that she'd noticed smoking a cigarette, wondered who it was," said Clara. "Did you see him, Adam?"

"I did, Clara. I was standing with Chrissy when she spotted him. And then he was gone."

"Oh, a bit of intrigue—how exciting," she said, rubbing her bony hands together as if they were cold.

"Well, I'm glad it made the funeral more fun for you," said Chrissy lightly, smiling her intention. It was about then that Chrissy's tea arrived on a tray and, more for something to do, she lifted the lid and stirred the pot's contents with a spoon.

Adam caught the eye of the barmaid and called across. "Any

chance of another cup?" The woman nodded and left in search of a cup for Adam.

"I think when we've drunk this we should head home, Chrissy. Is that okay with you? The boys will be waiting for us."

Clara perked up at the mention of the boys. "I notice they weren't here. Are they both okay?"

"Perfectly, thanks, Clara. They just opted not to attend."

"How very modern. Give them both a kiss from me when you see them, won't you? It's been too long since I last saw them. I bet they've grown!"

"I will," said Chrissy. "And yes, they have. They are of that age. They have a reason for everything, but as long as it makes sense we don't mind too much."

"Well, I've just seen your Uncle Tom come through the door so I'm going to go and say hello and leave you two lovebirds to it." Clara reached up and gave Chrissy and Adam each a peck on the cheek. They watched as she made her way over to a grey-haired gentleman that Chrissy hadn't seen before.

"I didn't know you had an Uncle Tom," said Adam.

"I've no idea who it is," said Chrissy. "But Clara seems to."

Chapter Eleven

Four days later, Chrissy found herself at her mother's place again. She'd stayed with Julie up until the funeral and for the first couple of nights afterwards, not really wanting to go home on her own. But two nights ago, she'd finally ventured back to her own place, to her own bed.

Both Julie and Chrissy had arranged to go around to their mother's house and start sorting out their father's belongings. Sandra had said very little since the funeral, and Chrissy hadn't prodded, sensing that something besides her husband's death was on her mind. She seemed angry. Julie had noticed it, too, and had voiced her concerns to Chrissy, who in turn had mentioned it to Adam, but there was little to be done until their mother decided to say something herself. If indeed there was indeed anything to be said at all.

So as Chrissy travelled to her mother's place via Uber again, she was hoping that soon everything would return back to normal. Adam was at work; he didn't need to take time off to support her. She was tough enough without his help, of course, but that didn't mean she didn't appreciate his offering. Julie, on the other hand, had played the perfect drama queen all the way through and continued to do so, draining every last ounce out of her performance. Richard, her husband, was keeping himself well away, it seemed. If Julie ever got herself a hobby it would be amateur dramatics. The thought amused Chrissy as the cab pulled into the driveway.

Julie was already in the doorway waiting, looking as immaculate as ever. Under her breath, Chrissy said, *"It must take her hours. Perhaps I should try harder."*

I doubt it. You look great as you are.

Really? Thanks!

Dressed in khaki shorts and a T-shirt, she was the polar opposite of Julie in her pale pink linen dress suit. The woman never took a break from her severe appearance. And what the hell—Chrissy had great legs and chose to show them off.

"You're looking summery," Julie quipped lightly. It was her way of saying "You're looking very casual today."

"And you look lovely, though you look like you're off to a wedding someplace. Have I missed out on an invitation?" It was Chrissy's way of giving her sister back a gentle dig. She made her way up the steps and into the cool area off from the porch, following Julie to the back of the house that she knew so well. Passing the lounge and the study, they headed down to the kitchen at the back of the house and on through to the conservatory. It was almost identical to her sister's own place. Julie's husband, Richard, was sitting in a wicker chair reading the morning's paper. He looked as highly polished and ready for a wedding as Julie did.

"Hey, Richard," Chrissy said. Richard looked over the top of his newspaper and his half-moon glasses and gave a weak smile as though he'd been interrupted.

"Hello, Chrissy," he said briefly, and went straight back into his newspaper. Sure that she couldn't be seen, Chrissy put her tongue out and wagged her head from side to side like a child would. Julie knew she did this, but never said anything mainly because she did it to her husband herself. Even though they dressed so differently, Julie and Chrissy had a lot in common—particularly their thoughts about Julie's husband.

Dull as dishwater.

"Tea or coffee?" Julie enquired.

"Is there any Earl Grey or maybe green?"

"Mum has some green. Fancy some of that?"

"Sounds good." Chrissy stepped over to the window at the back of the conservatory and peered out at the vast lawns behind the house. Julie had a gardener for her own place; she wasn't one for getting her painted fingernails dirty. Derek, the young gardener, went twice a week and Chrissy had often wondered just what happened in the little potting shed at the end of her sister's lawn.

She glanced over at Richard again. His bald patch was visible on the back of his head, a few stray wispy hairs combed over the top of it. Just as she'd always wanted to run her fingers through Julie's stiff waves, she'd always wanted to rustle those few fine hairs. He was so far away from Derek in the looks department, he was off the scale. She'd seen Derek the gardener herself. He was many women's hot dream, looking more like he'd stepped off Bondi Beach than Morecambe Beach. Chrissy could completely understand Julie's fascination.

Richard rustled the newspaper before closing it and folding it in half, placing it on the matching wicker table in front of him. Julie walked in the door carrying a tray of refreshments and proceeded to unload the tray onto the small table. There was green tea for Julie and herself and a cafeteria of coffee for Mr. Dull.

He glanced over the tray then looked up at Julie and asked, "Cream?"

Chrissy wanted to slap him and tell him to get his own and stop being such a lazy git, but she restrained herself. It was none of her business. Julie scurried off back to the kitchen and came back with a small jug. She hadn't been gone long enough to put arsenic into it, though Chrissy wondered if her sister had ever been tempted. She put the jug on the tray next to his cup and Chrissy watched, mesmerised, as Richard poured himself a mug full, topped it up with cream, picked it up and got to his feet without another word. She watched his back as he made his way to the door and off to the lounge down the hallway. She pulled her tongue out at him again.

"Stop it," urged Julie. "One day he'll catch you."

"Yeah, yeah. He reminds me of Dad—such a stiff. Whatever do you see in him?"

"He's a good man. A bit boring at times, but he provides for us well."

Well, that's all right then ... He keeps the moggie well fed and the spa bill paid.

Both women sat back and fell deep into thought.

When Julie finally spoke, she said, "We'll make a start as soon as we finish this." She hoisted her teacup. "Mum will be down soon. She's having a nap."

Chrissy closed her eyes for a moment and relished the warmth of the sunshine beaming through the window onto her forehead. She could have fancied a nap herself.

"Can't wait," she said.

Chapter Twelve

Chrissy was fed up with waiting. Julie had her perfect nose in a magazine and was deeply engrossed in a tale of woe. A celebrity had probably broken a nail and been rushed to Cedars-Sinai to get it fixed. She checked her own while she waited; they could do with some love and attention themselves. Chrissy huffed out noisily, encouraging Julie to peer over her magazine and look questioningly at her sister in a motion almost identical to Richard's greeting an hour ago. At least he was enjoying himself in another room down the hall or taking a nap, Chrissy thought miserably.

"Right. I'm bored now," she announced jumping to her feet. "If Mum's still sleeping, I'm going to make a start on his den."

"You can't start without her. That's neither nice nor fair."

"She doesn't want to do it anyway. Isn't that why we're both here?"

"Yes, I know but still."

"Still nothing. I've stuff to be doing. Are you going to come and give me a hand? Or sit and finish your reality trash magazine?"

Julie folded open the page she'd been reading, planning on returning to it later. Chrissy caught the main image, Meghan and Harry.

Dear Lord. Suits *will never be the same.*
You hate Suits?
Don't hate Harvey.

"I'll get the bin liners from the kitchen," Chrissy announced with authority as Julie finally found her legs and stood. The pins she wore as heels looked like they'd pierce a rhino's skin, they were so pointed. Chrissy preferred her flats; there'd be no bunions on her feet in the foreseeable future. The pins made a loud clacking sound as they followed Chrissy into the kitchen, though there was no need to. Chrissy was quite capable of retrieving the rubbish bags on her own. Still, at least she was helping.

They headed to their father's den, an ample-sized room towards the front of the house. As children, they'd avoided the place like the plague, though not for any other reason than that their father hated them going in there. It had been considered his sanctuary though the girls, as they'd grown up and understood more, had never actually found out what he had been seeking sanctuary from.

Chrissy pushed open the large oak door and both women stood in the doorway, looking in. It smelled musty, like it hadn't had the windows open in months, but the polished floor gleamed as if it had been freshly worked on yesterday, which they knew hadn't been the case. To their knowledge, no one had entered the room since their father's death. Chrissy marched over to the bay window and yanked at the catch to open it.

"It stinks in here, and it's hot."

The pins entered and clicked slowly towards the back of the room, where an ample leather desk chair sat behind an old wooden desk. Julie sat down and swivelled slightly from side to side, Chrissy looking on.

"I guess you're allowed to now," Chrissy said. "He'd turn in his urn if he could see you now." She couldn't stop the giggle that followed.

"You're so crass sometimes, Chrissy. Turn in his grave, I think you meant to say."

"Nope. Turn in his urn. That's where he is, right?"

Julie carried on swivelling as Chrissy took a black plastic bag from the roll and tore it off. It rattled as she shook it open and it filled with air. There was a large cupboard along the far wall and she headed towards it as Julie watched from her seat. Chrissy turned the key in the lock, the doors creaked open, and she saw inside a part of her father's world for the very first time. The entire cupboard was filled with shelves upon shelves of books, almost identical-looking from their spines. Chrissy peered in closer and pulled one out. It looked like a diary of sorts, and she flicked through the pages. It was almost a scrapbook. There were hand-written notes, cuttings, odd photos and what looked like memen-tos. She glanced back into the cupboard and roughly counted the number of similar-looking spines. There were at least forty of them. Had her father been keeping a record of his life?

"What have you got?" Julie asked, her feet now up on their father's old desk, pins kicked off. Even the underneath of her pale pink feet looked neat, Chrissy noted. She ruffled through another volume, stopped randomly at a page with handwriting on it and read it to herself.

"I think it's Dad's diaries. Look, listen to this:"

I hate it when we fall out but sometimes there's no reasoning with her. Everything needs to be about her. When will she learn?

"Mother, do you think?" Julie asked.

"I guess so." She replaced the book where she'd taken it from and pulled out another. She picked another random page with handwriting on it.

So far, so good. Maybe I'm on to something? I can't believe it's this easy.

She replaced it and picked out another random volume. Chrissy looked at the inside cover for a date—2015. There were only three more stacked after it. Placing it back in line, she retrieved what she assumed was the latest one and flipped it open. Turning to the last entry, she surmised it was. The last entry read: *My two girls are the best thing I've ever done in my life* ... but Chrissy was interrupted from reading any further.

"What the hell are you doing in here?" Their mother stood in the doorway, hands on hips, like she had done so many times in the past when either girl had upset or annoyed her for some reason. Julie's legs swung straight back down to the floor, feet finding their pins. Chrissy dropped the book she was holding as her mother's sudden and obviously stricken words assaulted her ears. She bent to pick it up.

"Leave it there!" her mother bellowed. Chrissy didn't think she'd ever heard her mother shout so loudly. So much for looking small and frail. Standing there with her face growing redder, Sandra Baker looked like could have taken on Tyson in the ring. Suddenly, Chrissy was a small girl again.

"Sorry, Mum," she said in a low voice. "We thought we'd better make a start on his things."

"Not in here, you don't!" Their mother's voice was high pitched, not at all like it usually sounded. A moment passed where nobody said a word. When she finally spoke again, at a volume like her normal self, she suggested, "If you want to help, why don't you start in the garden shed?" Her tone was conciliatory. The two sisters took the hint, scurrying off back down the hall and leaving their mother standing in the stuffy room.

Richard peered over his glasses from the lounge doorway as they hurried past. It seemed everyone was now fully awake.

Chapter Thirteen

Richard retreated back behind the closed door in the lounge, and Julie and Chrissy, chastised, retreated to the garden shed. At least it was warm outside. Julie brushed dirt off the seat of a director's chair, curling her nose up at the dust, before sitting her tiny backside down. Chrissy still carried the roll of black bin liners she'd hastily grabbed off the desk in passing, and she too pulled out a director's chair. They were now sitting at the bottom of the manicured lawn by Dad's old shed.

Out of the way.

"I didn't think Dad was the type to have a shed," Julie stated, pulling her sunglasses down from atop her head to cover her eyes.

"He wasn't. Mum was, a bit. I think this place is more for the hired help gardener to hang his hoe than anything else. She really wanted us out of the way."

"Hang his hoe?" Julie enquired, raising her sunglasses and looking across at Chrissy at the same time. "Isn't *hoe* a spiteful name for someone who sleeps around?"

"My god, Julie. You really have been reading too much trashy stuff. Hoe, as in garden hoe, as in tool to till the soil with. Hoe. To hang one's hoe. Nothing to do with anything else but digging and weeding. No pun intended."

Digging?

Weeding?

Julie rested back and turned her face towards the sun. Chrissy shook her head at her sister in despair but added nothing further on the subject. Instead, she announced she was going to start sorting the shed out or else she may as well head home for all the good they were doing.

"You sit there and work on your tan. I'll have a sort-out, though there won't be much in here to get rid of. Mum only wanted us out of the house. Odd, I thought, since we *are* here to help her sort stuff out. It was like we were twelve years old again, didn't you think?"

"Hmm," Julie said sleepily. Her eyes were closed behind her shades, no doubt. She wasn't paying any attention now.

With one last *tut*, Chrissy headed inside the shed and glanced around at the debris and garden utensils dotted around. Except for one big old once-comfy chair in the corner by the little window, there didn't appear to be a great deal else. The chair was covered in an equally ancient candlewick throw that Chrissy remembered being her bedspread when she was a youngster. She smiled to herself at the memory of a spilled glass of Ribena and the stain it had made. And the bother she'd got into. And the reason for the bedspread ending up in the shed. Faint pink was visible at one corner; the rest of the fabric was grubby from years of being used as a dust sheet. She grabbed a corner, gathered the cloth up into a wad with the years of dirt tucked inside it and placed it on the floor, then plunked herself down in the old chair. A stray spring nudged her buttock and she readjusted herself around it.

Through the small, grimy window, she could see the house; the back door was only slightly visible but most of the garden path was in full view. If you were hiding out in the shed, you'd certainly have privacy and be notified early on if someone approached. Maybe

Dad had a secret stash of booze nearby, a bottle of sherry like Trevor did in *No Place Like Home* when he was escaping Vera. But Dad would never have drunk sherry; single malt was his tipple. Nonetheless, she couldn't help glancing around for a hiding place. The shelves were empty save for half-full packs of fertiliser and odd plant pots, but a set of drawers at the rear of the shed caught her eye. An old tablecloth partially covered the top, its once-bright large pink and yellow checks as faded as the stain on the candlewick. A wooden knob was missing on the lower of the three drawers.

Chrissy was feeling inquisitive now: maybe there'd be a drop in the bottom. She pulled open the top drawer but was disappointed to find it empty, unless you counted the spider. The middle drawer contained some folded old yellowing newspapers. She checked the date on the top one; it was almost ten years old. She picked it up and opened it out. It was the *Financial Times*. She scanned the head-lines quickly, but the content was as appealing to her as a gardening book would be to Julie. Another spider crawled down the page and she put the paper back in the drawer and closed it again. The lower drawer only had one knob, so as she pulled it open, it stuck slightly on an angle. She tugged again; there was the dry scrape of wood groaning on wood.

"Damn it," she cursed, and bent to her hands and knees. If the drawer was going to come out, she'd have to ease it out with her hand from underneath. Getting in position, she pulled the knob with one hand and with her other, gently eased the drawer forward from underneath. When it had moved forward a couple of inches, she pulled the whole drawer open with her fingers.

Hello, darling. Chrissy smiled at the three-quarter-full bottle of golden liquid and picked it up. It was an 18-year-old bottle of Glen-fiddich, one of her father's favourites. She unscrewed the top and sniffed. There was a hint of sherry, she thought, and sniffed again, the strong vapours hitting the back of her nose in a pleasant way. She wiped the top on her T-shirt and raised the bottle to her pursed lips, allowing a tiny drop to seep into her mouth. It burned as pleasantly as the smell had a moment ago. She took another, much larger mouthful and played with it in her mouth, swishing it around like an expensive mouthwash before letting it warm the inside of her throat as it went to her stomach.

"Oh, that's nice," she said quietly to herself and took another mouthful, smaller this time, and savoured the taste. She wiped her lips with the back of her hand, looking more like sailor in a bar than a woman in her father's shed. She screwed the top back on and put the bottle on top of the set of drawers; there was no sense in putting it away.

The only other item in the drawer was an old biscuit tin. She pulled it out. "Huntley & Palmers Christmas Biscuits," she read. It had a picture of a boy with a snowball in his hand, hiding behind an old-style red post box, no doubt hiding from an incoming snowball thrown by a friend. It looked many years old, though there was no date on it that she could see. She shook the tin gently and felt something inside it move. Whatever it was, it didn't weigh much; the tin was light. She removed the lid.

Inside were a handful of photographs, in colour, but old and faded nonetheless. She sifted through them. They appeared to be old school pictures, each one of a young boy, and she estimated they were all in their early teens, maybe fourteen or so. There were seven of them. Picking out one randomly, she turned it over to check the back, but nothing was written, only the date it had been printed—June 1987. She checked each one in turn, but nothing was written on them either, only the mechanical printed date of developing. Chrissy shuffled through the pictures again, each of a young man smiling for the camera, each in what appeared to be school uniform, shirt and tie neatly done up. Chrissy stood for some time in the dusty shed and gazed out of the window, looking towards the house as though the answer would come marching down the path to her. When nothing happened, she looked at the photos in her hand again. On top was a fair-headed boy in thick-rimmed glasses looking back at her. He was smiling, as the others were.

"What on earth are your pictures doing in an old biscuit tin in Dad's shed?" she asked the empty space. "And more to the point, who are you?"

There was only one way to find out.

Chapter Fourteen

They'd filled precisely one rubbish bag with their Dad's things to take to the charity shop. While Julie had alternated between a shady spot and dappled sunshine, Chrissy had taken a liking to the bottle of single malt she'd found, and after polishing off almost half of it, had ended up nodding off in the other director's chair at the bottom of the garden. Chrissy hadn't said a word to her sister about the photographs, though she wasn't entirely sure why not. Something inside her had told her to keep it to herself for now.

It was nearly 4 PM when she eventually woke up with her mouth feeling like the bottom of a bird's cage. She tried to moisten her mouth with her tongue as she came to, but it was a far cry from a much-needed glass of cold water. Instinctively, her hand went to her brow then to her cheek. Her skin felt hot and she hoped she hadn't got sunburn. Opening both eyes fully and orienting herself, she realised she was sitting all alone. Julie had gone.

Gone entirely, 'gone home' gone? With Richard?

How would I know?

Go and have a look then.

The garden was peaceful as her mind wandered, the only sound a petrol-powered lawn mower chugging nearby. She stood, picked up the almost-empty whiskey bottle and made her way up the path towards the house. The photos were back in their tin and safely tucked away in the broken drawer with one knob. To take them out again now would only draw attention to them, she told herself, and since her father had obviously hidden them, they were better off left where they were. For now.

She was halfway back to the house when she had second thoughts.

"Sod it," she said under her breath and marched purposefully back to the shed. Knowing exactly what she was doing, she took the tin out of the drawer again and, using her phone, took a photo of each image individually as well as the date stamped on the back. When she had a copy of each of them, she put the whole lot back and closed the drawer yet again. The charity shop wouldn't be interested in a tin of faces, and she doubted her mother would be either.

But her inquisitive mind, the mind of a former intelligence officer, told her they were hidden for a reason. Her father must never have intended them to be found. Until she figured out what to do with them, the originals could stay put in their hiding place, out of harm's way. For now.

When Chrissy entered the cool house again, it was eerily quiet, as though she were all alone. But that was silly. Her mother would be inside somewhere, even if Julie and Richard had left while she'd slept. Chrissy hadn't realised she was so tired, but then she wasn't used to drinking hard spirits just after lunch. Not in the quantity she'd consumed today, anyway. She stopped in the kitchen and filled a glass with water, then drank the whole thing down greedily. She caught her breath with a gasp, then refilled the glass and carried it with her through to the front of the house to find her mother. Unless she'd gone back to sleep herself, of course.

She blushed as she remembered her mother's reaction to finding her and Julie going through Dad's cupboard full of notebooks. Maybe they had unwittingly intruded into something sacred?

Everyone was entitled to their own privacy, and while neither she nor Julie had even thought their father had diarised his life, she asked herself if she would she have been as intrigued if it been her mother's diaries. Her mind was over-reacting, surely; Dad had simply never seemed the type, and perhaps the unexpectedness of it was what made it interesting. Maybe she didn't know him as well as she thought she did. A small voice startled her as she passed the bottom of the staircase.

"I thought you'd left hours ago," her mother said, back to being tiny and frail again. Tyson had left the building.

"It seems I fell asleep in the garden. Julie must have let me be. You?" she enquired in a level voice. She didn't appreciate being treated like a twelve-year-old by anybody, including her mother. She was a grown woman, for heaven's sake.

"I napped, on and off."

She caught her mother's gaze; she was looking at Chrissy's hand. The remains of the whiskey.

"Oh—I found it in the shed. It's more than likely the reason I fell asleep. I had a couple of mouthfuls."

More than a couple—more like a third of a bottle.

"In the shed? Really?"

"Would you like some?" Chrissy offered, holding the bottle out. Her mother hadn't moved from her step halfway up but managed to nod yes. "Maybe come down. I'll get you a glass," Chrissy carried on.

As Chrissy turned back towards the kitchen, she heard her mother pad lightly down the hallway towards her as she selected a small tumbler and poured a couple of fingers in. Her mother seemed to have shrunk a foot since her outburst in the front room earlier and seemed a little sheepish.

When she'd taken a couple of sips, and presumably consumed enough courage, her mother apologised. "I think it's simply too soon. I'm sorry. Will you tell Julie?'

"I will if you want me to. It might be better if you did it your-self, though." There was a pause as Chrissy let her advice sink in, then she went on. "May I ask, did you know about the diaries, or the contents? I never really put Dad down as sentimental."

"Oh, he wasn't sentimental. Not sentimental at all. I expect there's all manner of private things in them, not for your eyes nor mine. And yes, I did know about them, though I only found out about them a few years ago, actually. They go all the way back to before we first met." She seemed sad suddenly, almost as though she had left the room, in spirit rather than body.

Chrissy felt the shift. "What was in them?"

"Nothing to concern you." Her mother tossed back the remaining whiskey and slammed the glass down on the drainer, making Chrissy jump in alarm.

Something was giving her mother dual persona: feisty one minute then decrepit the next. And it had to do with Dad, given her reaction to the diaries. Chrissy wondered if she knew about the photos too.

Diaries, secret tins of photos? Her naturally inquisitive mind chugged into motion like a grand old steam train starting out down a track.

Chapter Fifteen

The office of Banks & Crowley was situated in Abbot Kinney, a neighbourhood not far from Santa Monica. With small professional office blocks and trendy boutiques, Abbot Kinney was the hip place to be. Some called it the coolest block in America. Only a couple of miles down the road, though, was Venice Beach, considered hip by some and a dump by others. It was popular with those living on the streets. Since LA had an almost perfect climate for living rough, many homeless people found their way to the sands of Venice Beach and neighbouring towns to make their 'home.' Come Friday evening, its white sandy boardwalks would be filled with men and women panhandling. By Saturday morning, the same men and women would lie sprawled, fast asleep, sleeping off the booze.

Early-morning dog walkers and joggers would be treated to the acrid smell of vomit and urine; those who had the luxury of delaying their outings until after 9 AM would miss the mess. By then, the streets and boardwalk would be clean again and smelling of disinfectant, and the homeless would have drifted away to day programmes or the downtown.

Philip Banks lived nearby. As a keen runner, he knew the route down to Santa Monica Pier and back like the back of his hand. It was, after all, a straight run—literally. Bladers and cyclists moved in one clearly marked lane, runners and walkers in another, which kept traffic moving safely.

He was never alone on his run, even though he set out on his own. Even at six in the morning there were plenty of people doing exactly the same as he was. After all, this was LA, the land of the perfect body, the perfect tan, and pristine white teeth.

Beads of sweat had long ago turned into rivulets of salty water that ran down his face and neck, joining the growing wet patch on his shirt. He breathed hard; his heart pounded as his feet pummelled the pavement. As he did every morning, he was focusing on his time to beat. It was only ever going to be by seconds, but seconds counted; seconds mattered. Now, on his return journey towards home, sweat stinging his eyes, he was almost back at his start point and he gritted his teeth as he pushed towards his self-imposed finishing line: the store on the corner that sold cannabis on prescription.

As he raced up to its blue door, he pressed the 'stop' button on his watch to record the end of his run, then carried on a few steps at a much slower jog. As he caught his breath, he made his way across the grassy dunes towards the sea and, with his hands on his hips, waited for his breathing to return to near normal. He wiped his dripping face with his hand. Seagulls filled the sky, their cries multiplying as more and more birds appeared from all directions. In one giant swoop the mass hit the sand as one mob; somebody was throwing food for them. They were pests; it was the tourists that got pleasure from them. He squinted into the sunshine and even with sunglasses on, it was still bright.

Idly, as he stood there, he wondered about the family of Gerald Baker, and in particular his daughter. He hoped that being seen at the funeral was not going to cause any problems, though in reality, who would ever put two and two together? He was just a man paying his respects, like half the village had been doing that day, and there was no reason for anyone to think otherwise. It was never good losing someone close to you—he knew that from experience.

But Gerald Baker had had to be stopped. He had done enough damage already, and the only way to put an end to it was to take him out of the equation.

Alistair Crowley was the polar opposite of Philip Banks. But as happened on every good team, polar opposites worked. The two had known each other since childhood, having attended the same boarding school. Both were the sons of wealthy American parents with a dash of Scots on the Crowley side and had gone on to attend the same law school together. They'd worked together since they'd left law school, though not always from the offices in Abbot Kinney. They'd started out in Philip's basement, in an attempt to get going and practice law on a budget. Everyone left law school with huge loans, and they were no different.

When Philip had suggested early on that they try and make it on their own, their respective fathers had cleared their student loans off but told them they wouldn't finance their operation any further. The two young men had to prove themselves, which was fair enough. Ideally, in their parents' view, Philip and Alistair were meant to have secured jobs at reputed law firms and done the hard yards and gruelling hours like every other graduate. The two men, however, had other plans. They each had met the woman of their dreams and settled into the LA lifestyle, like their fathers before them. That had been a long time ago, and the women of their dreams hadn't hung around long enough to become permanent fixtures in their lives. Philip and Alistair were both single.

And polar opposites.

While Philip ran every morning, Alistair drank coffee and smoked cigarettes as his way of getting into gear. He knew he needed to lose some weight, but had never had the motivation that Philip had and had long ago given up trying to be anything but himself.

Alistair poured himself another mug of coffee and took it out onto the small balcony that overlooked the ocean. If he knew exactly where to look, he could probably have seen Philip out on his run, but instead he stood gazing at the rolling ocean, the morning sun warming his skin, the morning LA haze lifting with every minute that passed. His thoughts drifted, just like Philip's had, to Gerald Baker, to the man's family, but more importantly to his friends who had become victims.

Of Gerald Baker.

Now deceased.

Chapter Sixteen

Each morning at the same time, Philip and Alistair had a catch-up meeting to discuss current workload and what was going on in general. Today was no different, the men sitting at the glass table in Philips' office. Philip poured his first cup of coffee of the day and asked Alistair if he wanted a top-up. Alistair nodded his response, and Philip obliged, though he was probably on his fifth already and it was only just coming up to 9 AM. How the man functioned through the day with his nerves jangling with caffeine, he'd never know.

"How was your run, buddy?" Alistair asked, as he did most mornings.

"It never gets easier. You just get faster." It was the same response each time.

"What sort of answer is that? You tell me that every day."

"It's the truth, that's why. Felt like I was running with lead weights round my ankles this morning, but it's good to be back on familiar territory. I think I'm a bit jet-lagged, to tell you the truth."

"You saw him go, then." It wasn't really a question; more a statement of fact.

"I saw a wooden box go and assumed he was inside it, yes."

"Good riddance to bad rubbish, I say." Alistair pulled a donut out of the Dunkin' Donuts box and bit into it. Sprinkles dropped into his lap, tiny pieces of pink and yellow spattering the dark surface of his suit trousers. He brushed them away with the back of his hand, and Philip bent forward and offered his friend a serviette.

"Here, use that instead of making such a mess, would you?"

As though to set an example, Philip picked up an apple donut, tucked a napkin under it, and bit into his pastry without losing a crumb.

There was a knock at the door and their legal secretary, Carmen, a pretty woman in her early thirties with long, curly red hair, stuck her head round the frame.

"Philip, I've got Mr. Tillyard on the phone. He says it's important and wants to hold, though I told him you were busy in a meeting." She smiled knowingly at the box of donuts and then motioned to let Philip know he had sugar on his chin.

"Thanks," he said, brushing his face. "I'll be right there."

When Carmen had gone, Alistair gave one of his low whistles. "I swear she gets hotter every day." He licked his lips for good measure.

Philip ignored him, as he always did; Carmen was already spoken for. She preferred the perfect American male look, and Alistair didn't own it.

"Best not keep him waiting," said Alistair. "We need the money." He waggled two fingers to indicate that Philip should get on his way, and quickly. "Toodle-pip, as the Brits say."

"I'm going," Philip said with annoyance. Mr. Tillyard could be a giant pain in the ass at times, but the truth was they indeed needed the money. That money came in a constant stream of referrals via his long list of golfing buddies looking for reputable divorce lawyers, so Philip and Alistair looked after him well. He was an important pain in the ass that deserved their full attention.

While the practice had been going for some years, recent times had been tougher than usual and with the added stress and expense of their 'distraction,' as they referred to it, the two men were almost broke. Now their 'distraction' was finally dealt with, however, they could return to normal and concentrate on pulling the business back into shape.

Philip wiped his fingers on his napkin and tossed it into the bin as he left the room. The door clunked shut behind him, leaving Alistair to finish his donut off in peace. Even though it was Philips' office, he rested his feet upon the table in front of him, leaned his head back into the chair and closed his eyes for a moment. The 'distraction' had been draining for him as well as Philip, though he couldn't claim the added jet lag. Gerald Baker, and everything he stood for, was finally done, and Alistair was ready to move on. A cloud passed over the sun and he felt rather than saw the light dim over his head and shoulders. He waited a couple of beats, eyes still closed, for it to return.

He was still sitting in the same position when Philip walked in ten minutes later and woke him up. "I was resting my eyes," he said, sitting up with a start.

"With all the caffeine you consume, I'm not entirely sure how." Philip steepled his fingers in thought.

"Right. Caught, then. So, what did Tillyard want? Who's divorcing this week?"

Chapter Seventeen

Chrissy made it home safely. With nearly half a bottle of hooch in her stomach, she was thankful she'd not driven herself over. Although of course if she had done, she wouldn't have imbibed quite the quantity she had. The afternoon sun was still hot, and the back garden was bathed in its glow. The kitchen, however, felt cool; the windows were in the wrong place to catch the remains of the warmth for the day. Sunshine was always better in a kitchen in a morning, she thought.

She was sitting at the breakfast bar when Adam walked in. He bent and nuzzled the side of her neck.

"Mmm, you smell nice," he cooed contentedly. He straightened and walked over to the fridge, where he retrieved a beer and a bottle of white wine.

"Fancy a glass?" he enquired as he took the top off his beer. He waggled the bottle at her.

"Always," she smiled at him. It was her standard reply, and the reason he'd taken the bottle from the fridge. Adam knew his wife well.

"You're home early," she said.

"I thought I'd take my lover out to the pub for dinner for a change, if she fancies it."

"Oh, how nice for her. And what did your lover say?" It was their little joke. 'Lover' always sounded more exciting than referring to each other as husband and wife. It raised eyebrows occasionally when used in conversation with others, but of course that was all part of the fun.

Adam poured her a glass of wine and set it down by her elbow. Still standing, he slipped his tie off, opening the top button of his shirt at the same time. It reminded Chrissy of taking her bra off at the end of the day. That feeling of freedom and comfort, life's little restrictions removed.

"She said yes, of course," she replied, grinning. "Fancy joining us?" She watched him chug back a long mouthful of beer, his Adam's apple gently moving up and down. It was mesmerising.

"Absolutely," he said. "If we leave here at six-thirty, we can sit in the beer garden if it's still warm enough and everyone else hasn't had the same idea."

She swept up her glass and took a sip, then another, relishing the cold tartness in her throat. "Sounds perfect. In that case, I'm going to run a bath and soak for a while."

"You do that. You look a bit drained—understandably. We've plenty of time, so relax a little, unwind."

Smiling, Chrissy headed off upstairs to the bathroom. She placed her glass on the vanity, poured bubble bath under the running tap and stood for a moment watching the white foam form as the water hit the gel. The smell of rose petals filled the room, one of her favourite fragrances. It reminded her of the roses in full bloom in her mother's garden.

Was it now Mother's garden?

It's always been my parents' garden.

Your father's gone now.

Yes, I know.

You'll get used to it.

When the water reached the perfect level, she stripped off her shorts and T-shirt and slid in under the bubbles, making sure her shoulders were fully submerged. There was a slight sting on the skin under her collarbone where the sun had caught her earlier, likely when she'd had fallen asleep.

You'd drunk half a bottle of whiskey, remember?

How could she forget? She closed her eyes and tried to relax a little, but the first thing she saw was the old biscuit tin, the picture of the boy wrapped up warm against the snow on the front, snowball in hand. Odd that there were photos inside, and of boys. The questions rose again: Who were they? And what were they doing hidden away? Did her mother have any knowledge of who they were or why they were in the old tin? They should have been in Dad's cupboard, with his diaries.

Or perhaps not.

Chrissy slid completely under the water and held her breath, pinching her nose with her fingers so she didn't get water up her nostrils and scrunching her eyes shut. She could feel her hair floating around her head in the water, brushing her face gently like fine seaweed. Everything was much quieter under water; she could have stayed there for an hour. . .

She was vaguely aware of someone talking to her, of distorted, dull tones filtering through the water. Adam. She slithered back up, wiping her hair away from her eyes, and smiled at him. He smiled back.

"Enjoying yourself in there?" he enquired. He didn't wait for an answer. "I'm nipping out for a minute. The boys are stopping over at the Masons' place tonight and I'd forgotten all about it."

"Damn, so had I," she said, slapping her forehead with the palm of her hand. "Are they packed?"

"Apparently so. I'll be fifteen minutes, tops." He bent and gave her forehead a peck, then was gone. When she heard the front door bang shut behind them and his car pull away, Chrissy slithered back down into the tub, as far under the water as she could go, and practised holding her breath like she had in the old days. It had been part of her training back then.

Chapter Eighteen

Chrissy was towelling herself dry when she heard the front door slam shut and familiar footsteps on the stairs. Adam was back, right on time. She smiled to herself at how well she knew him.

After twenty years of marriage, you'd hope so.

I know my man.

"Are you still wallowing in the bath?" he shouted affectionately. Chrissy opened the bathroom door to prove she wasn't and stood there buck naked, posing like a Greek goddess statue, one arm in the air, the other draped across her torso, her face tilted to the ceiling, a slight smile on her lips.

"Holy moly," Adam said slowly. He took the steps two at a time, wrapped his strong arms around her waist and resting his hands on the tops of her buttocks.

She let one arm fall to his shoulders as she looked him in the eye and theatrically said, "Take me—I'm yours."

"Madame, I am happy to oblige," he said in a mock French accent. He scooped her up fully into his arms and carried her, unresisting, through to their bedroom.

. . .

The pub Adam had chosen was one of their locals. There were several to choose from, and even though the great British public houses were closing on a daily basis, the ones out in leafy affluent areas like Englefield Green were still doing a roaring trade. Folks liked "a ride out," as they termed it, and at weekends, the pubs could be chock-a-block full. Their choice this evening was a traditional but newly renovated country pub, with stone walls, a bright and airy feel, high levels of chatter and a menu Jamie Oliver would have been proud of producing. Pubs like these were actually restaurants in reality, with new owners keeping tradition alive, though with a different look than in days gone by. Still, it was good for the community and a profitable business for the owners.

They took their seats in the pub's restaurant, looking like two young lovers. Adam had chosen a corner spot indoors, since the warmth of the early evening sun had dissipated. And they were later arriving than they thought they'd be.

"We should move the boys out of the house more often," Chrissy quipped, with a coy smile. Adam winked in reply as their waitress arrived and handed them menus. They gave their drinks order to be going on with—more white wine for Chrissy and a pint for Adam. The waitress reappeared with their drinks then left them to study their menus.

"Same as usual?" Chrissy asked.

"Same as usual. I don't know why we bother looking."

"Me neither, but it's fun."

"I'll go and order then," said Adam, and headed over to the bar to order and pay. She watched him from her spot at the table, thinking back to not an hour ago as they had lain entwined with each other. She was going to miss him next week, but she also knew it was good for them both. Absence did indeed make the heart grow fonder. She sipped on her wine and watched him return. His narrow hips in faded jeans still mesmerised her. He caught her looking.

"You'll have to wait," he said. "I need sustenance first. I'm famished."

"I can do that." She smiled.

"Well, I'm going to change the subject before we both flee back home for the bedroom without getting fed," he said. "How did you get on today, sorting out with Julie and your mum?"

"Ah," she said putting her wine glass down. "It was a bit weird, actually. We both ended up getting told off, like we were kids again."

"Oh?"

"Mum went nutty when she found us in Dad's den, looking through a cupboard. She'd been asleep upstairs, so we'd made a start. Seems that wasn't the thing to do." Chrissy told him the rest of the story about the cupboard's contents but stopped short of her find in the shed. She wasn't entirely sure why, but her gut told her to keep the box of photos to herself—for now, at least. When she'd finished her tale, she noticed Adam's mood had changed slightly, a definite shift.

"What is it?" she enquired as two plates overflowing with crispy battered fish and chips were delivered. Adam asked the waitress for vinegar.

"I've been keeping something from you. I wasn't sure whether to mention it or not."

"Sounds like you're about to." She picked a chip up and bit into it while she waited.

"There was a letter. When we called to pick the flowers up before the funeral. I slipped it in my pocket."

"And?"

"The only thing on the front was 'Thief.' I took it so you wouldn't see it. I didn't want it to upset you."

Chrissy's eyes widened. "What was it about? What did it say?"

"I don't know who it was from, but it was threatening. Your dad had obviously angered someone. It seemed to be over lost money. There was reference to a scheme, though it was vague."

"Was it signed?"

"No. But I suspect it's not the first one your father received.

And if there are more letters. . ." He was silent for a moment. "What was your father up to, I wonder?"

Chrissy sat quietly, all thoughts of her food forgotten now, while she pieced the new information together with what she already knew.

And stuff you don't know about, remember?

Yeah, I know.

"Well, I don't know, but I'm sure we'll find out."

Chapter Nineteen

There were too many things whizzing about in her head. Chrissy had had hardly a wink of sleep, and it was nothing to do with the fish and chips. Adam had lain beside her, snoring gently, and she wished she'd been able to do the same. As she thought over events from the last few days, she realised there were far too many questions without answers, what with the diaries, the tin of faces and now the letter that Adam had informed her of only a few hours ago. He'd shown it to her when they'd arrived home. It didn't say much, really—just alluded to a scheme and money owing.

Oh, and a threat.

I'll not let you rest until I have back what is rightfully mine.

A threat that now would never materialise, since Gerald Baker was already dead. But it intrigued Chrissy nonetheless, because she hadn't known of her father being involved in any kind of shady financial scheme. His business had always run above board. Or so she'd believed.

And how do you know that for a fact, Chrissy?

Dad wouldn't scam people, that's why.

Sure about that?

And what about the man she'd seen standing by the car smoking a cigarette at the funeral? And what about the man she'd seen in the bar, someone Clara knew as Uncle Tom? He'd left soon after, and she'd never had a chance to chat, but he could well have been a genuine friend and not a foe. Her father, after all, had been a popular man; the church service turnout was proof of that. But there was something going on—of that, Chrissy was certain. The question now was what.

With Adam still gently snoring beside her, she pushed the quilt back, slipped into her slippers, grabbed her robe from behind the bedroom door and crept downstairs to the kitchen. The clock on the cooker was the only light, illuminating the room with a grey hue. It read 3:35 AM— far too early to be getting up. Silently, she tested the kettle for water and then topped it up to make tea. While she waited for it to boil, she sank down in the soft chair in the corner of the kitchen, a chair that she often took her morning tea in when the sun was streaming through the windows. She clicked the lamp switch and it casted a warm, peachy glow. It was chilly at such an early hour, so she pulled her robe in even tighter around her, kicked her slippers off and tucked her legs underneath her while she waited. The kettle eventually clicked off and the noise from the boiling water receded, but Chrissy was in no rush to fill her mug. She sat for a moment longer, turning the pieces of the puzzle over and over in her head.

Maybe Julie was right.

Maybe something had happened to their father, something more sinister than just a regular heart attack.

No sooner had she had the thought than Chrissy dismissed it for being stupid. What evidence did she have? None. A spiteful letter, a couple of folks she didn't know turning up at a public funeral, and a cabinet full of diaries did not make for a murder investigation. Neither did a biscuit tin with photographs of young boys in. Yes, she thought, it was probably just the old spook in her taking over.

Once a spook always a spook.

And Dad had had a heart problem anyway.

Chrissy always saw the intrigue, the bigger picture, in what others would term normal circumstances, she admitted. In her mind, there was always a more sinister angle. That's what she'd been trained to do: use her inquisitive mind, read between the lines of a situation, as it were. So, what was she going to do about this, then, if anything? Well, she had to satisfy her own curiosity if nothing else.

But right now, she needed tea. She padded in bare feet over to the work surface and opened the metal tea box to find a sachet of 'relaxing sleep' tea. She plunked it into her cup and poured hot water onto it. There was no point going for regular breakfast tea at this hour; she didn't need the caffeine if she was ever going to go back to sleep. And she certainly wasn't planning to stay up at 3:35 AM. As she waited for the teabag to steep, she made a mental list of all the things she'd need to do. First on the list was the tin of faces. Who were those boys, and why had their photos been hidden in the tin?

Something, a feeling in her stomach maybe, had told her not to tell anyone, not even Adam, about her find that day; if it turned out to be nothing, there was no point in upsetting anybody else. No, until she had something concrete to go on, she'd keep it close to her own chest. She tossed the hot teabag into the recycle bin and added a splash of cold water to her mug. Then she made her way back to her comfy chair and tucked her feet up underneath her again, sipping on her warm drink. In another two hours, Adam would be up, ready for his morning jog, and she hoped she'd be back in bed and back to sleep long before then.

When Chrissy did awaken again, it was 4:45 AM and she wasn't back in her bed. She'd fallen asleep in the kitchen chair; her still-full mug of tea on the floor beside her. At least she hadn't spilled it before dropping off. Her neck was stiff from sleeping at a strange angle, and she massaged it, trying to soothe the ache.

Something had woken her, and it wasn't the light from the lamp in the kitchen. There was movement upstairs: she could hear footsteps, and they sounded heavier than those of her two boys.

And the boys aren't in anyway, so it isn't them.

Must be Adam, then.

Her brain felt muddled from interrupted sleep, and she turned groggily towards the door as the footsteps began heading down the staircase. Yes, it was definitely Adam. She ran her fingers through her hair and stood, then walked over to refill the kettle and make them both a morning cup of tea. The door opened, and Adam entered, his own robe tied loosely around his waist, pyjama legs protruding from the bottom. His feet were bare, his hair ruffled at odd angles.

"I wondered where you'd gone," said Adam, "I woke up and you weren't there." His voice sounded petulant, like a 10-year-old version of himself.

"I think I ate too late," she said lamely, going to him and wrapping her arms around him. "I woke at three thirty and came down to make some tea, but I fell asleep in the chair. I hope I didn't disturb you?"

He stroked her head. "No, I needed the loo, but when you weren't there, I thought I'd better investigate." He was smiling as he said it.

"Well, you can call the cops off. I'm safe and sound in the kitchen. Want some tea?"

"Love some, please." Adam took her place in the old comfy chair and rested his head back. "Did I have a lot to drink last night?" he asked

"No, you only had a pint. Feeling rough?"

"My head is banging, and my mouth feels terrible. Mouth as dry as a hamster's cage floor." Smiling, Chrissy handed a mug of tea over. She perched on the chair arm and raised the subject of her father again.

"Do think there was anything in that note that was sent to Dad? I mean, any truth in it?"

"Maybe. Though if they did have any ill intentions, there's no point doing anything now."

She watched him raise his mug to his lips and sip thoughtfully. Was he convincing himself? Or Chrissy?

"And his heart issue was no surprise," he went on. "Can't fake a cardiac arrest to order."

Dr. Livingstone now, are we?

Chrissy wasn't convinced. And having spent most the night regurgitating everything she knew so far, far-fetched or not, there was no way she was going to leave it to lie. As soon as Adam was out of the house, she would make a plan to find out more about what she'd discovered so far.

She hoped with all her heart it was all a big non-story.

Chapter Twenty

Adam was in no rush to go. It seemed an age until he finally left the house for work, leaving her in peace and quiet for the rest of the day. The boys wouldn't be back until around 4 PM. As soon as he'd gone, she made fresh coffee, grabbed a half packet of biscuits and headed to her office upstairs. Keeping the attic room to herself had seemed the most obvious thing to do, given her previous profession. Citing her own need for privacy, no one had batted an eyelid. Adam had his office downstairs; she had hers in the roof.

Who was that mad fictional woman who was kept in an attic?

Your hair isn't long and grey, Chrissy.

She fired up her Mac and went straight to Google. She watched the cursor flicking like a car indicator while she decided what she would put in the search box.

Where the hell do I start?

At the beginning.

Deciding her father's name was probably as good a place as any, she typed in *Gerald Baker*. There were thousands of search results, and she clicked on the first one. It was an article from the local newspaper about the death of her father and the huge turnout at the local church. There was a lovely photograph of him taken some years back, his hair far thicker than it had been in recent months. And less grey.

"Where did they dig that one up from?" she mused. Scanning the article, she realised there was little she didn't already know, so she closed the page and went back to the search results. She scanned down the list, although she had no clear idea what she was looking for. When nothing of note grabbed her, she clicked 'next' at the bottom and loaded another page of results. Halfway down the page a headline caught her eye. From the URL it looked like someone's blog. It read: *Robbing Peter to pay Paul? Modern Robin Hood or Plain Thief?*

She clicked on the link, and there was another photograph of her father, this one more recent. She scrolled through the text, scanning, looking again for something to catch her eye. A paragraph about halfway down leapt out at her, and she read, and then re-read, the words with disbelief. The author of the blog post was accusing Gerald Baker of stealing £80,000 from his wealthy cousin. A Ponzi scheme, the writer called it, though he had no proof.

Chrissy sat back in her chair and rested her fingertips on her chin in thought. It wasn't the first time she'd heard the word "Ponzi" in the same sentence as her late father's name. And that meant there would be more articles about it—about *him*—she realised dully, though they might not be posting online like this guy was. She scrolled back to the top and read the whole article. The writer was careful with his wording so as not to directly accuse her father, but the sentiment was there in plain sight. And it wasn't as if Gerald Baker was going to sue for defamation; nor was his estate.

Opening another browser window, she typed *Gerald Baker Ponzi* and hit search. Her heart sank. It seemed there were more than a few other disgruntled people voicing their opinions.

"Why have I not heard anything?" she said out loud. Then she remembered a throwaway comment she'd heard some nights ago while at Julie's house. Her mother had been sitting stoically on the sofa while they were about to organise her father's funeral arrangements and had said she didn't care what they decided—after what he'd done.

After what he'd done.

The letter.

And then the other letter.

She topped up her mug with fresh coffee from the cafetière and mulled it over. If her father had been running a Ponzi scheme, there would surely have been records kept; he'd have had to know who had invested what and when, and when returns were due.

And that in itself posed another problem: those people, whoever they all were, would want what was due to them whether Gerald was deceased or not. And that brought her on to another thought—his will.

It hadn't been mentioned as yet. She reached for her phone and called Julie. It went to voice mail.

Spa time.

She dialled her mother with the excuse of seeing how she was.

"Darling," her mother said by way of greeting, not sounding nearly as frail as she had been. Chrissy was relieved to hear she was still speaking to her and not holding a grudge. It was too soon after her father's death for quarrelling.

"Hi, Mum. Thought I'd see how you're faring. You sound a lot brighter."

"I feel it—thank you. Must be the sunshine."

"Well, I'm glad. Listen, I wondered if Dad had left a will? He was always so orderly with his paperwork, so I figured he did." The line went as silent as a monastery at night. "Are you there, Mum?" Chrissy enquired, thinking they might have been disconnected.

"I'm here. Why do you want to know? Hoping for something left to you or the boys?" There was a certain snideness in her mother's voice, and Chrissy picked up on it immediately.

"Good Lord, no. I was merely thinking about you not needing the hassle if he died intestate. I couldn't care less whether he left me, or any of us, anything." The words came out in a rush, but it was true. Chrissy and Adam had both been careful and proactive in investing the money they earned.

I certainly don't need it.

"Then why the enquiry? Why do you wish to know?" her mother said, her voice still strangely testy.

In for a penny, in for a pound ... "I was thinking back to that letter, actually. The threatening one that you say you received, or Dad received. I didn't want any further angst on your part, worrying whether someone was planning on suing his estate."

"I'd hardly call it an estate," her mother said.

"It's still classed as his estate, no matter how small." Chrissy knew her mother was being deliberately obtuse, but let it pass. The conversation would probably have gone better in person, but since it wasn't to be, Chrissy boxed on.

"So, have you had any other correspondence about Dad being a crook?"

Choice of words, Chrissy!

"He's not a crook!" her mother screamed into the phone, loudly enough that Chrissy pulled it away from her eardrum.

"Well?" asked Chrissy, putting the phone back to her ear and ignoring her mother's obvious agitation.

"It's none of your business." The phone line went dead; her mother had hung up, leaving Chrissy staring at a blank screen and wondering how she was going to broach the subject again.

How odd, she thought uneasily. She'd clearly struck a nerve.

Chapter Twenty-One

Chrissy sat back in her chair, nonplussed. That certainly hadn't been the reaction she'd expected from her mother. She hoped things weren't going to get messy. Her father had clearly been involved in something, and had owed money. What she needed to ascertain was exactly how much, and whether it was individual debt or had been loaned against the house, making her mother jointly liable for repayment. Even though Gerald Baker was dead.

The thought was ghastly, but real nonetheless—her mother could well be forced to sell and turfed out if there wasn't enough cash available.

Chrissy needed time to think. Glancing at the clock on her computer screen, she was startled to see that time had wandered off without her. It was almost lunchtime.

"I need some air," she said. She closed her computer down, gathered the remains of the cold coffee and took the tray down to the kitchen to load the items into the dishwasher. Her mind was on overdrive, and the caffeine she'd consumed was making it worse. She filled a glass with water and gulped it down in one go. It felt cool and cleansing on her insides, though she was conscious it was hitting an empty stomach. She opened the fridge and pulled out margarine, ham, lettuce and mayo, then took a couple of slices from the loaf in the bread bin and made herself a sandwich and carried it out on to the patio. The lunchtime sun was high in the sky and the temperature was about right—not too hot to get burned and warm enough to sit in and enjoy the pleasantness without getting all sweaty.

You sound like your sister.

No one sounds like Julie.

Chrissy didn't mind sweat and worked hard keeping her body in shape, though she preferred the tarmac and pavements to germ-ridden gyms. Julie did neither, apart from occasional treadmill walks; she preferred to eat like a gerbil instead.

She chose a spot on the edge of a low retaining wall, sitting directly on the cool paving stones, her legs out in front of her on the grassy lawn. It was always peaceful in her garden out the back, the only sounds being birds or the odd lawn mower. Occasionally, a light aircraft flew over, a four-seater type of affair; the owners could have been any of a number of her neighbours, who certainly had the finances to own their own wings for trips out on a sunny day.

In another week, Chrissy thought, she'd be on an airplane herself, though larger and a whole lot more comfortable, sitting in business class with her feet up, a glass of bubbles at her elbow. She'd be away from Adam for a whole week at 'the conference,' a break that couldn't have come at a better time. Her ticket was purchased and tucked away on her smartphone, and ahead of her lay seven days of Californian lifestyle—her favourite alternative to the leafy suburbs of Surrey.

A sparrow nipped in close to her, daring itself to peck the few crumbs that Chrissy had let drop, and she watched it for a moment before tearing a small part off her crust and tossing it close by. The sparrow swooped in, grabbed it and took it to the relative safety of the edge of a geranium plant spilling baby pink flowers over onto the path. In a couple of beaks-full, the bread was gone. It turned back to her, its tiny inquisitive face hoping for more. Chrissy obliged with one last piece and let the bird have its way. A couple more had gathered in the trees nearby, as they often did. How did they always seem to know something was on offer to one of their feathered friends nearby? Seagulls were the same—toss a piece of bread on the beach and you'd be nearly knocked over in the stampede to get to it before another gull nearby did. They always knew.

Next week, her early-morning runs would take her along the beach, on a round trip journey from Santa Monica Pier to Venice Beach. Chrissy loved a dip in the ocean at the end of it; it was the most perfect way to cool down, bar none. The whole LA lifestyle was the polar opposite of leafy Englefield Green and her role as wife and mother—and, she knew, one she should have given away long ago when she'd retired from her life as a spook. Why she'd chosen to keep the pretence up she didn't really know, but it was too late to change it now. And she enjoyed the time away, so why not keep it? She wasn't doing any harm. It wasn't like she had a complete second life, used a different name and had another husband or family tucked away secretly. It was only a house.

Well, two actually, Chrissy. A place in France, too—remember?

And that came down to wise investments early on in her career and earning large chunks of cash on delicate assignments long before she'd ever met Adam. To tell him now would mean uncovering far too many stories to fill in the gaps, and Chrissy wasn't prepared to assume he'd understand her previous lifestyle. Having kept it from him for so many years, she knew he would, understandably, be pissed at her. She knew she would be at him if it were the other way around.

But LA and all the extremes that came with it was a few days away yet. In leafy Englefield Green, the sun was glorious. She kicked off her sandals and wriggled herself down onto the lawn, removed her T-shirt and lay in the sun wearing nothing but her shorts.

"The vitamin D will do me good," she murmured happily, and closed her eyes.

Chapter Twenty-Two

A nearly twelve-hour flight away in the early waking and sunny climes of Abbot Kinney, Philip was already up and about, running shoes on his feet but struggling to dig up the motivation needed to actually go out and do it. The blonde woman between the cotton sheets was starting to stir and he was drawn to her slow, languid movements. The top sheet was caught on her foot, and it slipped down to her waist as she turned, revealing a young, bronzed body of bikini-model proportions. He'd no clue as to her name, nor she to his.

The mystery woman opened her eyes and smiled up at him sheepishly. His body responded in the only way a man's would. Philip reached out a hand and gently teased his fingertips down the tanned, inviting thigh.

"Good morning." He smiled at the creature who, in turn, broadened her smile in reply. "Want some juice, maybe?"

"Maybe," she said coyly. "But I've a better idea. Why don't you join me back under here?" she enquired, lifting the top sheet fully so her entire naked body was open to his gaze. It didn't take Philip long to decide. He kicked off his running shoes and almost leapt out of his shorts back into bed, thoughts of his morning run all gone.

"Not like you to be a mid-morning stroll-in," Alistair said to his friend when Philip finally arrived.

"I got waylaid."

Alistair raised his eyebrows in question.

"Hot, was she?" He didn't wait for an answer. Philip had all the luck with the women. "Don't answer that. Anyway, what gives?"

"My sanity, I think."

"Eh?"

"Never mind."

Philip dropped his bag on the floor in the small kitchen area, which was essentially their place to brew coffee and refill their mugs. A small fridge under the counter held a few beers and Carmen's daily salad lunch but nothing else of any note. But then, it really wasn't big enough for anything else. Philip rubbed his right temple as he waited for a fresh pot to finish brewing and opened the nearby drawer in search of an Advil. Or two. Perhaps he should have drunk more water last night. Or had his morning run properly, as per usual. He smiled to himself; he never did ask her name as she'd slipped out of his place not an hour since. He doubted he'd see her again, as was often the case.

Alistair was keen to get his full attention, tapping his fingertips on the table while he watched the coffee being prepared. When he was sure that Philip was on the same planet as he was, he asked, "What's on your mind? Besides whatever you got up to this morning, that is."

Philip turned around and looked at his friend square on. "I guess you've forgotten, then?"

"Well, obviously, if I'm asking." He was often cocky, though jovial with it.

Philip wasn't going to make it easy for him. "Well, what's today the anniversary of, then?"

Alistair was sitting silently and Philip figured he was probably searching the filing cabinets of his brain, looking for a plausible answer.

When it popped into his head and recognition registered on his face, he groaned. "Ah, shit. The first anniversary of Stuart's death. My bad."

"Yes, your bad. The twins will be about two now. Do you think I should give Jo a call, see how she's doing? Or will that only bring it all up again?"

"I think the first anniversary alone will be the thing that brings it all back up again, to be frank. She'd going to hurt for some years to come, I expect. But we should call her anyway, let her know we're thinking of the three of them." He reached for his phone to check the time. "We're eight hours behind them, so it's early evening there. Shall we call her together, now?"

Philip fell silent for a moment while he decided what he wanted to do. He had planned to call Jo himself a bit later on, in private, but if Alistair wanted to say hello too, then why not.

"May as well," he conceded and pulled up a chair around the tiny table. The office phone, on speakerphone, in the centre. The screen glowed while they both waited for it to connect and after a few seconds, Jo's voice could be heard loud and clear.

"Hi Alistair," she answered. The benefits of caller ID.

"Hi, Jo. I have Philip here with me too," he said by way of explanation. He waited while Philip said his hellos. For some reason, he waved at the screen, not that she could see either of them, but it was a habit, something he did regularly. Jo greeted Philip too, then another voice, a much younger one filled the room and both men smiled.

"And Ben says hello, too," Jo said, "though you'd not know that's what he said obviously. Jerry, is fast asleep, unlike his brother here." She and Stuart had named the twins after Jo's out-of-control craving for ice cream while she'd been pregnant, and the names had stuck. Probably later on in life, when they started school, they'd suffer the mocking for it. And on their wedding days. Thankfully, both were a long way off. Ben ranted off another line of two-year-old talk; if nothing else, it filled the space with joy rather than sorrow.

Finally, though, it was time to say what was on their minds.

"We wanted to say hello, and say we are thinking of you," Alistair said gravely.

"Thanks lads. Stuart would be glad to know that, as am I and the boys. Twenty-seventeen will always be remembered as the year of Stuart's death, nothing else. But we're slowly on the mend now, though it's taken all this long to finally resume some sort of normal life again. And I think the two little ones have helped me get through each day, to heal and come to terms with what he did that day. He made me cross for a while, though, leaving us, but then we never stayed angry for long; we didn't do that. So yes, we're getting there. Each day is a little easier."

"Well, we're both glad to hear it," Philip said, speaking for the two of them. Alistair nodded in agreement. "And our offer stands, as always: if you ever feel the need for a little extra sunshine, there's always a free spot at either of our places if you want to come for a trip out."

"Thanks. I appreciate it; really, I do. Maybe when the boys are bigger, though. I can't see me managing an airplane and two screaming two-year-olds and carry-on luggage for us all. Not yet, anyway."

Philip grimaced at the thought; no one enjoyed screaming children at the best of times, and, confined to a big tin can in the sky with a set of hollering toddlers, anyone could be forgiven for murder. It was an inappropriate thought, but true nonetheless.

Alistair wrapped the brief conversation up. "Well, love to the boys, and love to you, Jo. Take care, and shout if you need anything, eh?"

"I will, and thanks again."

The two men said "Goodbye" together, and the back room at Banks & Crowley fell silent as each became lost in their own thoughts.

At length, Alistair turned to Philip. "Jo was obviously trying to hide her pain, even twelve months later. It can't be easy."

"No, it can't be. But at least the man who forced Stuart's hand to suicide has gone too."

"And good riddance."

Chapter Twenty-Three

She'd only lain there for fifteen minutes, long enough to bring a couple of extra freckles out on her cheeks. There was no way she was going to fall asleep in the sun this time. She opened her eyes and squinted towards the sky. Even though the sun was slightly behind her head, the day was as bright as an LED bulb shining directly at her, and she waited for her sight to adjust slightly before sitting back up. With no whiskey bottle at her side, she felt somewhat fresher than she had after her last sunny garden experience. Plus, she hadn't actually napped. She picked up her mug of tea, which was now only lukewarm, and headed back inside, tipping the liquid into the geranium by the patio. There wasn't a drought around her part of the country, but Chrissy hated wasting anything.

The kitchen was cool and dim, and once again her eyes adjusted to the lower level of light indoors. She placed her mug in the dishwasher and carried on through the house and upstairs to her office in the attic. The house was almost silent, and she breathed it in like a type of meditation as she climbed up to her private domain.

Her desk was up against the one dormer window so she could look out onto the back garden. There were two skylights that bathed the room with ample light, and Chrissy reached for the pole near the door that she used to open them with. It was a tad stuffy and she needed the warm air to circulate out and let some fresh in. Satisfied they were both open enough, she took her seat at her desk and turned on her Mac, then logged in.

By now, the photos she'd taken back at her father's shed would have uploaded themselves to a file in the sky and would be available for her to access on her computer. She clicked on 'camera uploads' in her Dropbox account and scrolled to the last batch she'd taken, all automatically timestamped with the date and time they'd been added. She thought back to the originals and the date stamps printed on the back of each photo. Technology certainly had changed since then, she mused. Clicking on each of the seven images in turn, she resized them so they fitted onto the screen in front of her, all together in two rows. Then she sat back to study them further, as a whole. A cloud passed over her room, diminishing some of the light as she examined the faces in front of her.

When the cloud moved on, the room was once again bathed in sunshine. Seven young teenaged boys looked out at her from the screen, tight smiles on their faces, as though they disliked being in front of the camera. From her own school photo experience, she knew the pupils lined up for the photographer, walked one by one to a backdrop, smiled, and snap! They were done. Then the next pupil. And then the next. A student had only seconds to get their grin right before the flash of light sealed it. Then your mother barked at you when she saw the pictures the following week and was expected to buy the package. "Look at your hair!" she'd snap, or "Call that a smile?" She'd dutifully hand over the money, of course, then keep the picture in a drawer where no one could see it. That had been Chrissy's experience, anyway, and probably loads of other kids' too.

She leaned in closer, studying each of the boys in turn. All in shirt and tie. All the *same* tie.

"So, you were all at the same school then," she murmured. "And all in the same year, I'm assuming. But which school? Where were you all together?" Zooming in, she looked at the crest on the ties, but it wasn't familiar to her. She selected and cropped the crest from the clearest photo, saved it, then brought up a browser page and did a reverse image search.

"Bingo!" she cried. "Glendene School, Berkshire. Thank you, Mr. Google. So that's where you all attended. Or did you?" Since British schools had no yearbooks like schools in the US did, there was no point in looking for one. That would have made the next job easier—finding out who the boys were.

Selecting the first face from the top of her screen, she did another reverse image search via Google and waited for the page to load. "A bit before the internet, but what the hell? It's worth a try." No hits. Chrissy tried a second image and waited. Nothing either.

With the fourth image, however, she finally found something— the boy's name. It was a group photo at what looked like a rugby tournament with another school, and there, kneeling down in the front row, was ... she tapped her forefinger across the row of names ... Stuart Townsend.

"Hello, Stuart Townsend," Chrissy said. "Mind telling me who your buddies are, please?" She changed the auto-date-stamped image name to *Stuart Townsend* and repeated the process for the next boy. It would have been too easy had they all been on that one rugby team, of course, but the next image drew another blank. That left two more to find, and she crossed her fingers hopefully.

"Bingo again," she said, peering closely at the screen once more. The photo was blurry, but it was undoubtedly the mystery boy from her collection. Cody Taylor's unmistakable blond curls would have been the envy of many women. It was a picture of a fundraising event in the nearby town of Hungerford, not far from where Glendene School was located, which made her even more sure it was him, though the curls were enough on their own. She wondered what they looked like now—would they be more grey than blond?

"Welcome, Cody Taylor," she said, and gave his image the rightful name. "One more to go." Entering the picture of a dark-haired boy with a goofy smile, she held her breath in hope. When a page opened with another image of the boy, she almost yelped out loud at her luck.

Three of the seven boys now had names. This latest one, sporting a bright, proud smile, was a district athletic day champion, and the last boy in the tin.

His name was Philip Banks.

Chapter Twenty-Four

Three out of seven wasn't bad. It was a start, something to work with. Since Glendene School appeared to be the link between the boys, she looked up the school's website. When they boys had attended back in the eighties, the internet hadn't been even thought up then, so she wasn't expecting to find anything of use about any of them on the school's site. It was worth a look, though; miracles did happen. Like finding the first of the three boys online. Perhaps there was a history or timeline page that could be of use.

The photo of the school and grounds looked as majestic as the bigger country houses around her own home, Chrissy thought, secluded behind high wrought iron railings and tall, faded brick walls. The school building itself was vast and ancient-looking—Harry Potter would have been proud to have attended—though the annexes looked more modern. The whole of the main building was covered in green ivy. Chrissy thought of the spiders that would make the vine their home.

"I'd never open a window," she said, shuddering.

There was a page tab titled 'Past and Present,' and she clicked it. A handful of ancient portraits of famous alumni was displayed, but made no impression on her. She didn't move in academic circles. Had the names included Donald Maclean or Kim Philby, ex– British intelligence officers who had been part of the so-called 'Cambridge Five,' she might had been a little more impressed. They had moved more in her old circle.

There was nothing more of note on the school's website, so she closed the tab. The obvious thing to do next was go back to Google and see what she could learn about each of the three names that she did have.

"Let's start with you, then, Stuart," she said as she typed his name into the search bar and clicked. There were fourteen million results. How the hell was she going to figure out which one was the individual she sought? There had to be a way of narrowing it down.

"If Glendene School was in Berkshire, he must be from the UK," she said. She added *UK* to the search and clicked again. Down to six million results.

"Okay, Google, let's add 'Glendene' into the equation." A mere 14,200 results. But was her Stuart Townsend one of them? Stuart may have gone to Glendene School, but did he still live in Berkshire as an adult? More than likely not. And since Glendene was also a boarding school as well as a day school, the young man could have been from anywhere in the world. The thought didn't help her. Chrissy drummed her fingers on the desk while she pondered what to do next.

Out of sheer force of habit, she closed her eyes and repositioned herself mentally in a basement office where she'd worked for so many years.

You had more tools then, Chrissy.

What would her next move have been, back then when technology wasn't as it was now?

"You'd have picked the phone up and traced the headmaster, that's what you'd have done," she said to the empty room. She opened her eyes and brought the school's website back up, then searched for the staff and principals of past and present. She silently praised the school for having the list readily available. The names and dates listed went back to 1910 when the ivy-covered school had first been built. Scrolling down the list, she remarked to herself that the names all sounded like something from a Shakespearean novel, each one steeped in a family history all its own. Being a teacher or headmaster at such a school seemed a family tradition, given the many duplicate surnames: brothers, maybe, or fathers and sons. There were, of course, scant few female names.

Tradition, eh?

Women were still chained to the sink, remember?

Finally, she found what she was looking for: Frederick Browning, headmaster at the time the boys would have been pupils. Annoyingly, he'd retired some twenty years ago, and another headmaster was now running the school. Still, it was worth calling to see if the man was still alive. She dialled the number and waited. A receptionist answered in a bright and extremely high-pitched voice. Chrissy had to stop herself from spluttering with laughter. She had a friend who sounded identical to a donkey hee-hawing when she laughed, which invariably stopped nearby pub conversations dead. Awkward... She felt sorry for them both.

"Hi, Mrs. Livingstone here," she said, refocusing, keeping her voice direct yet still pleasant; best to stay on the right side of whoever she was about to deal with, but show some authority at the same time. "I'm doing a spot of research for an article in 'Horse & Hound' magazine," she went on, "and I wonder if you could tell me if Mr. Frederick Browning is still living locally, by chance?"

Horse & Hound Magazine *had worked for Hugh Grant in* Notting Hill, *right?*

Yeah, but this isn't the movies ....

The voice on the other end almost burst Chrissy's eardrum with a squeal of high-pitched, excited laughter.

"Oh, my favourite magazine, totally," she enthused. Chrissy hoped she wasn't going to ask her any pertinent questions in return, ones she couldn't answer confidently anyway.

"I'm so glad. Then you'll know all about what we do." Changing the subject back quickly, she asked, "So is Mr. Browning close by, then?" She waited.

"Yes, he is. He still lives here, actually, in a small cottage on the edge of the grounds. Is the story about him, then?"

"Kind of. Do you have a telephone number I can call him on?" She wasn't expecting the girl to hand it out to her, of course, but no matter: she now knew where the old man still lived. "It'll be so helpful if you do. I'm sure he'd love to be featured." She stayed silent, not filling the gap in conversation. When she heard a low exhale of breath, she knew she had her.

"You didn't get it from me, though, okay? I'll get in trouble." The perkiness in the young woman's voice had diminished a little, and Chrissy wondered if she spoke at such a high pitch all the time or if this, heaven forbid, was her 'telephone' voice.

"Not a problem. You've been extremely helpful. He's going to love this! And what is the number, please?"

Chrissy scribbled the digits down and thanked the high-pitched woman again for her time.

"Oh, before you go," the woman said. "He'll not be home now. Best leave it until about four p.m. He's a creature of habit."

Chrissy wondered what kind of habits the elderly man would have that kept him out until 4 PM each day, but declined to ask.

"I will, and thanks for your time." She hung up before the woman could ask any awkward questions. Rule number one: get out when you've got what you came in for.

Since it was only a little before 3 PM, there was no point calling Browning now, so she put the number to one side. On second thought, she reasoned, maybe paying the old man a visit in person would be more fruitful than a telephone call. Sure, it would be easier to chat over the phone and ask him if he remembered any of the three boys, the ones she had names for, but if she drove out to his place, maybe she could show him the photos and he could throw some light on the remaining four at the same time. Yes, she thought resolutely, a drive out to his cottage seemed the sensible thing to do. She hoped this Frederick Browning would be receptive to her.

In another hour or so, she'd make the call and find out. With any luck, he could give her a few more answers.

Chapter Twenty-Five

Four PM came and went. Adam had skipped his weekly squash game and arrived home earlier than he usually did, opting instead for a cold beer and some catch-up work in his own study. After making sure he was occupied for a while and the boys were playing kick-about along with a neighbour's son, Chrissy finally climbed the stairs back up to her attic room and stared at the telephone number on the desk in front of her.

"Are you sure you want to start digging up the past? Because once you've got their names, you'll be like a dog with a full packet of biscuits. Things could get messy," she warned herself. "Dad kept the pictures hidden for a reason." She looked up through the skylight for the answer, though it gave her only gathering slate-grey clouds; rain was on its way. She dialled the number and waited to be connected. Eventually, as she was about to hang up, he answered.

Must be slow on his feet

He's probably ancient, remember?

Frederick Browning had a gravelly voice; he sounded almost decrepit as he tried to speak. As he cleared his throat down her eardrum, she winced.

"Hello, is that Mr. Browning?" She had to be sure it was him, of course.

"Yes? Who's calling?"

"My name is Chrissy, and I'm doing a story for a magazine. I wondered if I might take a drive out sometime tomorrow and have a chat to you about the school some years back, and a couple of your ex-pupils. A kind of 'then and now' feature, as it were."

Liar, liar, pants on fire.

"Oh? What sort of story is it?" Talking caused him to gasp for oxygen; the simple act of breathing sounded like hard work for the old man.

"More local interest, really. A look at the school over the years. I'm also trying to trace a couple of the boys, and since you were their headmaster back in the late eighties, you'd be a good place to start. Would you be free to chat? Maybe I could buy you lunch, at a pub perhaps?" She heard a sort of chuckle as he spoke again. He seemed to like that idea. She wondered if he'd survive the first pint.

"Yes, that would be nice, though come to my cottage first. No sense in us both driving." Chrissy smiled at the man's cheek; it was fair exchange, though. She couldn't image the old boy in control of a vehicle if his frailty over the phone was anything to go by. The roads would be safer without him on them. He gave her his address, and she promised to be there for twelve noon the following day. If he was still on this earth. It was only an hour away in the car, a drive down the M4 from Slough, so not particularly scenic, though functional. Still, it was easier than the train; the old headmaster's cottage wasn't going to be anywhere near a station.

So far so good. Chrissy hung up, satisfied she'd made the right decision to go. After all, what harm could it possibly do?

Frederick Browning had an inkling what the woman was going to be interested in; he wasn't stupid. Retrieving his walking stick from the side of his chair, he pressed a button on the control panel for the chair to raise him forward to a standing position and steadied himself on the cane. It took him several slow steps to reach the window, where he stood looking outside at the world and focusing on nothing in particular. Common birds flitted in and out of the garden; brightly coloured bedding plants moved gently with a light breeze. Only two things had happened in the late eighties that the woman would want to talk about.

And they had both happened on the same godawful day, the day the town of Hungerford had become famous for all the wrong reasons.

First, sixteen people had lost their lives when Britain's first mass shooting had happened, and about the same number were badly injured. The gunman had even shot his own mother, once in the leg to slow her down, then two more bullets into her back for good measure. The man had been found later, holed up in a school, his own bullet in his skull, from his own hand. The incident had rocked not only the town but the whole nation, and changed Britain's gun laws forever. It had been a dark day indeed.

But he suspected Chrissy would already know that story; it was part of the town's dreadful history now. No, if she wanted to know more about ex-pupils of his, that meant she had just one story on her mind. And he didn't relish bringing that topic back up either. He coughed a little, his emphysema sending his lungs into a spasm of helpless hacking as he struggled to breathe and control himself. He knew he was getting worse, that soon enough he'd be relying on a canister and mask for air, but he'd pushed back against, it deciding he'd rather have some quality of life before he finally went into his coffin. Sitting with a mask on all day was not an idea he relished; he still had so much to do before then. He coughed into his handkerchief and waited until he was able to move again safely, without falling over, before returning to his chair.

The coughing left him exhausted. Maybe he didn't have as much time as he thought he might. Maybe the woman calling tomorrow should be told the truth of what had happened that day. Frederick closed his eyes and rested for a while, his head drooping forward, deep in thought. Would it do any good now, to tell the story? Who

would it serve—would it merely be a way to ease his own
conscience? Or would it open old wounds and cause distress all over
again? Those affected had carried on with their lives, surely, and had
gotten through okay and moved on. Was there any point, he
wondered, if it only served his own selfish needs? He'd be gone
himself soon enough; maybe the events of that day, the secrets,
should go into the ground with him, alongside his brittle old body.

He'd sleep on it. And decide what he'd do when he met this
Chrissy Livingstone person for lunch the following day.

Chapter Twenty-Six

She'd tossed and turned for a good portion of the night, again. But instead of getting up and making tea, she lay in bed, stared at the ceiling in the pale glow from the moon, and listened to Adam's steady breathing. She was glad he wasn't a regular snorer, but there was plenty of time for him to develop the habit. What would they both be like when they got old?

The sound of the old headmaster's straining voice echoed in her head. Maybe he was ill, dying even; it sounded like breathing was hard work for him, and she prayed that serious illness kept away from her own family's door. The clock glowed a green 4.34 AM; it was over an hour since she'd first awoken and still at least an hour until Adam rose. But Chrissy was bored, and she knew sleep would never return before breakfast.

She slipped noiselessly out from under the sheets and crept around the room to grab her robe, then padded silently downstairs on her bare toes. The house was morgue quiet, and as cool as one at such an early hour. The only light was from the distant moon as she passed through the house towards the kitchen, her chair and the kettle.

Déjà vu, eh?

An hour later than last time, though.

She found chamomile tea in the cupboard and made herself a cup. There was no movement overhead, no footsteps padding around; she'd obviously been quiet as a mouse and was glad she hadn't disturbed Adam or the boys. She took her mug and sitting back in her chair, rested her head back and closed her eyes briefly. Later on today, she would meet with the old headmaster and possibly learn what had gone on back then, why her father had kept a tin of photographs from such a long time ago. It wasn't normal.

The chamomile did the trick in relaxing her mind; not fifteen minutes later, Chrissy fell sound asleep in her favourite chair in the corner with her feet curled up underneath her. It was only when Adam came down after his alarm had gone off that she awoke. Dawn was breaking nicely outside, sending an eerie pink glow throughout the kitchen as the sun stretched itself and awakened. In the distance, light filtered between houses on parallel streets, seeming to caress each building as it squeezed between them.

She felt Adam before she heard him. The light touch of his fingertips on her bare knees startled her, but as soon as she realised who it was, she relaxed and smiled up sheepishly.

"You seem to be making a habit of this. Are you feeling okay?" Adam asked.

Chrissy rubbed her eyes like a tired child and smiled up at him.

"Seems like it, doesn't it?" she said. "But no. I just couldn't sleep again. My head seems to be full of garbage for some reason, useless stuff floating around and taking up space. Maybe I should start drinking chamomile *before* I go to bed rather than when I wake up. Or maybe it's the hormones; I'm getting old, after all."

She stood awkwardly; her legs were numb with pins and needles from sitting on them. The circulation slowly returned as she hobbled across to the kettle. Without asking, she placed a teabag in a mug for Adam and another for herself and waited.

"What have you got planned today?" he asked as he seated himself at the breakfast bar.

"I've got work to do in my office, and then I'm going to see a man about a dog, actually," she said. It wasn't far from the truth, and it would do for now.

"And what about you?" she said, changing the subject swiftly. "What does your day hold?"

"Same old same old, though I won't be late home. Fancy going out again tonight?" he said, winking. "Shall we get rid of the boys?"

He gave her another wink, and Chrissy giggled. She turned her back to him as she poured the water on their teabags, thinking about her secret rendezvous with a man who could be her great-grandfather's age by the sound of him.

"I have a better idea—why don't I cook us something nice, something we haven't had for ages, and maybe we'll go for a walk after dinner? Are you up for that? It would be nice to spend a bit more quality time with you before I leave."

"Ah, I'd forgotten you're away soon. Bummer. Where is it this time, again?"

"Santa Monica, so at least it's not a great long plane journey. Why don't you come with me and hang out? The beach would be great; you could do with the break." She knew he never would, which was why she was asking him in the first place. Taking time off work at short notice was never an option in his game. He was never tempted to play hooky.

"I would if I could, but it wouldn't be much fun waiting on my own for you all day. Though I'm sure the babes on the beach would keep me distracted." He winked at her again. "Or I could bird watch, perhaps."

"You must have something in your eye," she chided him. "Anyway, it's only a week. Could be worse."

Chrissy would have liked to be away longer, but with everything that had gone on recently, including her father's death, she felt one week would have to suffice this time. No doubt she'd squeeze in another week away later on in the year. And then another.

"Right," said Chrissy decidedly. "I'm going up for a shower while you drink your tea. I've got a stack of things to do before I head out."

Adam didn't reply; he had his head firmly in his phone, distracted with something. Maybe it was work; maybe it was play. She didn't know. She picked her mug up and left him to his own world while she headed off upstairs to get ready. In reality she had all morning to kill, but didn't want to face any further questions.

She had plenty of her own.

Chapter Twenty-Seven

The drive was uneventful. It had taken her a little over an hour, though she'd allowed more so she could stop for a coffee in Hungerford beforehand. She wanted to drive around, have a look at some of the surrounding area to familiarise herself; it felt like the right thing to do.

Hungerford was an historic market town, though there was no market on today. It was also infamous, she knew, for the mass shooting that had occurred there in 1987. When she'd first realised she was going to Hungerford, an eerie chill had crept down her spine. She'd heard the stories and, later, read the headlines, though she was too young to remember them herself. England wasn't used to having mass shootings, and she doubted the town's name would ever be spoken without causing chills and uneasiness.

The address the headmaster had given her was actually in a village called Inkpen, a little outside of Hungerford; its name seemed apt given the man's vocation. And so, filled with coffee, she set off towards Inkpen. Most of the surrounding land was cultivated fields, some empty and brown; some green with freshly planted crops—she had no idea what. There was also scattered woodland that had once been part of the Savernake forest. She drove on to the tiny village centre—if you blinked too quickly, she mused, you'd miss it. She cruised slowly past an antique church. The sign out front read St. Michael's, and the date plaque informed her it had been built in the thirteenth century, though she thought parts of it looked newer; probably additions over the years, she guessed.

The village had an Iron Age or even Stone Age feel about it; maybe the Romans had even settled here at one time. Chrissy didn't know for sure, but she was aware that she was driving through deepest rural England: Stonehenge itself was only up the road as the crow flies.

The lanes were quiet; there was not a lot of late morning traffic, not a lot of traffic in general. There were plenty of birds about, though, and Chrissy rolled her window down to hear their cheerful, busy little songs; it was a busy day for feathered travellers. Driving slowly, Chrissy took the opportunity for a good snoop around. She passed the village hall, with its crumbly faded red brick; the old post office already permanently closed, as was one of the only two pubs. That left the one focal point of the village, besides St. Michaels, of course: The Crown & Garter, which was obviously where she and Mr. Browning would be heading later for an early lunch.

Sun umbrellas sat on the patio outside, shading the traditional faded wooden tables and chairs. A few terracotta pots filled with plants sat nearby. Its exterior was faded red brick, though lovingly restored to 'shabby chic.' There was a neatly mown lawn out front, perfect for cyclists and ramblers alike. Smiling, Chrissy suspected the menu would be more than pie and chips: the place practically screamed 'Modern fayre! Come and try something a little bit out of the ordinary.' Chicken livers, she expected, along with trendy and unusual boutique brewery beers. All in all, it looked a lovely place to share lunch with someone. Perhaps she'd bring Adam one day.

She parked up in the small car park and sat for a moment, taking in the peace and quiet. Even when she'd opened her door to let the warm fresh air circulate around her, there was only the sound of birdsong and the faint murmur of human voices in the distance, coming from inside the pub itself. She spotted a few early customers on foot, as well as staff getting ready for a full day ahead. Another car pulled into the car park, loose chippings crunching as it came to a standstill and parked under a nearby tree. A man in his thirties got out; he retrieved his briefcase from the back seat, walked purposefully towards the front door and slipped inside. A rep, Chrissy surmised from his formal dress, maybe from a brewery or a food supplier. There would be few formal business meetings planned all this way out, she knew; Hungerford itself would have been a more likely place for those, as it was closer to the motorway for easy access.

Her phone clock read 11.30 AM. She had thirty minutes to travel maybe a kilometre, so she had time to kill.

The photos were still on her phone, though she'd printed a copy out to show the old man. She'd written the three names she already knew under each photo in blue pen: Stuart Townsend, Cody Taylor and Philip Banks.

"I'm hoping to find the rest of your names. And even better, I'm hoping to find out what you might be doing now, so I can trace you all properly," she said to the empty car. A nearby blackbird heard her and tweeted a birdsong reply. She wondered if maybe she should nip into the pub now, before her meeting, and see if anyone in there might recognise the boys' faces; perhaps they were still living locally. She rejected the idea, since she had seen only one person entering the pub; it was much too early yet. No, she'd see what Frederick Browning had to say first; he'd agreed to meet her, after all. The car was getting warm as the sun climbed in the sky.

"Sod, it," she said and started the engine. "I may as well drive round." She checked the address again, followed the map app's instructions, and found herself outside a small cottage a minute or two later. The little house sported leaded windows with tiny triangles of glass; she imagined him peering through them as she arrived

—if he'd heard her, of course. Not bothering to lock her door, she slowly wandered up his front path and admired his garden. He must have been watching.

The door opened before she'd reached the front porch.

Chapter Twenty-Eight

Frederick Browning stood unsteadily in his doorway, his stick at his side. He was obviously infirm, Chrissy noted, and he appeared to shake slightly, like a flower in a light breeze. Parkinson's disease, maybe. He coughed as she approached, as if to confirm his frailty.

"Good morning, Mr Browning," Chrissy shouted heartily as she reached the door.

"And good morning to you, though there is no need to shout. I might be old, but I'm not deaf."

He smiled to signal that he wasn't offended and Chrissy matched it with one of her own. She held a hand out to shake, and Frederick Browning took it. While his skin was paper thin like her own mother's, he had far more sunspots, those telltale brown circular marks on the back of his hand, than she had, most likely from years outdoors in the garden. He had a surprisingly strong handshake, though his bony fingers were barely covered with flesh. It was like shaking hands with a warm skeleton.

His eyes, in contrast, were more than alive, crystal clear in fact, and she sensed he was as bright as a button up top. While his skin might be worn with his years, his brain no doubt was not.

"You're early. I like that," he said. "It gives us time to chat. Since it's such a beautiful day, we should sit outside at the pub. There is usually a spare umbrella at lunchtime." He paused for breath but with a kind of stammer to fill the space. "It's not as crowded at this time of day, but it will be tonight. Everyone turns out from the city, looking for somewhere nice to sit and drink a pint." Chrissy waited for him to finish his sentence so she could agree but he joined it straight up to another one, even though it seemed a struggle to speak. "It's been good business for the village, and sunny days like these can be a goldmine for the owners." Then he instantly changed the subject. "Shall we go?" he said, wheezing slightly. Chrissy forgot about trying to get a word in; maybe he didn't receive many visitors to talk to. He held out his arm for Chrissy to take, though of course, given his age, it would be Chrissy supporting him. In another time his chivalry would have been commonplace, but today their roles were reversed.

He pulled the door closed with his other arm and the lock clicked almost silently behind them. Chrissy assumed he already had his door keys in his pocket; she didn't fancy breaking in through one of the small lead windows to get the old man back inside. Slowly, they made their way down to her car. Chrissy opened the passenger side for him, waiting patiently while he supported himself on the car rim. He finally got in and made himself comfortable. It was hot already inside the car, even with the windows open a little. She climbed in on the other side and waited until he'd secured his seatbelt.

"I gather we're going to the Crown and Garter?"

"You've been doing your homework, young lady," he said breathlessly, and she caught the twinkle in his eye.

"I must've been a detective in a previous life," she said. "I like to know where I'm going, and since it's a small village it didn't take me long to find my bearings."

"There used to be two pubs," he said," but the village isn't big enough to sustain two anymore, which is a shame really. But business is business."

Browning was already out of breath again, as he had been

yesterday on the telephone. She could still hear that slight wheeze, which sounded painful. Conscious that it was hard for him to breathe and talk at the same time, she decided to save her questions until they were at the pub.

Loose chippings crunched under her own tyres for a second time in the pub's car park, and she noticed that the assumed sales rep's car was absent from its previous spot under the tree. She pulled up close to the door, quickly unhooked herself and hurried around to the passenger side door to open it for her guest. With trembling hands, Browning unhooked his own seatbelt and she put a supporting arm out for him to hold on to, helping him out with a slight pull. Once he stood on the gravel, she leant back in and gathered his cane. Then, with him as the pace setter, she followed quietly and steadily indoors.

If he came here every day as part of his routine, she mused, god only knew how he drove himself each day. Perhaps he didn't, though; perhaps he used a driving service? It would make more sense.

Once inside, Browning headed to a quiet corner, even though he had previously suggested dining outside. Maybe his short-term memory wasn't what it used to be; Chrissy hoped his long-term memory was in better shape. After all, that's why she was there. When he was seated, she enquired what he would like to drink.

"I'll have half a mild .... and a whiskey chaser if I may, please."

It wasn't really a question. Chrissy smiled and walked over to the bar to place their order. The lunchtime menus were stacked in a neat pile, and she picked two up before ordering their drinks. She ordered a white wine spritzer for herself, as she was driving. The man behind the bar said he would bring the drinks over and take their order then. He seemed pleasant enough, and Chrissy quite rightly suspected that he was the owner; he had the starting of a beer gut around his middle. Chrissy thanked him and walked back to their table.

"He'll bring them over," she said, and handed the old man a menu. From the inside of his tweed jacket pocket he produced a pair of half-moon reading glasses and propped them on the end of his nose. He reminded her of Richard, Julie's husband, peering over the top of his spectacles like a schoolteacher. At least the man in front of her had a legitimate excuse—he was both a schoolteacher and old.

He closed his menu and looked straight at Chrissy.

"I can highly recommend the pork pie and salad, though it's not on the menu. I have it almost every day. I guess you'd call me a creature of habit," he wheezed. "I've had about eighty-odd years to perfect my habits, and in my time of life, I don't care about the cholesteryl content. I figure the salad balances it out."

Chrissy smiled; no doubt she'd be the same when she got into her eighties. Although she hoped she wouldn't be suffering like the man in front of her was.

"Then I'll have the same," she said as the barman brought over their drinks. Chrissy placed the food order for them both and the man left, and then it was time to move on to the business that had brought her here. She wasn't entirely sure where to start the conversation, but she felt it would be impolite to start with pleasantries. It seemed false somehow, chatting about the weather. She needn't have worried, though, because the old man took the decision out of her hands.

"So, you said you wanted to talk to me about some pupils from the late eighties."

Inwardly she sighed with relief. She imagined he'd been just as businesslike as a headmaster, before taking the cane to some unruly child's backside. Swiftly. Get it over with. She bent to her bag and pulled out the printout of the boys' photos and slid it in front of the old man. She waited, wondering if he'd say anything else before she probed. He didn't. But she watched his face like a hawk would watch a mouse. The signs of recognition were there if you knew where to look. And Chrissy did.

Frederick Browning's worst fears had come true. He'd kept these images out of his mind for nearly 30 years, and yet here they were, flat out in front of his face with a stranger asking questions. He'd told himself the previous night that if it was about the incident, he wouldn't tell her; he wouldn't resurrect the hurt and the angst it would cause to those involved all over again.

Whatever the woman's motive was, as nice as she might seem, he'd decided not to tell, to keep the secret a while longer. But seeing the pictures again in front of him unearthed something deep down, and he was once again unsure of what to do.

All he could do was let out a sigh and pretend to be thinking.

Which he was. But his eyes welled up, giving his sadness away.

Chapter Twenty-Nine

The old man's reaction wasn't lost on Chrissy. She was silent, giving him time to collect himself. The old man's breathing sounded even more shallow, but still she waited patiently.

She was interested in what he had to say. As the headmaster of the school there was no reason why he wouldn't know the boys. The question burning in Chrissy's mind, was what was so significant about these boys, why were all their pictures hidden away in the tin? And why was he crying?

"I'm sorry," she said reaching a hand out to cover his. Thick blue veins were visible through his papery skin. He felt warm. "I don't mean to upset you."

He wiped a tear away and smiled weakly. "Thank you. I'm fine."

Their food arrived and the old man seemed thankful for the interruption; he picked up his utensils and tucked in.

But after a long moment, she couldn't contain the urge to say something, she couldn't wait any longer. Carefully, she raised the subject again, this time in a more soothing tone. The last thing she wanted was to upset him again.

"Since you were the headmaster when these boys were at

school, you obviously know who they are, I mean, I expect you knew each of the boys at the school?"

"I remember their faces well," he conceded. He didn't elaborate any further, which was frustrating, but Chrissy tried her best not to show it. The old man was quick to recover himself, and picked up his knife and fork as if pretending that they were doing nothing other than having a friendly lunch together and had not seen the photographs in front of them. Chrissy, on the other hand, ignored her meal and pointed slowly to the first picture, on the top left-hand side of the page, tapping her finger gently at it.

"I think I have three of the boys' names already. I've written them under the photos, as you can see. Can you confirm if I'm right so far?" Chrissy was pointing to one she knew—Stuart Townsend. "Can you confirm this is Stuart?"

The old man put his knife and fork down and chewed thought-fully but still didn't say anything. What was going on in his head? she wondered. Why was he not forthcoming? It was an age before he spoke again.

"Yes, that's Stuart." He glanced at the other names. "And yes, that's Cody and that's Philip. You've got those correct. It's a long time ago now. My brain is a bit rusty, but seeing their names—yes, I remember them."

"So how about this one?" Chrissy pointed to the second image, one of the ones with no name underneath. "Can you remember his name?" The old man simply stared, didn't say a word, though he did look like he was concentrating. Chrissy pressed on. "Or how about this one here?" She indicated the photo of a boy with short ginger hair.

"Like I said, my mind is a bit rusty; it's been a long time. But they do look familiar." Another silent interval as he caught his breath and organised his words. "Give me a minute; I'm sure I can figure something out. See if I can remember something. Do you have even a first name to go on? That might help."

"Nothing at all at the moment," she said. "What I've found out so far, I managed to get from Google, but as you've said, it was a long time ago, and there wasn't any internet back in the eighties." She smiled, trying to break the tension. She picked her own knife and fork up and cut into her pie. Taking a small mouthful, she chewed thoughtfully, though what she was doing was giving the headmaster some more breathing space.

The old man picked the paper up and held it closer to his face, as if doing so would stimulate his brain to recover memories from a long time ago.

"Robert," he said suddenly. "Robert something. Yes, I'm pretty sure he's called Robert." His gnarly finger moved along to another photo with no name under it. "Stephen—Steve, I think he was called. Yes, that's right. Steve. Steve Marks, from memory."

Chrissy took out her pen out of her bag and hurriedly scribbled the names underneath the images; she hoped that seeing their names there would spur him on to remember the surname of the boy with the ginger hair. There were two more names to be found now, two more photographs that she had nothing on. She picked her knife and fork back up and carried on eating again, to give the old man more time. At last he made an "aha" sound; it seemed to be working.

"I think this one is called Alistair," he said, though sounding slightly unsure. "He was American, and so was this other fellow," he said, pointing back to Philip Banks's picture. "I don't recall why they were both in the country, but they were American. They were quite pally, so if you've already found Philip Banks he might remember more about Alistair."

Chrissy wrote 'American' under both photographs; at least it was something to add into another Google search later. But still there was one missing. Chrissy once again pointed to the last photograph and said, "What can you remember about this young man?" Once more, she resumed eating though she really wasn't that hungry. She noticed the old man had barely touched his food at all, nor sipped at his half pint. Again, it was tempting to fill the empty space with more questions but Chrissy resisted. Finally, the old man came up with a morsel of the boy's name.

"Moore, with an E on the end," he said. "That was his surname."

"Would there be a listing back at the school so I could get his first name? I'm guessing they were all in the same year, maybe the same class?"

"The same year from memory, yes, but the same class? I couldn't tell you. May I ask why you want the names of these boys?"

It was a question Chrissy had been expecting, and she had the answer ready, though not entirely a truthful one. She noticed he'd avoided her question about a class list back at the school.

Maybe the receptionist can help you with that.

The squeaky woman?

Yep.

"I'm writing a story about another boy from back then. I believe these boys were his friends, and I figured I could talk to them and get more background for my article." The old man's clear eyes latched on to Chrissy's, and she could see him trying to read her face, perhaps not trusting exactly what she was saying. He had good reason; it was all a pack of lies.

"Oh? Who is the other boy? I might be able to help there."

"His name is Richard Stokes," she said, quoting her brother-in-law's name and knowing full well the old man would not remember him. Why would he? Richard had never gone to Glendene School, but it fitted her story; he would be about the same age.

The old man scratched what bits of thinning white hair he had left, looking perplexed, and said, "I don't recall the name. Was he in the same year?"

"I believe so, but I'm not entirely sure myself."

"What is the story that you're writing. What is it about?"

Chrissy had that covered too. "Richard is quite a whiz at investment banking and I'm doing a story about what type of person it takes to be so successful in the industry. Nothing more than that, really," she said brightly hoping to relax the old man away from thinking it was something more sinister. Which, of course, it was. In her mind, at any rate. But having watched the old man's reaction to the photos, she was now certain there was much more to it, that something, well, *sinister*, had gone on back then.

He seemed to relax a little and resumed eating his meal. Chrissy changed the subject, hoping to put him further at ease. They chatted about mundane subjects such as the weather and how long he'd lived in the area and how he filled his day: safe topics, stress-free topics. After an hour or so Chrissy ordered coffee for them both and tried one last time for answers to her questions. It was time she was leaving.

"So," she said "have you thought any more about the names of these boys? It would be really helpful if I could find out who they are." She slowly slipped the sheet of paper back in front of his nose and was quiet while she let the old man pore over it. She watched his face for the slightest movement, the slightest twitch, anything at all that would give the game away, tell her that he knew who the boys really were.

"Samuel," he said with certainty. "That's the boy. Samuel Moore —yes. Samuel Moore. Sam for short."

Chrissy wrote it down under the relevant picture and sat back. She had almost all the information she needed now. It was almost like filling in a crossword puzzle, though there were still a few gaps and very little in the way of clues.

Browning also sat back in his chair, with a look on his face that said 'That's all you're getting.'

Chrissy picked up on it and wisely left it there. Time to go.

"I have to thank you, Mr Browning. Thank you for agreeing to see me and thank you for being so helpful. It's been an absolute pleasure." She smiled her brightest smile and his face crinkled as he smiled back, and nodded gracefully, though his eyes didn't twinkle quite the same as they had when she'd first arrived. Chrissy knew there was more to the story; probably a lot more.

"I should get you home, or would you like me to leave you here? I don't want to interrupt your routine," she said, smiling. He looked a little sad, she thought, but she waited for a reply nonetheless. She wasn't surprised at his answer.

"I think I'll stay here a while. I can get a lift home later; it's not far. It was nice talking to you."

Chrissy stood and shook the old man's hand, thanked him again, and went to the bar to pay the bill. She doubted he'd meant the last bit. Before she left, she turned back in his direction to wave, but he wasn't looking her way.

He had his head bowed, and she could have sworn his eyes were closed.

She doubted he was asleep.

Chapter Thirty

Chrissy was sitting in her hot car with the door open, the lunchtime sunshine streaming in. She didn't start the engine. Not yet. She spent the time regurgitating what she'd learned so far in her experience with the old headmaster. It was obvious to her that he knew an awful lot more than he was letting on. Yes, he was old; she felt sorry for his health issues, and so had resisted probing further, pushing the old man into telling the truth. She wasn't an agent in the field now, after all; she wasn't a detective either, of course, but she was a woman on a mission. And she was now more motivated than ever to find out about the boys in the tin, and vowed not to stop until she got to the bottom of it.

She'd got most of the names, and two of them were American. though she wasn't sure why that was relevant to anything at this stage. Her thoughts immediately sprang forward to her upcoming trip to the US. Depending on where the boys, now adults, resided in the US, she might be able to look them up and pay one or both a visit.

She secured her seatbelt, closed the door and started the engine. The tires crunched on the loose chips as she left the car park. Pulling out into the quiet country lane, she headed back through

Inkpen and on to Hungerford, regurgitating the discussion she'd just had and trying to piece things together. By the time she was back over the river and the railway lines and onto the M4 towards home, she was feeling pleased with her morning's achievements.

While she drove, she debated whether to mention it to Julie at all. While they were sisters and as close as siblings could be, they didn't share the same interests. Chrissy doubted Julie would be the slightest bit interested; she didn't have the same inquisitive mind. But for some reason, Chrissy yearned to talk to her sister. It concerned their father, after all. Her thoughts drifted to his diaries. Did they play a part in all this?

She asked Siri to call Julie, and a moment later her sister's voice filled the car.

"Darling Chrissy," she exclaimed in her high-pitched, welcoming voice. Julie had never used to be snobby but when she'd started dating Richard, she'd decided to fit into the pantomime of wannabe celebrity status; she'd fit right in on a reality housewife TV show. Chrissy found it false, but there was no point in saying anything; as long as Julie was happy, that's all that mattered. Each to their own.

"Hey, sis. What are you up to?"

"Not a lot. How about you? You sound like you're in the car. Where are you?"

Chrissy debated whether to tell her exact location and decided to go with generic. "Just headed home, actually. Thought I might drive over if it's convenient? Richard's still at work, I'm assuming?"

"Don't be like that," Julie said. "Richard is all right. You should get to know him better." There was a pause, then Julie carried on. "Yes, come on over, and yes, Richard is still at work."

Chrissy could only do with Richard in tiny doses, like cough medicine. He bored her senseless. "I am about an hour away so I'll see you then."

"I'll be here. Is it a social visit, or did you want something in particular?" Julie asked.

Chrissy once again debated how much to tell her sister and decided to keep quiet, for now anyway. "I just thought I would pop in and see how my favourite sister was doing—and yes, I know you're my only sister. Anyway, like I said, I'll be there in about an hour. Talk to you then."

Chrissy disconnected via a button on the steering wheel, probably a wee bit abruptly, and carried on concentrating on the drive back towards Julie's place. While she was itching to get back to her office and look up the names she'd been given, she wanted to ask Julie about the diaries they'd found, to find out if her mother had mentioned them further. Their mother was closer to Julie than Chrissy was. She may well have confided in her, and since Julie wouldn't know to put two and two together, she wouldn't think anything of it. If their mother hadn't mentioned the diaries again, though, Chrissy would have to somehow get back into her father's study and take another look for herself at the year in question. That might net her some answers for her many unanswered questions.

Assuming the faces in the tin had been put there by her father, of course.

Back in the Crown and Garter, Fredrick Browning was sitting all alone with his eyes closed. He wasn't asleep, but he was deep in thought. He had been somewhat surprised that the woman had the photos; she'd been busy, he thought. And it was clear, going by the names that she had hadn't got, how little she knew. And for small mercies he was grateful. He'd kept his own side of the bargain that he'd made with himself last night and not told her about the events that had happened that day. She quite clearly didn't know about them anyway, although she was clearly fishing. But he wasn't going to be helpful by supplying the missing details for her. Seeing those boys' faces again, all together in front of him, had nearly stopped his heart.

They hadn't been strong enough at the time. They had been young, only fifteen years old, and death leaves its impression on everyone differently. He knew what the boys' names were; of course he did. He'd helped in the healing process. And he'd followed their progress through life. And, for some of them, their own deaths.

He knew this Chrissy person wasn't writing an article about Richard Stokes, whoever Richard was. It was all a ruse, a ruse that he'd seen through straight away, because he knew the truth. He'd given her just enough to send her on her way, no doubt feeling she'd been successful, when, in fact, it was he who had been successful.

If she continued to fish, she'd need a different rod.

He wondered what her real interest was, and kicked himself for not finding out her full name. But no matter: he felt sure she'd be back—particularly when she got closer to the truth.

He suspected he'd be gone by then.

Chapter Thirty-One

The traffic was tedious, and it was only early afternoon. Though when were Greater London's motorways ever clear? It was a common complaint from those that lived around the counties and used the road network every day. That's why the trains and the tube were so much more convenient, even though they cost an arm and a leg during peak times. There really wasn't any choice. Sitting on the M25, London's biggest 'moving' car park, was a whole lot more stressful. At least you could read while travelling on public transport.

Chrissy was glad she didn't have to do it regularly; her ample office in the attic was all she needed to run her fake business. But looking up at Julie's sizeable home from her position at the entry gate, she was reminded again that it said volumes about why people did commute such vast times each day. Money. And lots of it.

She pressed the keypad entry code. Nothing. Julie had probably changed the code again. She pushed the buzzer.

"It's me," she said in a singsong voice.

"Come on in," Julie said in return, sounding somewhat more relaxed than usual, Chrissy thought. Perhaps she'd been laid out relaxing at a spa all morning. Or the gardener had been round.

Wicked!

You've seen Richard!

She loves him...

Chrissy parked out front as usual and made her way to the door, where Julie was now standing, looking stunning as always, dressed once again in a beautiful cream linen number. The short shift dress complimented her stunning legs; her spray tan was just the right shade of Ibiza. Chrissy was a tiny bit jealous, but she knew she'd have her own tan after a few days relaxing properly in the LA sun.

"Darling," Julie greeted her. She air-kissed her, gently holding her at arm's length so as not to crease her dress. "What a lovely surprise. Thanks for dropping in. Can I get you some iced tea, perhaps? Is it too early for a glass of wine?"

"I'd love one, but not with the car, thanks." Chrissy followed her sister through to the back where she had been sitting in the warm conservatory, blinds half drawn. A copy of *Hello! Magazine* was open on the small side table, a tall glass with the remains of an ice cube and a slice of lime by its side. Julie's life would bore her silly, but then Chrissy wasn't Julie.

"Iced tea please, with lemon if you have some," she said, eyeing the green citrus circle. "Or I'll have lime, if it's easier." She kicked her sandals off and sank down on one of the huge wicker chairs, the quilted seat enveloping her like quicksand. Julie left her to it for a moment, and Chrissy took the opportunity to sit in the tranquillity and close her eyes. The sound of ice rattling in her drink as it was placed on a matching wicker side table caused her to open them again.

"Was you passing?" Julie enquired, sipping from another glass of something tall and clear.

"I had a spot of business and wanted to ask you something, actually."

"Oh? Sounds intriguing."

"Remember when we found those diaries in Dad's den? And Mum went loopy?"

"How could I forget?"

"Has she mentioned them again since? I mean, she talks more to you than me, so she'd be more likely to say something."

"You always say that, and it's really not true." Chrissy gave her a look that said, 'Yeah, right.' Julie continued. "But since you asked, yes, she has mentioned them." Julie sipped her drink without making eye contact, suddenly finding the flooring of great interest.

"Told you!" Chrissy almost shrieked. "What did she say, exactly?"

"Tell me why you want to know first."

"It's nothing, really. I simply want to know—call me nosey."

"Then there must be a reason. What is it? Then I'll tell you."

They'd grown up together; Chrissy knew how Julie worked, and when she got like this, there'd be no pushing her to get the answer out.

"I'd like to read a couple of them, that's why. I think it would be interesting, now Dad's gone." She was making it up on the hoof, and hoping Julie wouldn't see through the story. "I miss him," she added, for good measure. "I'm sure he wouldn't mind, now he's moved on to another world."

"I've a confession to make," Julie said sheepishly. "I've seen inside a couple of them. Mother was throwing them out, ready for the incinerator, I expect. And I picked one out when she wasn't looking."

Chrissy couldn't believe her ears, but hid her excitement.

"And? What sort of thing was in them?"

"Nothing much. A bit of a let-down, actually. Finances mostly. I tried another but that wasn't any more exciting either."

"And where are they now?"

"The last I saw of them was Mother filling a black bin liner with them. Then she put the bag by the back door. Like I said, I expect the incinerator at the bottom of the garden has had them by now. That was two days ago." Julie sipped delicately from her glass, a slice of lime tapping at her top lip.

"Oh well. I guess I'm too late." Thinking again, she asked, "Do you think Mum has read them?"

"I wouldn't know, but from what I saw, they'd be fairly dull. Hardly a Mills and Boone story, Dad's old finances."

With that Chrissy had to agree. Maybe she'd drive over, take another look in the shed at the bottom of the garden again in the hope the bag still sitting there, waiting to be burned. The Sandra Bakers of this world didn't light fires; someone else did the dirty jobs for them. The old family house wasn't far out of her way. As was her habit, Chrissy didn't let on her thoughts.

"Oh well, I guess I'm too late," she said defeatedly, and changed the subject. Nodding her head at the open magazine, she asked, "What's the gossip, then? Who's sleeping with whom this week?"

"Well, you'll never guess who's getting a divorce!" Julie said excitedly. Chrissy mused at how shallow her sister could be sometimes, but played along anyway.

Rolling her eyes, she said, "I've no idea. Tell me."

Chapter Thirty-Two

Philip looked to Alistair for clarification. "You're kidding me, right?" he asked incredulously.

"Absolutely not. Pretty juicy, eh?" Alistair replied.

Philip was mulling it over, thinking of the ramifications and, more importantly, of the possible payday. They most certainly needed the funds; their bank account contained fewer crumbs than the bottom of a biscuit barrel.

"When are you meeting him?" Philip asked.

"On the golf course—where else? Though in the bar, not on the green. At four PM, to be precise, no doubt with a gin and tonic in one hand and a fat cigar in the other."

"Well, I can't fault his choice in divorce lawyers. Do you know who our opponent is? And who his wife has chosen?"

"No doubt he'll tell me when I see him later, but I expect them to be tough. He will not want her to have anything because he's a tight-arse, and she will be out for what she can get because she's the trophy wife and has put up with his fat belly on top of her for far too long. Who wouldn't want compensation for living with him? His cigar breath alone could be cause for divorce."

"Well, this is LA, so anything is possible," said Philip. "I'm intrigued to know who the opposition would be, though, just because I'm curious."

"Patience, my friend," Alistair said. "You'll just have to wait." He stood as he spoke and walked to the small window that looked out over the busy street below. As usual, the bright LA sunshine was glaring at midday and, down below, California's hot and trendy people went about their daily business dressed in anything from teeny-tiny shorts to top-of-the-range designer workwear. The majority of them sported long blonde hair—a prerequisite to living in one of the coolest suburbs of the United States. Neither Philip nor Alistair fitted in in that respect, but from Alistair's observations it only applied to the females. The pressure was all theirs. He felt Philip get up from his chair behind him and wander over to stand beside him.

"Are you thinking what I'm thinking?" Philip asked

"Well, that kind of depends on what you're thinking," said Alistair.

"Well, with him being such a high-profile personality, there's going to be a lot of gossip and a lot of fallout, not to mention a lot of work for us, and this could drag on for months, if not years. Have we got the resources to handle it?" Philip sounded a little tired, Alistair thought. Probably delayed jet lag.

"I guess there's not a lot we can do until I meet with him and he's signed us up. Everyone knows who he is, and I bet his phone has been ringing off the hook with offers to represent coming in. And there will be dirt flying all over the place from him and from her."

"I guess we'll soon see, but I've got work to do," Philip went on. He checked his watch, and went back to his desk, leaving Alistair gazing at the blonde heads and tanned brown legs of the locals below.

It was a few moments before 4 PM when Alistair strolled into the bar at the Bellevue Golf Club, one of LA's finest courses and country homes. The waiting list to join was said to be in excess of ten years, which was a crazy amount of time to wait to whack a ball around immaculate lawns in the sunshine with your buddies. But such was LA and just being on the waitlist was all the social proof some people needed that they were indeed part of the elite club. A celeb in the waiting.

The man he sought was standing at the bar holding court, his podgy face animated and somewhat orange from the tan lamp that he was said to keep by his bed. Why the man needed it Alistair had no idea; the natural stuff was readily available. And the results were a whole lot more natural-looking. He wore pale chino pants with a sharp crease down the front and a long-sleeved button-down shirt open at the neck. Stray, fair hair poured out from the top. The man obviously wasn't keen on being waxed. Or didn't feel the need for chest hair control. Alistair wondered if his back was equally hairy, and if that was another reason for the divorce. Hairy body and cigar breath—not many women's dream.

Four younger men in their forties were gathered around him, hanging on to his every word and listening to a story—of what, Alistair had no idea. Judging by their faces, they were waiting for a punchline, their smiles growing slowly as he headed towards the climax. Like sycophants, each one guffawed as expected, keeping up the pretence that they liked the man they were stood with: they were hanging out with their buddy.

Alistair waited for the punchline to be delivered before he joined them. The man with the escaping chest hair held out a beefy hand and Alistair took it, catching and holding the man's eyes at the same time.

"Good afternoon, Mr. Jamieson. Alistair Crowley."

The four men, sensing they were no longer, needed briefly said their goodbyes and shifted along the bar, leaving the big man with Alistair. Whether he imagined it or not, Alistair sensed his prospective new client sizing him up. While he wasn't obvious in doing so, Alistair nonetheless felt the fine needles prickle down the back of his neck as he was summed up. First impressions and all that.

"Good to meet you, Alistair. Thanks for coming out at such short notice."

The two men seated themselves on deeply tinted wooden bar stools, the seats themselves covered in matching soft leather.

The big man carried on. "Divorce can be a real bitch. I should know; I married her," he said, and threw his head back, laughing at his own joke.

Alister followed suit to be polite, though not as raucously. Yes, divorce could be a bitch; he'd heard the joke many times before and everyone always thought it was themselves delivering the line first. So as not to appear rude, he always chuckled along with it.

"And that's why you called me," Alistair said confidently, avoiding commenting further on 'bitch.' He leaned in and asked, "Do you want to talk here or do you want to walk out on the patio? Walls have ears sometimes."

Understanding what Alistair was implying, the big man nodded his approval and picked up his tumbler by way of agreement.

"Let's get you a drink and we'll head out," he said, catching the bartender's eye and raising his glass and two fingers. It seemed Alistair didn't get a say in what he was about to drink. The men slowly made their way to the door and out onto the patio that overlooked the green expanse of immaculately mown lawn. There were tiny flags dotted about, but they were perfectly still, as there was no breeze. The bartender would find them outside.

When he was confident there was no one close enough to eavesdrop, Alistair was keen to take the lead. "I'm sure you're aware, Mr. Jamieson," he began, "that this could get messy, like most LA divorces invariably do. You're just as famous as she is, so we need to keep this under wraps as much as possible and get it settled as quickly as possible. Do you know who her lawyer is yet, who she's appointed?"

"Yes, I do, but that's not why I called you." Jamieson took the last mouthful from his original tumbler and placed it on the low wall nearby. Alistair waited a beat while the man composed what he was about to say next. It was obvious from his face it was going to be a little out of the ordinary.

"I'm looking for a different solution, actually," Jamieson said casually, "one that will save me a hell of a lot of money in the long run." The man's pale blue eyes bored into Alistair's as though he was trying to read the inside of his head. Alistair felt the pinpricks again, or did he imagine it?

"I'm not entirely sure I follow," said Alistair. The bartender interrupted his train of thought by delivering two fresh tumblers of clear liquid; each man took one. The interruption gave him something to do while he thought. He took a sip; the heat from the alcohol both warmed and refreshed his throat.

"I believe your partner Philip has just had a quick trip to the UK, to a funeral I believe."

Something passed over Alistair and it didn't feel good. "He did, yes. Someone from his old school days, I believe."

The big man smiled in a way that said 'I wasn't born yesterday,' and added, "A rather sudden death, though, I'd heard. Such a shame when death occurs unexpectedly."

Alistair knew exactly what the big man was insinuating, and it turned his stomach. They weren't in the market for taking care of other people's problems.

"I think you have the wrong man, Mr. Jamieson. I'm a divorce lawyer, nothing more."

"Oh, I think I have the right man, Mr. Crowley. The question is, how much do you want my business? And since I already know the answer to that question, I'd say quite a lot." The big man raised his tumbler at Alistair as if to say cheers, a sinister half smile on his lips that made him look like a cartoon character.

Alistair fought to keep his face neutral: How the hell could this man in front of him possibly know about Philip's trip to the UK and the state of their finances? He needed to get out of this whatever this was, fast. He put his tumbler down on the wall next to the other empty glass and said, "I think you'll need to find somebody else. Thank you for the drink." He turned and proceeded to walk away, hoping Jamieson didn't call him back. That could get embarrassing.

Alistair didn't look back as he left the patio and marched back through into the bar. He caught the eye of one of the four men who had been previously stood with his prospective client. Neither smiled, but the man's eyes followed Alistair. For a split second, he wondered if the man knew about the conversation he'd just had. He picked up his pace and strode straight out the front entrance towards the car park, his heart beating rapidly in his chest. When he was safely out of the building, he turned around to make sure nobody had followed him, then slowed his pace as he approached his vehicle. The experience had been surreal. And frightening.

If one man knew exactly why Philip had been to the UK, then others probably did too.

Chapter Thirty-Three

For the second time that day, Philip said, "Come again?"

"It's a worry, isn't it? The fact that he knows why you went to the UK. I mean, what are the chances that he would know? How could he have known?"

Alistair had eventually called Philip from his car on the way back from the golf course. There was little point in going back to the office, so he was headed straight home. But he felt he needed to fill Philip in; Philip was his partner, after all. He was stuck in the afternoon traffic now with everyone else in LA going home after work; it was going to be a long journey home. The airwaves between them went quiet while both men thought about their predicament. A car horn blared in one of the lanes nearby. Alistair was itching to get back to his apartment, get out of his work clothes and crack open a cold beer. He needed time to think; he needed time to go over what had happened back in the bar. As someone cut in front of him, slipping into a gap that you'd have been hard-pushed to manoeuvre a scooter into, Alistair put his own hand on his own horn and screamed at the open-topped sports car now directly in front of him. Philip caught the outburst over the car's speakers.

"Heavens, Alistair!" Philip said, just as loudly as Alistair had cursed.

"I'm not in the mood for pricks, and since a prick has just pulled in front of me when there wasn't a gap, I want to rip his head off and shove it up his..."

"I get the picture, but ranting at the dickhead isn't going to get you very far. What are your plans for this evening?" he said, changing the subject.

"I'm getting pissed first off, then I'll see after that. Why? What are you doing?"

"I kind of have a date, but I think this is a whole lot more urgent than me getting laid. I propose I come over to your place, bring a couple of beers, maybe a pizza, and we try and figure out what to do next. For all we know, someone could be listening to this conversation."

"You think it's that serious?"

"Well, if somebody found out why I went to London, I can't think how they would have done that unless they'd overheard a conversation. Only you, me and Carmen knew I was even going, never mind *why* I was going. That only leaves you and me, and I didn't tell anybody else. Did you?"

"I'm not even going to answer that—of course I didn't."

"You just did answer that." Philip chuckled, trying to lighten his friend's mood.

"You know I didn't tell anyone. No story to tell."

Now that the idea that someone could be listening had been planted in their minds, both men suddenly became careful with their words.

Alistair continued, "You bring the beers, and I will order pizza when you get here. But I warn you now—looking at this traffic, I could be a while yet. The place is jammed."

"Well, I'll see you when I see you, then." Philip hung up, leaving Alistair to slowly chug along with the rest of Los Angeles.

· · ·

Philip was sure nobody had known anything about that trip, never mind what he had been going to do when he got there, and it puzzled him how a well-known movie mogul would have had that snippet of information in the first place. And even more importantly, *why* he'd have the information. It didn't make any sense at all. All thoughts of a nice payday from a juicy celebrity divorce had flown out the window. Now, the only way they were going to get a payday off this gig was if they...

What, exactly?

They weren't hit men. They weren't contract killers—they were divorce lawyers. While not everyone liked divorce lawyers, they were certainly several rungs higher up than the aforementioned on the ladder of life's occupations. Now, not only did they need to drum up more business, but they had the added stress of someone knowing their little secret. How could Philip and Alistair trust what Jamieson had on them, to keep it to himself, to keep quiet? They couldn't. And just like in the movies—probably one of the man's own movies, Philip thought, groaning inwardly—that would mean being in his pocket for life. It was like a scene out of *The Godfather*. Philip wasn't prepared to go there, and he knew Alistair would feel the same.

But they couldn't get rid of the problem that easily; the genie was out of the bottle. As Philip approached his apartment, he wondered who they might be able to talk to without letting that person in on exactly what had happened on his trip to the UK. Not many people would understand that sometimes taking a life was actually an okay thing to do.

Not even a priest would understand that one.

Philip slipped the key into the lock and opened his front door. Immediately, a tingle ran up his spine; something didn't feel right. Instinctively, he turned around and scanned the walkways, looking for someone watching him. But at this time of day, the immediate outside area was a hive of activity, with dog walkers and runners and everyone in between. Was he being paranoid? Maybe, especially since that conversation about possibly being overheard. Satisfied there was no one obvious loitering nearby, he slipped inside and closed the door behind him, slamming it harder than he meant to. The noise rattled around the lounge and vibrated his nerves just a little more. His senses fired again. There was a definite feel to his place, and it felt out of sorts.

He wanted to go for a run. But he'd just agreed to have a beer with Alistair, and they needed to talk. There would be time for a run later. Dropping his keys on the table, he went through to his bedroom and got changed anyway. Just getting out of his work clothes felt better, and he slipped on his running gear so he could be ready to go after his meeting with Alistair. It was while he was hanging his trousers up that he noticed something out of the ordinary. Something had been moved. The alarm clock was just a little out of place. He scanned the room. The blinds had very definitely been moved. He didn't say a word out loud, but walked through to the bathroom, then the kitchen and then back to the lounge, his eyes covering every surface to see what else was out of place. Since Philip was an exceptionally tidy individual to the point of being OCD, he appreciated and expected things to be and stay just so. But he found more anomalies. The fruit bowl's contents were stacked out of order, the TV remote control had been moved slightly on the coffee table and the basil plant on the kitchen windowsill wasn't perfectly dead centre.

Someone had very definitely been inside his apartment.

Moving things.

Looking for something.

He grabbed some change and his door key and headed out. There was no point meeting Alistair at his place now. They needed a different location.

There were still plenty of payphones dotted around, and Philip found one nearby and fed in the relevant change. A homeless man was sitting in the sand nearby, two empty beer cans by his side. He smiled a toothless grin. Philip dialled Alistair's number and was wondering if he would pick up when his phone flashed: no caller ID. Alistair would let it go to voice mail, no doubt. Finally, Alistair picked up. Philip dove straight in.

"Change of plan: I'll meet you at Muscle Beach. I'm going for a run first, so I'll meet you there at seven." Philip blurted the words out in a rush, hoping Alistair wouldn't ask any questions. If he wondered why he was being called from something other than Philip's mobile phone, he never asked. But Alistair was a smart man and didn't question it.

"Roger that," he said brightly. "I'll see you later." He hung up.

As Philip left the phone booth, he wondered if anyone had seen him make the call. It felt ridiculous, but since things didn't move around his apartment on their own, perhaps it wasn't. He made a note to look around when he met Alistair later and see if he noticed anybody that he'd already seen once today; he'd wouldn't be surprised. He tossed the remaining change to the man with most of his front teeth missing.

Joining in with a small group of runners as they passed by, he hung on the back and matched their stride, settling in to try and enjoy his run.

Chapter Thirty-Four

Chrissy was tempted to call in at her mother's on the way home. If Julie was right, and those diaries had been burned, there wouldn't be an awful lot left to find, possibly rendering the whole exercise a waste of time. Again, she hoped that burning rubbish wasn't high on her mother's agenda.

Her thoughts were interrupted by her phone ringing; glancing at her console, she noted it was Adam. He often called throughout the day, just for a chat when he had five minutes, but since it was later on in the afternoon he was probably home already. She clicked select on her steering wheel and waited for his voice to fill the car. She loved the sound of it and could listen to him all day without getting bored.

"Hey, you still working?" he asked.

"Nearly home, gorgeous. A bit longer day than I expected. The boys home?"

"I'm not sure. I'm not home myself yet. I was just ringing to tell you I am going to be late and not to worry. I'll get a bite to eat in town while I'm out, unless you have something planned, of course, that I'm not aware of?"

"Well, I did say I'd cook ..."

"Ah. Forgot."

"Don't be silly. You go and enjoy yourself. I'll take the boys, go get burgers. I'll be home in five anyway."

"Right. I should be back by nine at the latest. I've got an early start in the morning, so you enjoy yourselves and I'll see you later." Chrissy smiled at the windscreen as if Adam could see her and clicked 'end' on her steering wheel. She'd not been grocery shopping anyway, so not having to cook dinner was an added bonus. While she wasn't far away from home, she was further out than five minutes, though that didn't matter because Adam wasn't home to see her arrive. She glanced more closely at her surroundings and did a double-take. Weirdly, without her realising it, while she been driving along and chatting, she'd absentmindedly steered towards her mother's place.

"I guess that's fate. Obviously, I'm meant to go to Mum's," she said when she'd realised her mistake. Or was it a mistake? It was a worry that it had happened while driving her car, almost like she'd been on autopilot. No wonder accidents happened, she thought ruefully.

She turned her attention more closely to the road and wondered what her excuse she would give her mother about why she was calling; she had seen her mother more in recent days and she had in recent months and weeks. But funerals did that to people, she knew; you saw more of some than others.

"Anyway, she might not even be in," Chrissy said to herself.

Ten minutes later she pulled up in front of the familiar house. For a moment she stayed in the car, looking up at the door, thinking of her father. She missed him; not that they'd been particularly close, but when something was gone forever you often craved it more than when it had been readily available. She knew that at some time in the future she'd need her dad's advice, and he was no longer around to give it. The thought filled her with a fresh wave of sadness.

"Come on, then, Chrissy," she said encouragingly, trying to snap herself out of her maudlin mood. "Let's go see if she's still got them." She climbed out of the car and headed to the front door, but before she reached the top, her mother, small and frail as she was, seemed to fill the doorway. She had a tight smile on her face, but that was nothing new. Sandra Baker had never appeared to be a jovial spirit.

"Hi, Mum," Chrissy said chirpily, feeling like she was putting it on, which in fact she was. She watched her mother's wrinkled face for signs of her mood.

Tyson or frail?

"Hello, darling. I wasn't expecting to see you this afternoon. What a pleasant surprise." If she was surprised or it was indeed pleasant, she certainly didn't sound or look like it. It was more like she was saying it by rote. Her mother was also on autopilot, it seemed. But there was no sense in saying anything about it, so she let it lie. After all these years, her mother was certainly not going to change now.

"I thought I'd just drop by and see how you're doing. I wasn't far away." It wasn't entirely a lie, and as she reached in to give her mother a light hug, she hoped her actions were a bit more convincing than her mother's had just been. Her mother opened the door wider and Chrissy stepped inside and headed down the hallway towards the back of the house. In her head, Chrissy still wasn't exactly sure how she was going to get to the subject of the diaries without causing a fracas. Last time the diaries had been mentioned, she had almost been banished from the house; she didn't fancy a repeat of that.

"I would have thought you'd be home making dinner for Adam by this hour." Her mother had always had an annoying habit of making Chrissy feel inadequate as a wife and mother. It was as if she always had to get her dig in; she never understood that Chrissy worked for a living.

Well, you used to, anyway.

My investments still provide, don't they?

Sandra Baker had only ever known running a home and family, and she had never been employed as far as Chrissy could remember. Unfortunately, that meant that she judged everybody by her own standards, and that meant all wives and mothers should perform each and every one of their tasks like she herself had done. Without going out to work. Keeping a job and trying to run a family and home was not acceptable, in Sandra Baker's book.

"He's working late. I'm taking the boys out for burgers as soon as I get home."

Her mother curled her nose up. "Burgers are not particularly nutritious. Can't you go out for sushi instead?"

Chrissy kept quiet and let the barbed comment flow over her head as they both sat down at the breakfast bar in the kitchen. Her mother offered her a glass of wine, and Chrissy declined, stating it was a flying visit.

"Did you want something specific, then?"

Chrissy was tempted to say yes but stifled the urge. If the diaries had been dumped in the black bag, she thought, they'd be back down the shed waiting for the incinerator and the gardener. That's what she would have done, and she was banking on her mother having done the same.

"I think I left something in the shed when I was here last. I just need to pop down to see if it's there."

"Oh?"

Damn—why is she wanting to dig? Of all the things to dig into.

"Do you mind if I just pop down? I'll only be a moment," she said, and, not waiting for a response, made a move towards the back door, handbag draped over her shoulder. Even at her age, Chrissy still felt she needed to ask permission, and since she was at her mother's house... There was a pause in the conversation and Chrissy assumed that her mother was thinking about what to answer. Manners had never been Chrissy's strong point, so she opened the door in anticipation anyway.

"But it's jam packed with bags for the charity shop," her mother protested. "Your father's old clothes and the like. And I didn't see anything when I was last in there."

Was she trying to stall Chrissy? Not waiting to find out, she headed out the back door and down the path to the bottom.

She was going into that garden shed, permission or not.

Chapter Thirty-Five

Chrissy almost felt bad about dominating her mother, but it was important that she get inside the shed and, more importantly, into the bags that were stored there. She'd sensed her mother's hesitation in letting her enter, but since she'd stood with the back door open, Chrissy had simply made her own way and ignored her mother's protests. She'd get over it.

The door was unlocked as usual, and Chrissy slipped inside the dusty old wooden building, and then stood aghast. Her mother had been right about one thing: it was filled with bags. It was going to take an age to find the bag she needed. Well, there was nothing for it. Chrissy got to work quickly, feeling the outside of each one to see whether it contained the hard edges of books or the soft edges of her father's clothing. There were probably about fifteen bags stuffed into the small space, and Chrissy moved things around to create a system of which bags she'd felt and which bags she still needed to investigate.

Finally, she hit pay dirt—or so she hoped. She carefully untied the knot at the top of the bag even though it would have been quicker to rip through the plastic. Since she wasn't supposed to be looking in the bags at all, she needed to leave them just as she'd found them so as not to raise any further suspicion. Carefully folding the top back, she pulled a diary out. The year on the cover was 1985; not what she was looking for. She pulled another out: 1984. She pulled out another, and another, adding each one to the growing pile beside her.

When the last diary was out of the bag, she rested back on her heels in thought. The diary she wanted was missing. And so were two others, from the years on either side of 1987. Now that was odd. Where were they? There wasn't time to go through the other bags, and she peered through the small shed window to check her mother wasn't on her way down the path. That would leave some explaining to do.

"Damn!" she muttered, and began placing them all back into the same bin liner they'd come from. As she worked, her mind sifted through various explanations for why the three diaries she was interested in were missing. As an afterthought, she plucked a random year from the bin liner and slipped it into her own bag.

Quickly she retied the bag, figuring she was about out of time, and lifted some of the other bags on top of the one she been rummaging in. If her mother was about to instruct the gardener to burn them, they'd be back where she had originally left them. She felt like a thief, taking something that wasn't exactly hers, though she reconciled it in her own head as further research. She checked round the small shed and when she was satisfied it was roughly how she'd found it, she walked back up to the house.

She was not surprised to see her mother stood in the doorway again, with her arms crossed and looking annoyed. Chrissy ignored her mood and said, "I knew I'd left my other glasses somewhere. I just didn't know where."

"I never noticed them when I was in there last, but at least you've found them now." Her mother's lips were pursed, the words tight as they left her mouth. Or was Chrissy imagining it?

Not wanting to hang around for her mother's inquisitive ques-tions and not wanting to lie to her any further, she quickly air-kissed her mother's cheek and explained she'd better get back for the boys, didn't want to keep them waiting. With a breezy goodbye, Chrissy once again left her mother in the front doorway as she set off back to Englefield Green and burgers with her boys.

The house was empty when she got home, though there was a note on the side in the kitchen that simply read "Having dinner at Gary's place. His mum has made sushi." Chrissy read the note out loud and laughed to herself. She must be a terrible mother to force burgers on her children. Her own mother had inadvertently got her own way: the more nutritious sushi had won out after all.

She dropped her bag on the work surface next to the note, grabbed a wine glass from the drawer and headed to the fridge, where she knew there was a bottle of white wine chilling. She pulled out a bottle of Pinot Gris, unscrewed the top, poured a large glass and took two long mouthfuls before topping the glass back up. The coolness felt good on her throat; it always did. She retrieved the diary from her bag along with her reading glasses and took a seat in the soft old chair in the corner of the room. With Adam and the boys out doing other things, she made herself comfortable, took another sip of her wine and opened the book. The random one she'd taken was dated 2014.

At the sight of her father's handwriting, she instinctively moved her fingers over the words as if they were embossed, raised up, and she could feel him through them. She took a moment to remember him before she started to read. If he was watching her now while she looked into his diary, what he would be thinking of her? Would he be cross, anxious even? Or would he be happy that she was taking such an interest after he had left this earth?

She hoped it was the latter, though she knew inside she was prying.

Chapter Thirty-Six

If you've ever been to Venice Beach, you'll know about Muscle Beach, the place where the big guys, with tanned, bulging biceps, like to show off their bodies, and where folks go to watch them lift weights of gargantuan proportions, or swing with ease like monkeys on giant metal frames, or push out press-ups by the dozen in the sand below. Some go for fitness; some go for show. But either way, it's hard not to stand and stare at hard-worked-on bodies glistening in sweat as you wander by.

The beach itself attracted a certain kind of person to train there. Venice Beach hasn't always claimed the title of Muscle Beach; the original Muscle Beach was south of Santa Monica Pier, though there are only a few frames and apparatus there now. The new Muscle Beach Venice was where it was at. A raw, outdoor gym, it attracted mainly male gym bucks, though not many bunnies, with an emphasis on minimal clothing. Working out while working on your tan was the preferred form of multi-tasking.

A man with skin the colour of an aged walnut headed towards Philip. He was dressed in nothing but a red Speedo and rollerblades. A greying ponytail hung down his glistening back; deep brown shades, *Top Gun*–style, covered his eyes. His abs were like granite, his body a hard statue. On wheels. He didn't stand out particularly; in fact, he fitted right in. Nobody was ever out of place here on Venice Beach.

Philip looked at his sports watch for the umpteenth time. Alistair would arrive at any moment and wonder why the clandestine meeting. His sweat was drying in the late sun; he'd shower when he got back to his place.

Philip was spooked; he'd never had anyone go through his stuff before, had never been burgled. There'd never been a reason for anyone to intrude in the past; this was all new to him now. And he didn't like the feeling. Moreover, he didn't like the fact that someone could be listening, or watching, and he didn't know which was worse. There was only one reason he could think of for the recent events.

And that was Frank Jamieson and his veiled threat. Jamieson knew too much.

The man had money and power, and, Philip suspected, a mean streak, given their conversation at the pub. Under his breath, Philip muttered "sick greedy bastard."

In the distance, an arm waved high in the air. It was Alistair. Philip watched him approach and noted his friend's head turning each time a pretty blonde or brunette passed by. At one point, he raised his shades off his eyes for a better look. The man was too obvious for words, though the woman was oblivious. He waved again, and Philip raised his own arm in reply.

When the two men were finally side by side, Alistair asked, "What's going on?"

"Let's walk. I'll tell you as we go."

They started walking slowly north through the crowds towards Santa Monica Pier. Alistair, sensing something was adrift, had the good sense to keep quiet and wait for Philip to fill in.

"Someone's been rifling through my place," Philip finally said. "Nothing seems to have been taken, so it's not a burglary, but things have been moved. Things have been shifted slightly."

Alistair turned to Philip as they carried on walking. "How do you know? What's been moved?"

"I noticed my alarm clock has been moved slightly, and when I noticed that, I paid a bit more attention to the rest of my surroundings. And you know how tidy and meticulous I am, everything is in its place. Except things aren't in their place. And that started me looking further. Nothing's been taken. Things have just been moved."

Alistair was quick to catch on. "And you now think it's connected with our latest client."

"He's no client of ours," Philip said, a bit more brusquely than he intended.

"I grant you, it's not what we would have expected, no, but he *could* be a client."

Philip stood stock still now, and Alistair paced past him a step before realising Philip wasn't moving. He backed up a little.

"Are you serious?" Philip asked incredulously. "We're divorce lawyers—end of story. I'm not getting mixed up in dodgy dealings. It was bad enough what I went to do in the UK. If anyone ever finds out about me being there, it's me that's up to my neck in it, not you." Even though he'd said the words quietly enough, Philip still checked his immediate vicinity, his eyes switching from side to side to see if anybody had heard his little outburst. When he was satisfied that no one had, he carried on. "Look, I don't know what we do now, but it's fair to say Jamieson and his tricks have rattled me. I don't know if that was his intention, but he's rattled me nonetheless."

Alistair tried to calm him. "Take it easy, buddy. It's only suspicion at this stage. There's no evidence, and there could be a clear explanation for it that you don't realise yet." He put his arm around his friend's shoulder and they resumed walking, carrying on slowly towards the pier. While Alistair wouldn't admit it to Philip, he wasn't surprised at what had happened to Philip's apartment.

Because he'd decided to stop at home before their meet.

And he'd had the exact same experience.

Chapter Thirty-Seven

Alistair knew he'd have to say something, but right now wasn't the time. The two men walked silently, each deep in thought. When they reached a bar, Alistair suggested they pulled in for a swift one and Philip readily agreed. They chose a seat in the outdoor area and a waitress wandered over, a bright smile plastered on her face. Like many of the wait staff in LA, she'd be hoping to make her fortune, be discovered, and waiting tables would do in the meantime. It would leave her time for attending auditions when they came up. Alistair thought about asking whether she was an actress or a singer, out of common curiosity and for no other reason—not that he could help in any way. He greeted her warmly; maybe he'd get lucky if he played his cards right.

"A couple of Sol beers, please," he said, smiling a bit too broadly.

The waitress, obviously keen on working her tip, replied "Sure thing, hon." Then she was gone.

Alistair smiled at Philip and Philip shook his head slowly, not impressed. "You never stop trying, do you, Alistair?" he said.

"Never. I don't want to, either. And judging by your face, my friend, an orgasm would do you the world of good."

Philip nodded, though he wasn't really paying attention, and instead turned to watch the boardwalk. Three older teenage girls, wearing only bikinis and rollerblades, slowly made their way past, making a show of themselves, probably looking for a modelling part. Everyone was looking for something—someone to make their career, someone to show themselves off to.

Their two beers arrived, pulling Philip away from his view and back to their table and the discussion ahead. Alistair carried on in his quest to steer the conversation, first checking over his shoulders to see if anyone was listening. It was early yet by LA standards, and the bar was nearly empty.

"Listen, Philip, don't let this rattle you. But let me fill you in on something else." Philip looked at Alistair as if to say 'Go on.' "I've just been debating whether to mention it to you, but since we're in this together, it's only fair." Alistair checked around again just to be sure. Philip wondered uneasily just what he was about to say.

"Someone's been in my place too. The same as you, I expect— just something moved, nothing taken—but I was only in a moment or two so I'm not sure. I called at home just before I came out to meet you. I guess if you've been rifled through as well, any doubt I had about my place has vanished." He let it sink in a moment to see what Philip would say, how he'd react. If they'd both been rifled through, this was serious stuff.

"Shit! Who do they think we are? And why didn't you say something earlier?" Philip asked, in an urgent but hushed voice.

Alistair shrugged. "Well, something a little more than two divorce lawyers trying to earn a crust, I'd say. And to answer your second question, I didn't want to believe it, I suppose." He took a long pull from his beer and looked thoughtfully off into the distance again at nothing in particular.

"So, what do you think we should do?" Philip asked. "Leave things as they are and hope we're not being bugged or watched?"

"I think it's a bit extreme to think we've been bugged. They were more likely just looking for something—not that there's anything to find. But they don't know that, so they searched us both. And since they didn't find anything, that's probably the end of it, I'd say."

"I wish I could be so sure," Philip replied. "It doesn't feel like that. And that Jamieson has got his fingers in all sorts of pies, not just movies, and I don't trust him. Any man who wants to get his wife knocked off to avoid a costly divorce is on another level entirely. Which leaves us a problem: he obviously thinks we are up to something; otherwise he wouldn't risk asking us about it. I can't think who else would be behind our places being searched."

Philip had a point, but Alistair didn't have a ready answer. "And me neither, to be perfectly honest," he said. "All we can do is be careful, like we're doing right now. I suggest that, until we get to the bottom of this, we don't mention his name or the UK at all at the office or on mobile phones or in our apartments. And with regard to his specific request, I suggest we ignore that too, wait for him to come back to us. That will give us a bit of breathing space, and we can decide how to handle it when and if the problem arises again. We've said we are not interested. Let's hope that's enough for now." Alistair picked his beer up and examined the label with great curiosity. It was a Mexican brand, and he began to smile.

"What's funny?"

"If the shit hits the fan, we could always run away to Mexico."

Philip frowned. "Let's hope it doesn't come to that. I hate Mexican food."

Chapter Thirty-Eight

The men didn't have to wait too long. It was nearing lunchtime the following day when Frank Jamieson again made contact. He asked for Alistair, but Alistair was away from the office, so he'd then asked for Philip. Carmen asked him if she should put the call through, but Philip told her to put Jamieson off. Unfortunately, the man had been insistent. Philip stared at the flashing light on the handset. Jamieson was on hold. If he didn't pick the call up, he'd only call back, and Philip would spend half his afternoon avoiding him and being distracted by it.

At last, Philip snatched at the receiver and resisted the temptation to bark down it. It would do no good to show his true feelings, so he paused for a moment before saying, "Good morning. Philip Banks here." He might as well be polite, he figured, even though inside he wanted to tell the man to go to hell.

"Frank Jamieson here, Philip. I hope I'm not interrupting you too much?" The man sounded cordial enough, and Philip carried on being the polite divorce lawyer as if nothing had happened.

Not much, to be fair. Except his belongings moving about.

"Not at all, Mr. Jamieson. What can I do for you?" Philip's voice was level, even; nothing out of place.

"Now that's what I like to hear. There is most definitely something you can do for me. Shame your partner doesn't feel the same way. I gather you know about our conversation yesterday?"

Philip debated whether to act dumb or not but it seemed pointless. "Alistair filled me in. Yes, I'm aware of your particular. . ." He searched for the correct word. ". . .needs. And I think my partner mentioned that's not something we specialise in. We tend to stick to divorce law, with the emphasis on *law*." Philip didn't mean for his comment to sound snarky, but it came out that way and he heard Jamieson's sharp intake of breath. Philip said nothing and waited.

"Well, that is a shame, though I think it would be worth your while if perhaps we met, the two of us, to see if we can't come to some agreement. I think you'll find my terms very reasonable. And you do need the business, from what I have gleaned."

Philip didn't like the sound of where this was going, and he took a deep breath and held it in his chest for a moment before releasing it. He hoped Jamieson couldn't hear it down the telephone line. He'd never met the man, though he knew a lot about him, and he wasn't sure if it was gory interest or sheer stupidity. Even though LA was vast, at times it was a village, a village that was fuelled by gossip. Philip found himself relenting, although he hated bullies. He gathered energy and prized it into his voice like one too many pairs of jeans into an overstuffed suitcase.

"Even though it's a waste of my time, I will agree to meet. When and where?" He heard the man chortle lightly at the other end of the phone and Philip wondered if Jamieson was chalking one up on his imaginary scoreboard with his forefinger. Philip had another suggestion for that same finger.

"That's more like it. I'll come your way, shall I? I'll come to your offices, say at three PM?"

Did Philip really want him at his office? Did he want people seeing Jamieson enter? Although maybe, on the other hand, a sizeable chunk of change walking in the door might not do them and their reputation any harm. He didn't need to check his schedule; Philip already knew it was empty.

"That will be fine. I assume you know where to find us. I'll see you at three." Philip didn't wait for the man to say anything further and ended the call. He kept his hand on the handset for a long moment, staring at his own flesh still in situ. It was beginning to look wrinkly, probably from too much sun. He should use more sunscreen.

Carmen knocked and opened the door straight away; her beautiful head of hair looked stunning as always. She had one hand resting on the door frame above her head and the other on her hip. If anyone could be a model, Carmen could. She'd look right at home in a *Marie Claire* magazine shoot.

"Was that THE Frank Jamieson? Don't tell me he's looking for a divorce lawyer and we're it? I saw he was splitting up from his wife —it's been in all the magazines." She said it almost proudly, though Philip couldn't see Carmen being interested in local gossip. Maybe he didn't know her as well as he thought he did. Somewhat irritated at Jamieson getting his way, he snapped back at her unintentionally.

"You must have something better to do than gossip, Carmen." His fiery eyes locked with hers, though hers were full of confusion at his outburst. But he wasn't about to apologise, not yet. She took the hint and left, closing the door rather noisily in her wake. Philip leant forward and put his head in his hands. His shoulders ached from a sleepless night, worrying whether someone was watching or listening to his every move. He'd even cut his morning bathroom routine short for that same reason.

His office suddenly felt claustrophobic; he needed air, so he stood and headed out into the hot street, not really knowing where he was going. It was stifling. He longed to be wearing only his shorts and T-shirt, and he rolled up the sleeves of his dress shirt as he paced forward amongst shoppers and tourists alike. The searing sun scorched down on his head and stung his eyes, and he squinted. He wished he had his sunglasses, but they were back at his desk.

He ducked inside a small café and took a seat at the back, relaxing slightly as he readjusted to the dim interior. He picked up the menu for something to do, not because he was hungry, and found himself gazing at the selection of ice creams, of all things. An ever-present smiling waitress hovered by his elbow and he ordered a triple scoop of chocolate with sprinkles on top.

"Sure thing, hon," she said. He looked up as he recognised the same words he'd heard spoken recently. She was the same waitress from the bar last night. She must work two jobs, he deduced. If she remembered him, she never let on; she was gone as quickly as she'd arrived. Had Alistair been there with him, he'd have been excited at the prospect of being waited on by her a second time. He enjoyed probability, and two instances would mean an omen. To Philip, however, it simply meant she worked two jobs.

He picked up a sachet of sugar and fiddled with it to give his fingers something to do while he waited, and began searching the other faces inside the café. He'd never bothered taking an interest before, but with recent events, and the notion that he was being observed, he thought it prudent. Apart from the waitress, there was no one else he had seen before, not recently anyway. He awaited his ice-cream.

Philip had decided he wouldn't phone Alistair and let him know that Jamieson would be descending on their offices at 3 PM. Alistair was out for the rest of the day, but more to the point, if anyone was listening, Philip didn't want them being privy to the conversation.

It was almost 3 PM and the only person excited for Jamieson's arrival was Carmen. He heard the laughter coming through his door. She sounded delighted, if not a little fan-struck. Philip expected a knock at the door any second and wasn't disappointed. He called for him to come on in. He thought it best if he received his unwanted guest, for want of a better word, while standing. It was an alpha male thing, like who had the strongest handshake or managed to put their other hand on the opposite fellow's arm first.

As Jamieson strode into his office, Philip forced himself to make eye contact with him, but couldn't get past his rather bulbous nose. He tried harder to meet the man's eyes but found he was drawn, once again, back down to the incredible nose. He knew he was being rude and wondered if his opponent had noticed. He offered Jamieson a seat and sat down opposite him in the other of the two client armchairs.

"What can I get you to drink? Something cold, perhaps?"

"Nothing, thank you. I won't take up much of your time. I wanted to meet you, to meet the other half of Banks & Crowley, and hope that you can help me out with my. . . situation." He gave Philip a cloying smile.

Philip was desperate to keep control of this meeting, and not let Jamieson run roughshod over his ethics. He was a divorce lawyer, nothing more. "We can certainly help with your divorce, Mr. Jamieson, as I'm sure Alistair will have mentioned to you, and we would be delighted to take on your business. But that is where our expertise finishes. We only specialise in divorce law."

Philip watched Jamieson uncross his legs in his seat and re-cross them in the opposite way, leaving his right foot resting on his left knee. The cuff of the man's trousers rode up a few inches, exposing grey socks and a swatch of hairy white leg. And an ankle holster for a concealed weapon.

It was empty, but the message was there, all right. Jamieson smiled as Philip's eyes widened.

"Think on it some more, Mr. Banks. I know you'll find my terms worth your while in the long run. I'll see myself out."

Chapter Thirty-Nine

The words echoed around Philip's head: *"Think on it some more, Mr. Banks. I know you'll find my terms worth your while in the long run."*

Philip had thought of little else since Jamieson had closed the door behind him a few hours ago. He needed to find out what they had on him, or what they *thought* they had on him, because he was getting more scared by the hour. It was one thing knowing someone has been through your belongings, but coming to your office and making veiled threats was something else. Empty holster or not, Jamieson would find another way to intimidate him into doing what he wanted.

Philip had done what he usually did when something was on his mind, and that was go for a run. But he didn't want to be crowded in; he felt like he needed to stretch his legs where there weren't so many people milling about to get in his way. So, he headed north again, towards Santa Monica Pier, and figured he'd go on from there — though where exactly that might be, he wasn't sure. It was a hell of a long way to Malibu, not the ideal place to run to, but since he was heading in that direction, he figured he'd run as far as he could go. He made his way off the boardwalk just before the pier and down to the water's edge, where the sand was a little firmer and there were fewer people to dodge.

He did his best thinking when he was running, and even though sometimes it hurt like hell, the feeling he got when he'd finished the run always made it worthwhile. As he picked up pace along the water's edge, Philip could feel his sweat running down his temples, liquid that would ultimately run to his chest and soak into his running vest. The more he sweated, the more motivated he was to carry on, which made running in LA all the easier. It was hard not to get soaked when the sun shone most days of the year. He liked to run with music in his ears, but right now he needed a clear head and time to think, so he'd left his music at home, though his phone was tucked safely in the pouch wrapped around his bicep, just in case. The further away from Santa Monica he got, the more the crowds thinned out, and the more alone he started to feel. If anyone was watching him now, he'd be vulnerable, but he didn't think the situation was that serious. He wasn't a defecting spy, after all; he was a simple divorce lawyer caught up in a misunderstanding. Jamieson was just trying to scare him because he wanted Philip to do a job for him, a job that he wasn't going to do.

Because Philip wasn't the killer.

Well, not intentionally, anyway.

Yes, Philip had gone to Gerald Baker's house that day, with the intention of first talking to him, getting him to see sense after both he and Alistair had realised what the man was up to, and then killing him. He'd done his research and had figured out a way to make things look like a heart attack, even had a doctor friend confirm it would work for him. But the day's events had turned a little odd, and before Philip could administer the drug he'd crushed up in preparation, the old man had keeled over all by himself.

Obviously, Jamieson now thought Philip had been responsible somehow, and Philip had debated whether to tell him the truth. But telling the truth would be admitting that he had been there, that he'd been in Gerald's house and that they'd argued.

Philip was the last person to see him alive.

And he hadn't helped save him.

He'd let him die.

The old man was a fraud. He'd developed a financial scheme that they'd fallen prey to, but more importantly, Gerald Baker had caused the deaths of at least three other individuals that they knew about. And maybe more outside their circle. And since the three victims had been friends of both Philip and Alistair, they'd sought to get their revenge. Teach the man a lesson. But it's funny how life's events turn out: Mother Nature had intervened and got the job done herself. And while Philip had been witness to the episode, he certainly hadn't helped the guy.

Did that make him a killer?

Regardless, somehow Jamieson had known that he was there, that Gerald Baker was now dead, and had assumed that Philip had been instrumental in this.

And now he wanted Philip to do the same to his wife.

No doubt there would be a fee involved, and while the money was tempting and they sure could use it, it would mean Philip would have to officially cross a line. Was money worth it? Or was a clean conscience a better price? He'd had a lucky escape with Gerald Baker; he hadn't got his death on his hands, though he'd come close. But what if Jamieson wouldn't take no for an answer? How would Philip explain away that he had been at Baker's house, and then that he'd been at the funeral? That last idea had been a giant mistake, but it had been a double check, just to make sure that the old bugger had been put in the ground and hadn't suddenly come back to life in a mortuary refrigerator. No, he'd seen him go, all right; Gerald Baker was good and gone.

Philip decided he'd had enough running; he'd still got the return journey to do. He jogged to a halt at a rocky outcrop, turned to face the ocean and was tempted to get in for a dip, cool himself, and wash some of the sweat off his body. He looked like he'd already been in the sea; he was saturated, and tiny rivers of salty sweat ran down his head and arms.

The water was tranquil and calm, small waves breaking easily at the shoreline just a couple of feet away from where he stood. There was nobody else around; he had the beach to himself. He bent to undo his laces, kicked off his trainers and removed his armband, leaving them all in a tidy pile out of the water's reach. Barefoot, he waded out until he was waist high in seawater, the salt from his sweat mixing with the salt from the ocean. He dipped down and stuck his head and shoulders under the water to rinse, holding his breath while he stayed in place, quite still, feeling the water move around his body, swirling around his head until he was almost out of breath. He popped back up and took a gulp of air to refill his lungs, then dipped back down under the water.

The cooler water did wonders to lower his body temperature, and when his lungs were almost empty again, he broke back through the surface to breathe but kept his tanned shoulders tucked under. It was wonderfully refreshing, and he lifted his legs beneath him and trod the water like a dog paddling. He rested his head back in the water and closed his eyes for a moment, feeling the sun warm his face, doing its best to dry the salty sea water. He stayed there, eyes closed, just floating in the water, letting the stress loosen from his shoulders while he could. It was the escape he needed.

But he couldn't stay there all night. With a sigh, he made his way back to the shore and his trainers. As he sloshed back up onto the shore, his running shorts hung loosely around his hips, water cascading in long tapering rivers down his legs. He picked up his phone and trainers and started to walk back towards home, water still dripping down his tanned body. The run had done him good, the soak even more so, and he felt a little clearer in his own mind. He wasn't interested in Jamieson's offer; he wasn't interested in the man's money. No, he was interested in his own moral compass—and being on the right side of it. If that meant telling Jamieson the truth about what had happened that day, then so be it; he'd suffer the consequences. But he wasn't going to put himself in that position again. Something had intervened that day. Philip had never been meant to kill the man—that deed had been taken out of his hands.

It was best he should leave things that way.

Chapter Forty

Tuesday 4th August 1987

I'm finding this so hard to deal with and, cliché or not, I simply have no clue what to do for the best. My life as I know it would turn upside down if anyone knew what I'm doing, and I couldn't bear to hurt them. But how can you love more than one woman at the same time? My feelings for Sylvia won't go away and I'm addicted to her presence; I can't keep away from her. I miss everything about her—her smile, her perfume, her easy-going ways. She makes me feel so alive again. Yes, I know, another cliché, but she does. She puts a smile on my face. And I know I must stop before someone suspects something. The question is, how can I keep away from the woman I'm so drawn to, so addicted to, so in love with?

Chapter Forty-One

Chrissy couldn't work out if she was disappointed or not. She'd started out with the 2014 diary, looking for some clue, into what she yet had no idea. And the year was the wrong one; she needed 1987. But it was all she had to go on, all she had of her father's private life, which she knew nothing about. Alas, all the diary contained was a few entries about his feelings and a few business and social events that he'd attended—birthdays or christenings or similar events. There were, as expected, a few financial notes that made no sense to her at all, with what appeared to be some sort of code written next to them. Weird, but certainly not interesting.

She sipped on her wine while she read and when the glass was empty for the second time, she got up to refill it again. Swaying a little as she stood, she caught herself with the arm of her chair. She was beginning to feel little woozy; she needed food in her empty stomach before the boys got home.

They're not coming home for dinner, silly.

Healthy sushi at Gary's place, remember?

I'm a terrible mother.

It was perhaps a good job they were being fed elsewhere; she couldn't have driven them for burgers or sushi. Even if she didn't drink any more wine, she needed to soak up what was already sloshing around in her empty stomach. She opened the fridge again and took out items to make a sandwich; it would do, although her creation would not have garnered points on *Britain's Best Home Cook*. Mayonnaise oozed precariously down the side of the bread. Cooking was not one of her stronger points; no wonder Adam had chosen to stay out for dinner. She took her hastily made sandwich back to her corner chair and put her feet up on the small side table rather than tucking them underneath her. It was easier to eat that way.

"What was going on, Dad?" she asked the otherwise empty room as she picked up his diary again. "And why is the diary from 1987 missing? And the years either side of it? Who's got them?"

Even with the three books missing, there was no way she was going to let this puzzle go now; it was getting more mysterious as the days clicked over. Maybe she would fare better with the information she'd gleaned from the old headmaster, she thought. At least he'd managed to give her parts of names; maybe she could Google the rest of them now. With nothing left to learn from the 2014 diary, she took the remains of her sandwich and glass of wine up to her attic office and her computer.

It was always peaceful in her attic office; she liked it up there. Smiling, she reached up to open one of the skylights. The temperature in the room was still warm, and the air was a bit stuffy from the late afternoon sun shining through. She could hear the chatter of birds in the trees nearby and she stood for a moment under the window to listen, enjoying the birdsong. It could be incredibly relaxing. When a cloud passed over and changed the light in the room, she took her seat once again in front of her laptop and pulled up a webpage to start her search on the name she'd been given. Philip Banks she'd already got, but now she knew something more about him, namely that he was American, and so was his friend Alistair; that should narrow things down a bit. She wrote their names down on a pad in front of her to come back to.

She decided to start with one whose full name she knew, and

typed *Samuel Moore* into the search bar. Samuel Moore, Moor with an E on the end. She added *1987*, figuring there would be hundreds of thousands of Samuel Moores. It turned out to be a good move. Up came a picture of the boy, looking similar to the one in the biscuit tin, though whoever had posted it online had omitted the E on the end of his surname. It was a clear likeness to the picture she already had. Finally, she was getting a bit further. She clicked on the link to read more about the boy from thirty years ago.

There wasn't much to be gleaned; it was mundane school stuff, nothing to get excited about, so she went back to the search results and look further on for a more adult Samuel Moore. With an E on the end. Reading the headlines, she scrolled down the first and second pages. Nothing particularly grabbed her attention. On the third page of the search results, she stopped, hovered her mouse over the link and groaned. It was an announcement of the death of Samuel Moore; the age listed looked about right. The deceased man would have just turned 45.

The small hairs on the back of her neck prickled slightly as she read that Samuel Moore had taken an overdose twelve months previously and was found by his family in his home. It went on to say that friends and family had no idea why such a happy man would have taken his own life; there seemed to be no reason for it. A shock to them all. He'd left two small children and his wife behind.

Chrissy studied the photograph of the man and then flipped through to the other webpage she still had open, where a younger Samuel Moore looked back at her. She checked the boy's eyes against the man's eyes, the boy's mouth against the man's mouth, and made adjustments for fading hair over the years. In her opinion, the two photographs were of the same person at different stages in life.

She'd found the right Samuel Moore, but too late, it seemed.

"One down," she said to herself, and opened another browser tab for the next search. She had two more that she had full names for: Stuart Townsend and Steve Marks. She picked the latter, entered his name in the search bar, and pressed search. With just his name alone there were over 100 million results, so she tried her trick again and added *1987*. That brought the figure down to 16 million, still far too many to wade through. She thought for a moment and then added Glendene into the mix. It didn't do much good, but she scanned the first few pages of headlines just in case something grabbed her like it had with Samuel. There was nothing obvious, nothing worthy of investigating, nothing that piqued her interest one iota.

"Damn. I thought it might have worked a second time. I must've just got lucky." She stared across at her screen, wondering what to try next.

"What if Philip and Alistair were friends as kids?" she thought, sitting forward again. "I wonder if they stayed friends as adults, being that they are both American." She hurriedly typed in *Philip Banks* plus *Alistair* plus *America* and waited for the results to come back.

She couldn't believe her luck.

Smiling, she clicked on the top listing, the URL for a firm of lawyers in the LA suburbs, not that far from Santa Monica.

"Well, would you look at that? What are the chances that they are in Santa Monica, and that I'm going there too?" She raised her eyes to the ceiling, her hands in front of her as if praying, and said, "Thank you." Now she was excited: finally, she was getting some-where, and the stars were aligning on her side. She clicked on to their 'About Us' page and read the brief corporate descriptions of Alistair Crowley and Philip Banks. Both were divorce lawyers, both working in Abbot Kinney at their own practice.

But the thing that really caught her interest was their photographs on the page. Even though they were on the formal side, something sparked inside of her.

She was sure she'd seen Philip's face before. But where?

Chapter Forty-Two

Chrissy peered a bit more closely at the picture on her computer screen. Although Philip's shirt and tie made him look older, stuffy and corporate, she was certain now that she'd seen him before, although she still couldn't be sure where—if it indeed had been him. She'd never used a lawyer in LA, so it couldn't have been that, and she certainly didn't socialise when she was out there, preferring her own company, peace and relaxation. Her time away. Sure, she had a few friends, but they were passing acquaintances and she was sure he wasn't the partner of any of them. And since he wasn't from around Englefield Green either; that couldn't be it. She put the thought to the back of her mind to come back to later, then carried on with her search.

Getting results spurred her on. She checked the time via the clock on her computer screen and figured what the hell, she'd keep looking. But her mind kept drifting back to Philip and Alistair, their law practice and the fact that they were literally around the corner from where her LA place was. Clearly, she had some decisions to make. But first, she wanted to find out more about Stuart Townsend, another boy whose name she had but hadn't been able to find much information on. Figuring that all the boys had gone to the same school and that two—Philip and Alistair—were lawyers, she wondered now if maybe there were other lawyers amongst them.

She typed in *Stuart Townsend* and *lawyer*, and waited. There was still over a million results, but the Wikipedia result at the top of the page caught her eye and she clicked on that as a starting point. No good. Unless the Stuart she was looking for was an Irish actor, and she doubted that, it was the wrong guy. She scrolled down, looking for something else that might stand out. She'd no idea at this point if she was in fact actually scrolling over useful posts or not, but she hadn't the time to go through every single link—she'd be searching all year.

It was page six when something eventually popped out at her, and she decided to click. It was on a UK law website, in the news section and it was a brief story about how Stuart Townsend had been found dead at his home in Richmond, Surrey. He'd left a wife, Jo, and two twin boys, Ben and Jerry, behind. She read a brief outline of Stuart's accolades and achievements, that he had been a talented lawyer in his prime and that his suicide had been a massive shock to all. There was no mention of how he'd taken his own life, but immediately Chrissy heard alarm bells ringing.

That was two on her list who had committed suicide—Samuel Moore and Stuart Townsend—and that was too much of a coincidence. Would any more turn up dead, she wondered. With a sinking feeling, she turned her attention back to Cody Taylor now, putting his name in the search bar again and adding *lawyer*. Nothing. But adding *suicide* brought up what she needed.

"Shit!" she exclaimed. Cody Taylor, a businessman in infrastructure, was also listed as having died of suicide. That made three. Her pulse started to race. There wasn't much more now that she needed to find out: she needed to find out a surname for Robert, and she didn't have a fat lot on Steve Marks either. Adding *suicide* to *Steve Marks* turned up nothing of interest. So, Steve could still be alive, but what of Robert? Sitting back in her chair she pondered for a moment; the light around had begun to dim slightly as the sun slid down the sky to the horizon. She flicked on the desk lamp and sat thinking for a moment in the quiet of her attic office.

Her head was buzzing. Buzzing with what she had found out so far: the fact that two of the boys in the tin were alive and well, and had their business at Abbot Kinney, and the horrible fact that three of the others had committed suicide, and only fairly recently, in the last year or so. All of those three had had young families at the time of their deaths, so whatever it was that had encouraged them to take their own lives must've been pretty rough. Chrissy was never of the opinion that those who committed suicide were cowards. More the opposite: to be able to take your own life, to swallow those pills or put a noose around your own neck or any of the other ways that people chose to take their own lives, must be incredibly frightening. It would take a lot of guts to accomplish. Leaving a small family along with a loving wife must be devastatingly difficult to contemplate, never mind act on. She wondered what that something was that had encouraged them to do such thing. Was it connected to her puzzle?

The wine and the sandwich weren't doing much for her concentration now, so she made her way back downstairs. Once back down in the coolness of the kitchen, she flicked the kettle on to make some tea, hoping to dilute the couple of glasses of wine dulling her senses. The sandwich hadn't been sufficient, so she took a pizza out of the freezer, unwrapped it from the cellophane and placed it in the oven on high. Pizza wasn't normally her thing. She kept them in for her boys, but since neither one was home and she was hungry, she considered it a treat. She wasn't going to beat herself up over it; she was sure pizza had some vital nutrients in it somewhere— maybe in the sliced vegetables on top? 'Everything in moderation' was her guideline; there was no need to deprive yourself when you really desired something. Instantly, however, she thought of Julie's waiflike body.

She must be permanently hungry.
I should cook her a proper meal.
With my cooking skills? Maybe not.

She let her head run free while she waited for the pizza to cook, her brain filtering through all she'd learned while she was upstairs in her office. Now she had to put it into some sort of order and figure out what the link was other than that the boys had all gone to school together and a good proportion of them were lawyers.

Or dead.

The more she delved, the more she found out, the more she wanted to know. It was a shame her father wasn't around to tell her more.

He'd hidden that tin for a reason.

"And where the hell are the three missing diaries? Why would someone take them? And who? Did they even exist?" The more she thought of the missing diaries, the more she realised they had to hold the key to whatever it was that was being concealed. Of course they existed: her father had been too meticulous over the years to not have kept the three in question. And whoever had them now surely was involved. She couldn't see either Julie or her mother being that person. What motive could they have?

But somebody had a motive; somebody was hiding them from her.

The timer dinged. As she slid the pizza out of the oven, she wondered what else the old headmaster hadn't told her. He was definitely somebody else who held clues. There was a story he wasn't telling her. She'd have to go back and pay him another visit, ask about the suicides and about Robert, the boy without a surname. And since she was leaving for LA the day after tomorrow, she didn't have much time to see the old man again.

Chapter Forty-Three

They were hidden for safekeeping. Nobody should ever know the truth; there was little point. It served no purpose now that Gerald was dead. Enough people had died already, and if the full story ever came out there would be shame added to the hurt. Shame on those that were involved; shame on those that were left behind. How those photographs had ever come to be found at all was a mystery. But now Chrissy was snooping; only time would tell if she was savvy enough to piece it together and bring the story to light.

Unless the story was stopped, of course. But that would mean stopping Chrissy—not an easy task.

The diary paper sounded crinkly, thin, like parchment paper almost, and it was covered with the man's inky scrawl; he had used a fountain pen to create the distinctive calligraphy on each page. There were everyday notes, there were business dealings, and then there were his love notes. They had stayed in the diaries, never been delivered, and so they were there to read, Gerald Baker pouring out his heart and soul into his private writing. Maybe he re-read them to himself, relived them even. From the content he'd written, it was obvious quite how in love the man was—with a woman he couldn't have. The passion in his words showed how it pulled at his soul.

Another page turned, another day devoured, another story learned.

There'd been a rumour that Gerald had had an affair, but no one had ever seen any proof. No one realised just how deep in he had been until the diaries had come to light.

They'd always been there, locked away in the cupboard in his den, but the key had been hidden, keeping the cupboard's contents safely away from prying eyes. But now Gerald was dead and buried, and it seemed only right that his sordid secret should stay with him.

The three diaries were slipped back inside the safe for safekeeping, far away from searching, prying eyes.

Chapter Forty-Four

Chrissy seemed to be making a habit of getting up before dawn, she thought, sighing with frustration. Knowing full well there was no point lying there any longer, she slipped out of bed once again. It was just coming up to 5 AM, almost dawn. Instead of going down to the kitchen, she went up to her attic office as quietly as she could so as not to wake the rest of the household, who were still peacefully sleeping. The boys had got home later than expected and would welcome the sleep-in. Chrissy would drop them at school herself to save them time. Adam would be up shortly; she'd wait for her morning cup of tea until then. But first she wanted to find out if a hunch she'd had during the night would pay off. There were still two names that she had virtually nothing on—Robert somebody and Steve Marks. If she put all the names into one Google search at the same time, would anything rise to the surface, something they all had in common, perhaps? It was worth a try.

Making herself comfortable at her desk, she opened her laptop and waited for the WiFi to connect. She entered each of the boys' names, adding a plus sign between each one, and threw in *Glendene* for good measure. She clicked search and waited.

Nothing.

"Damn," she said to herself. She took *Glendene* out and tried a second time without it. She stared at the screen, willing it to give her an answer, but once again, nothing was forthcoming. She sat back, tapping a finger on her chin. What would she have done in a previous life? How could she have found out more with just a first name to go on, for a boy that she knew had existed back in 1987?

Legwork. She had to talk to people on that list who had known the boy, but the only ones still alive both lived in LA. Three more were deceased. There was the old headmaster, of course, but she'd drawn a blank there yesterday, so unless he'd had a miraculous memory explosion since she'd left him in the pub, that was a dead end.

"I guess first I need to go back to Inkpen, see if the school secretary will talk to me. Maybe she's been there a while and can help." She remembered the bright, breezy voice of the girl she'd spoken to on the phone, the one she'd lied to about working for *Horse and Hound.* Maybe she could bribe her somehow to gain access to the boys' records. All she needed was this Robert's surname, and maybe where he'd moved on to if they kept that information, and then she'd follow it up herself. Or maybe the school had an address, and Robert's parents still lived there, and she could call in on them. Either way, she had to do the legwork; there was no other way.

And she only had today.

She heard the faint sounds of movement from the floor below her and figured Adam was up. She flipped the lid of the laptop shut and went down to join him.

"Good morning. Want some tea?" she said brightly as she entered the kitchen.

"Three mornings in a row you beat me to it. I hope you're not ailing for something," he said. Adam wrapped his arms around Chrissy as he pulled her close and kissed her forehead tenderly. "You do feel a bit warm." Chrissy enjoyed the comfort of his arms; she'd miss them in the coming days, but knew that she would look forward to his embrace even more when she returned. Absence made the heart grow fonder.

"I'm fine," she said. "I'm just cramming, trying to get everything tidied up before I go. A bit on my mind. But thanks for asking."

"I'll miss you, you know. I'm not fond of when you go away." He tightened his grip ever so slightly and nuzzled into her neck. If she were a cat, Chrissy would have purred. He smelled of sleep; his face was rough with stubble and he had a severe case of bed head. Her stomach growled. Her own evening meal the night before had not exactly hit the spot.

"Why don't I make us both scrambled eggs for breakfast, before the boys get up? And a pot of coffee?" she said, looking up at him expectantly. "You always enjoy my eggs."

"That's because it's hard to ruin them, unless you leave them on too long and burn the toast." She slapped him lightly across his chest and he restrained her further in a tight bear hug until she squealed out. "Ssh, you'll wake the boys," he said.

"Then stop teasing about my cooking skills. Eggs or not? You'll wish I was here to make them next week," she said in a singsong voice. Knowing he'd succumb, she unwrapped his grip and gathered the utensils she'd need, taking eggs from the fridge.

Adam added bread to the toaster for them both. "I'll be in charge of the toast," he informed her, a knowing look in his eye. "That way, I know it will be done to perfection."

Chrissy raised her wooden spoon in the air at him, mock threatening. Changing the subject away from her cooking skills, she said, "I leave tomorrow night. Are you sure you won't come out for a couple of days?"

"I can't really," he said. "And what about the boys? Your mother is in no state yet to look after them. She's still grieving. And we can't ask Gary's mum again. They were only round there last night, eating her out of house and home, I shouldn't wonder."

None of this was news to Chrissy, and she knew he'd never head out with her. But in asking, it made it feel like it was his choice not to tag along rather than her choice to leave in the first place. One day, he might surprise her and say yes. But she'd deal with that if the situation ever arose.

Scooping scrambled eggs out onto perfectly cooked toast, she handed him a plate and they sat down to eat.

"Look at that," she said. "Perfect eggs. Who said I can't cook?"

Chapter Forty-Five

After she'd had a long hot shower and Adam and the boys had left for the day, Chrissy called Glendene School again. The same bright and extremely high-pitched voice answered her call, and Chrissy did her utmost once again not to laugh. She idly wondered if surgery might have been responsible for the woman's peculiar tone. Bubble from *Absolutely Fabulous* sprang to mind. Perhaps this woman dressed similarly too.

"Hi. It's Chrissy Livingstone here. You—"

There was no need to go on. The bright voice talked straight over the top of her. Rather excitedly.

"Hi!" she squealed. "*Horse & Hound Magazine* lady!"

Chrissy left a moment of silence empty in case there was more to follow. When the coast was clear, Chrissy went on. "Yes. What a great memory you have."

"Thanks! Do you need something else? I guess you've heard?" Incredibly, the woman's voice suddenly dropped several octaves as she asked the last part of her question. The bubbles sounded like the gas had left them.

"Heard?" she enquired. "I spoke to Mr. Browning yesterday at lunch. Have I missed something?"

"Oh," the woman replied. The syllable was tinged with sadness. Chrissy waited, then pressed on. "What's happened?"

"Mr. Browning fell terribly ill yesterday, I'm afraid. A taxi took him home after lunch, but the driver ended up taking him straight to the hospital. His breathing. He's in intensive care, and it doesn't sound good by all accounts. It's awfully sad."

Chrissy couldn't quite believe her ears. Only yesterday she'd been eating pork pie with him while he sipped on his half pint. And she'd badgered him with questions from the past, about boys whom he quite obviously knew. About a secret he was never going to let her in on. And now he was gravely ill. He'd take what he knew to his resting place.

But had Chrissy contributed to his anxiety, bringing up whatever it was that he'd been keeping secret? She was conscious of the woman's voice on the other end of the telephone. The light fog cleared around her thoughts and she said, "I'm so sorry. That's terrible."

"Thank you. Everyone here is quite upset. Mr. Browning is a well-respected man. He did so much for the school, and now he's almost gone." Her tone changed upwards again, thoughts of the man's illness evaporating rapidly, Chrissy assumed. "So, what can I do for you?" Back to gas-filled bubbles.

"Actually, I'm trying to trace another chap for my story. He attended the school in 1987, so he'd have been around fifteen then. Robert was his first name. Would you be able to tell me his surname, perhaps?"

"Oh. I wouldn't be able to, I'm afraid. I wasn't here then."

Chrissy rolled her eyes. My goodness, but this woman was dim.

"I realise that," she said politely. "Would you be able to look up his surname for me? I can't think there'd be too many Roberts attending in 1987. I'll know it when I hear it, and then I can get hold of him." Chrissy figured she'd write all the names down as the woman reeled them off, then fake excitement at the last one. It had worked in the past.

"I'll have to check with the secretary," Bubble said, though she sounded nervous about it. *Damn.* Chrissy couldn't afford to lose another lead, and she knew that the secretary would not divulge the information. They were worse than the old ward sisters in protecting their patients. She needed to rescue the situation before all was lost and she left empty handed. Chrissy decided to go out on a limb, though a fake one.

"Well, how about when I've finished this article, I get the photographer to pop on over and grab some shots of you in the grounds perhaps? And I'll make sure you're in the magazine, since you've been such a big help already. We're looking at the Christmas edition currently. Maybe you could wear red that day?"

There was a delighted but low squeal, and Chrissy pushed the phone away from her ear until it passed.

"Well. . ."

"If you read the handful out, I'll know which one I'm looking for. I'm pretty sure his parents are still around Berkshire." Chrissy cringed at her own untruths.

May your mouth turn black.

There was a light clackety-clack from fingers tapping a keyboard, then, "Here you go." Chrissy had her pen poised, ready. "There are six. Jones, Harvey, Newsome, Smithson, Turner and Vegar. Do you recognise the one you need?"

"Wonderful! Thank you so much—yes. You've been extremely helpful. And I'll not tell a soul."

"Well, let me know what day I should wear red, won't you?"

"Of course. I'll be in touch. Thanks again." Chrissy disconnected before the woman asked any more questions. She doubted she'd be able to call for anything else in the future. Looking at the paper in front of her, she smiled at the six names. It was time to get back to more digging.

The rest of her search was tedious work and took her up until lunchtime, but she only had to get halfway through the list to find what she needed.

Robert Newsome was the boy, now the man, she was looking for.

And thankfully, Dr. Robert Newsome appeared to be alive and presumably well.

Chapter Forty-Six

There wasn't a whole lot of time to go and see the doctor. Dr. Robert Newsome would not be getting a visit from Chrissy before she left for LA the following day, but that didn't mean he would be forgotten about. It was bad timing—or was it good timing? To be scheduled and going to LA at all was fortuitous. Or an omen. But there were things she needed to do before she left, things for her family, and they were far more important than her own private investigation.

Since Chrissy had never been known for her cooking skills and the family regularly groaned when she attempted to create something, she often used a cooking service, meals she ordered online that were then delivered vacuum packed and ready to be warmed up. They weren't bad. In fact, some would say they were better than what she produced herself, and so she relied heavily on them. Scrolling through the order page, she clicked on various meals for the three hungry males in her life, ordering enough for the next ten days and adding a few desserts in as special treats. She'd only be gone a week, but it didn't hurt to have excess in the freezer to give everyone a bit of choice. Her mother would have grimaced if she saw what Chrissy was doing, but at least the lads were getting fed and would not be living on sandwiches or takeaway crap.

Or sushi.

Or burgers.

She added all the items to her account—no need for credit card details, as they were already preloaded—and printed out her order so that Adam could easily see what was available. There would be no need for him to rummage in the bowels of the freezer. He was a busy man, too, and mundane things like eating during the week had to be made as simple as possible all round. The food order service was a godsend and a time saver.

Satisfied everything was sorted for their nourishment needs, she made her way downstairs and gathering her handbag, slipped on sandals and left the house. She had errands to run before she left, things that couldn't be avoided, like picking up Adam's dry-cleaning and her prescription from the pharmacy. She unlocked her car, climbed in and set off in the direction of Egham, only a couple of miles down the road, a town she could in fact have walked to on any other day.

On a day she fancied a long walk.

Her stomach growled, sounding like water gurgling down an outside grid, as she drove the short distance, so much so that Chrissy herself commented in the emptiness of her car.

"I'd better make lunch my first stop," she said as she pulled into a parking space in the small car park five minutes later. There was a café that she liked to frequent just around the corner and, gathering her belongings off the passenger seat, she made her way round.

It was a little after 1 PM and the place was heaving. Peering towards the back of the café, she spotted a vacant table for two and made a beeline for it before somebody else saw it and swooped in. There was a tall, skinny, well-thumbed menu propped against the cruet, though she knew the entire contents of the list without needing to read it. There was always a slight possibility she might try something new, but it was the same thing each time. She'd been there only a moment when the waitress came over.

"What can I get you from the kitchen?" she enquired. Efficient and polite enough.

"I'll have the bubble and squeak with poached eggs, please, and a chamomile tea," she ordered. The young woman wrote it down without saying another word and Chrissy watched as she headed over to the till to input her order. She wondered about the young woman, about her life; she wondered if she was happy.

Chrissy often watched people. It was a habit from a previous life and one that she carried on with because people fascinated her. She turned in her own seat so that she could watch the front door better, always interested in who was coming or going. What secrets did they hold? What went on behind their closed doors? Were they happy? Did they have a special someone somewhere? It wasn't as though Chrissy wasn't happy; she was—how could she not be? She 'worked' for herself as a HR contractor and that took hardly any of her time up. She was free to come and go as she pleased, and that included overseas travel. To a point, though. She had to be careful not to raise suspicion.

A man in a suit walked in. He looked like any other forty-something businessman, and Chrissy watched him as he approached the counter and ordered what she assumed would be his lunch. While he waited for it to be prepared, he took out his smartphone and scrolled. She watched his fingers moving up and down as he scanned, looking for something to engage his attention. When something did just that, he stood, stooped at the shoulders, and read what was on his tiny screen intently. It could have been a news article, it could have an email, it could have been his Facebook newsfeed; who knew? But watching him reminded her of Philip, whom she was going to look up when she got to LA. He had the same aura about him, from what she'd deduced from the 'About Us' page. Maybe this guy was a divorce lawyer too. He could easily have been Philip Banks or his partner Alistair Crowley.

How would that go, exactly? She couldn't just go barging into their office and say "Hello. Why is your face in a tin with some other boys' pictures? And how do you know my father?" She'd come across as a nutter. No, she'd be a little bit more covert than that. She knew he was a divorce lawyer—nothing spectacular there. And there was a connection to her father; of that she was sure. The same was likely true of all the boys in the tin; otherwise, why would her father have hidden them in the shed? No, her father knew them, all right.

The man at the counter picked up a brown paper bag that contained his order, uttered a couple of words, most likely his thanks, and made his way back towards the door. From behind, he could have been Adam. Same height, same sort of close-cropped hair, same navy suit. A moment later her own lunch arrived, and she tucked in hungrily, bright orange-yellow egg yolk spilling out onto her plate after her knife pierced it. The eggs in LA always seemed paler by comparison, more like pale custard made from a packet, like her grandma used to make. It was a small observation, nothing important at all, but over the years noticing tiny things had become second nature, to her, each one filed away. Maybe it would be recalled later, maybe not, but she knew from experience that omitting detail could get you in trouble. Or out of it.

When Chrissy had finished her lunch, she sipped on her chamomile tea and carried on her lazy surveillance of the small café for no other reason than to fill her time. The lunchtime crowd had thinned now, and a waitress cleared tables, including Chrissy's own, apart from her tea. There were only two tables plus her own that were occupied now, and the inhabitants of the others both had their heads in books.

Feeling suddenly anxious, though she couldn't understand why, she left the remains of her tea, grabbed her bag and left the café at a pace, like she had a destination to get to. A feeling of restlessness filled her body as she headed out into the warmth of the afternoon, stalking purposefully towards the drycleaners, though she couldn't put her finger on why. Normally, the day before she was going away, she was calm, looking forward to going and having some alone time, but this time it didn't feel that way. Maybe it was because she had slipped back into her old ways, from her previous life, and had a target firmly set in her sights. Maybe it was a strange sort of thrill that was rippling through her body, not restlessness at all. Maybe it was the excitement, the idea of something she could get her teeth into, something other than her everyday life.

This time tomorrow, she'd be hanging out in the trendy part of LA, at Abbot Kinney, watching and waiting for two faces from the tin.

Chapter Forty-Seven

Monday 10th August 1987

We had simply the best day down by the river. Our river—that's how I'll always think of it. Not our spot, but our river. The tranquillity of it was so like her, as we lay entwined in each other's arms, the ferocity of it on other days an equal match to her passion when we make love. So gentle, yet so rapid. I should call her my river—yes, it sounds so like her. My river Sylvia: bubbling, vivacious, calming, tranquil, transparent yet deep. All the words I think of to describe her also describe the river that runs by our feet.

She brought sandwiches today, cut into squares rather than triangles, which is her all over—different. Why do people make triangles when squares work as easily? The simplicity of her drives me mad with desire, and today I got frustrated with myself that I couldn't find a release, not there, not then. We are more than sex—there is a lot more to our relationship—but I know I'll never be able to show the world. There would be too much pain. And right now, there is only my own to contain.

Chapter Forty-Eight

Flying was not something Chrissy neither looked forward to nor loathed. It was a means of getting somewhere, the whole experience neither pleasurable nor non-pleasurable, only ho-hum. And maybe a little bit tedious. The flight out to LA took up the full day and then some, even though the time change made up for it, making it seem like you'd only had a handful of hours in the air. Not likely—eleven hours was fidget worthy. Even in business class. Her personal bar selection held no appeal, though she noticed others had all but drained theirs. Should she offer her own as a pleasant gesture? And everyone seemed to be keeping themselves to themselves; there was not much chattering going on. Many had their heads buried in laptops. Everyone was in the navy suit brigade, as the man getting his lunch yesterday in the café had been. There were just two women plus herself; everyone else in the cabin was male. Was that representative of business people nowadays, she wondered? Or simply of those who could get away? Wanted to get away? They'd all have their reasons, though Chrissy doubted any would be as intriguing as her own.

Carrying on a previous lifestyle.

Is that what you call it?

So what if it is?

She checked her watch, which she'd put on LA time when the aircraft had taken off. It helped to get her body clock adjusted quicker, she believed; she did the same thing in reverse on the return trip to London. The dial read almost noon; three more hours to go. She'd decided that as soon as she'd got to her apartment and showered, a walk would be in order. A walk that would take her by the offices of Banks & Crowley. If she was in luck with her timing, she'd see them leave for the evening. Should she follow them, maybe? Perhaps they liked to go for a drink after work, or tennis perhaps. Were they even in the office today?

A flight attendant broke into her thoughts and asked if she could fetch her anything. After ordering another coffee and a couple of biscuits, Chrissy closed her eyes, put her head back, and tried to relax a little. It would be a long time until bedtime in Santa Monica.

The congestion around the airport was nothing new, but Chrissy managed to find her Uber driver without a hitch. She was grateful he wasn't a chatterbox; no need to ask him to be quiet. Some drivers picked up on their fare's mood, but others carried on, seemingly on autopilot. She always felt ungrateful asking drivers to leave her in peace, but since she was paying, she wanted what she wanted.

Being back in the bustle and congestion that was LA felt both exhilarating and relaxing at the same time, and she felt at home instantly in her unfamiliar surroundings. She knew that by tomorrow, she would feel like she'd never left. Englefield Green and Santa Monica were two completely different places, worlds apart. The driver entered Wilshire Boulevard and Chrissy felt a tingling sensation inside her stomach; for some reason she felt a little nervous. But why? She'd arrived here on her own dozens of times before but couldn't recall ever having had such a feeling. She put it down to slight nerves at being on a mission of sorts. It had been a long while.

Another couple of minutes on and she was parked outside her place on Yale Street, a smart weatherboard craftsman-style home, somewhat secluded with thick green bushes and shrubs, though not overgrown. The gardener, Joseph, took care of that while she was away, and on her return, he invariably met her at the house and flung the patio doors open, freshening the place out. There'd be a few basic items in the fridge too. And coffee. Tea in England, coffee in the States. How very English of her.

With her bags on the pavement and the sound of car doors slamming, a bronzed, open-shirted elderly man appeared on the front steps, his smile as big and bright as a Colgate advert. He wasted no time in greeting her as he rushed forward.

"Miss Chrissy, it's so good to see you again," he said enthusiastically. "Good trip?"

"Great, thanks, Joseph. Glad to be back. Are you well?" She picked up one bag, and Joseph picked up the other. While Chrissy was more than capable of handling her own luggage, the elderly man would have been offended had she taken them both. He slung the lighter bag over his shoulder as they went up the front steps and indoors.

The ceiling fan was spinning full tilt, sending a cool breeze wafting through the place tinged with both the smell of both LA and the ocean. After her bags were deposited on the wooden floor, Chrissy headed straight out onto the patio, where she stood stock still, head tilted towards the sunshine, eyes firmly closed. The sun was relaxing on her tired body and she wondered if she'd make it until bedtime without a nap. The clinking of ice cubes against the inside of a glass caught her attention, and she opened her eyes to see Joseph coming towards her, bearing a tall jug of fresh home-made lemonade on a tray, alongside a tall glass. There was also a tiny bowl of mixed fruit and nuts to nibble on. He'd been doing the same routine for as long as she could remember. She took a seat on the lounger, and Joseph set the tray on the low stone table by her side.

"Thanks, Joseph," she said taking a long mouthful of chilled nectar. "Will you be coming back this week? I thought we might go out for lunch if you're free." They did the same thing each visit—like they did the lemonade.

"Then I will be around. Thank you. You know where to find me," he said, bowing slightly as he left her to it, his Colgate smile wide and bright.

Flipping her legs up on the sun lounger in the dappled shade, she waved and thanked him again. She kicked her shoes off and let them fall to the deck, then wiggled her pink-painted toes, thankful for their freedom and the light breeze caressing them. There'd be sand between each of them later on when she hit the beach before dinner. Until then, with her head back and the lingering sweetness of lemonade on her lips, she felt herself drift off to sleep, like being carried off to a soft cloud in the sky, the local sounds of a foreign town propelling her to her destination.

It was close to 7 PM when she awoke again; the sun behind her was lower in the sky. Realising the time, she groaned, then resigned herself to the fact she'd have missed any chance of seeing Philip Banks or Alistair Crowley leaving their office for the day.

"No matter," she said. "There's always tomorrow morning." Pouring another glass of lemonade, she drank it down, quenching her parched mouth. No matter what class you flew, dehydration and jet lag were something that invariably arrived in their own time.

The ice had long ago melted, but the drink still tasted good and the sugar hit was a welcome addition. Since she'd promised her toes some sand, she quickly changed into shorts and a T-shirt, stuffing a few dollar bills and her credit card into a pocket.

Chrissy Livingstone was hot to trot.

Chapter Forty-Nine

Her longer-than-expected afternoon nap the previous day had meant an early rise. There was only so much sleep your body could consume, and when you lay there wide awake at odd hours knowing that sleep was not about to return, it was just as well to get up. Joseph had organised fresh juice, which she'd sipped watching the sun rise, then progressed to making a pot of fresh coffee as her energy returned. She needed the caffeine if she was going to go for a quick run; right now, her body felt more like an old snail carrying its house on its back than that of a regular runner. By her second mugful, she felt better; fuel was surging around her veins. She took out her running kit and trainers then added her armband pouch that contained her phone and playlists. By 6.30 AM, she was out and hitting the pavement, destination the boardwalk than ran south to Venice Beach. And Abbot Kinney.

As usual, a crowd was already out—those getting their exercise fix in before work, and those getting it out of the way before their day began, depending on how they looked at it. Not everyone enjoyed running, or exercise, Chrissy knew; most tolerated it as a way to eat more of the things they enjoyed or to keep up a level of fitness. For Chrissy, it was both. Calories in meant calories had to leave, too, if she wanted to maintain a healthy weight and a decent a level of fitness. In a previous life, she'd been a good deal more serious about it and had attended a gym daily for strengthening exercises, but since her 'retirement,' she'd dropped that entirely.

By the time she'd got to the concrete track, the surf breaking gently on her right, her face was already covered with a wet film of sweat that would soon turn into tear-like trickles that would run down to her cleavage and soak into her crop top. She liked to think that each trickle was the crap leaving her body. Her cloth cap kept the liquid from stinging her eyes.

In the distance, she could see the street cleaning machine long before she heard it, but then Taylor Swift was dominating her eardrums through her headphones. She fixed on it as she moved forward. It slowly made its way towards her, meandering in and out of the recesses of the boardwalk, past benches that still contained sleeping bodies, shopping trollies full of belongings by their side. A running group headed towards her, the pacer at the front keeping them up to speed. As the group drew closer, Chrissy smiled good morning to the pacer, who blanked her completely. As did the front row of her charges.

Welcome back to LA, Chrissy.

She'd adjust by the time she was due to leave. The culture was somewhat different than lush and leafy Englefield Green, where greetings were warm. In LA, the sun was warm, the greetings few and far between. It could, at times, be a lonely city.

By the time she'd got to Muscle Beach, she was soaked and panting hard. She pulled up to a walk and sauntered over to an empty bench. The toilet block behind her was being hosed out. Water ran in narrow rivers towards the drain; the building would be saturated inside, but clean for the day ahead. Chrissy adjusted her soaked running cap slightly and wiped her sunglasses on the edge of her shorts before shielding her eyes with them again. With constant sunshine came constant brightness. Noticing the water fountain a few feet further along, she ambled over, her breathing almost back to normal, and bent to take a sip. It was slightly warm, but it was better than nothing. Wiping her mouth with the back of her hand, she went back to her bench to watch the world go by.

Chapter Fifty

Philip had slept fitfully again and woke up to his alarm clock blaring. His hand reached out and turned it off, then flopped back down onto the bed. He groaned to himself, then turned over onto his stomach and buried his face in the pillow. Memories of his placed being rifled through stomped into his head like a marching band and he groaned out loud. An image of Frank Jamieson's face popped into his head, adding to the mayhem. Today, he'd organise someone to sweep his and Alistair's apartments, to put their minds at rest that no one was watching them in the shower. They could ill afford it, but sleep was more important. He hated sleeping in boxer shorts, but under the circumstances, he'd made an exception. As he slipped out from under his sheets, he was glad he'd worn them. He valued his privacy, and liked to share only on his own terms.

Even though his energy level was trailing around the floor line somewhere, he changed discreetly into his running gear and headed out. At least the sunshine would lift his spirits. He grabbed a bunch of dollar bills and slipped them into his phone pouch to buy a breakfast muffin on his way back.

He headed south towards Santa Monica Pier. His body felt heavy as he tried to get into his stride; the rhythm felt out of sync somehow. He was clearly sleep-deprived. He slowed right down and tried to find his groove as a small group trotted comfortably past like an army unit out on a drill. He counted their rhythm in his head: 'one, two, three, four. One, two, three, four.' Then, on a whim, he slipped into the back, unnoticed, and began to run with them. After a couple of minutes, he relaxed into it, and when he felt comfortable again, he dropped away from them to concentrate on his own workout.

He passed a bench, where he noticed a woman dressed in running gear similar to his own, soaked with sweat from her own run, plus a bright pink cap. He carried on forward.

Chrissy was sitting on the bench watching a male runner in a bright green cap awkwardly trying to find a rhythm. Her eyes followed him until he settled, found his stride and separated himself from his group. She'd had days like that herself, when she hadn't slept well or something was on her mind. Chrissy stayed for another couple of minutes before setting out on her journey home; the other runners were now a long way in front of her.

She needed to hustle if she was going to get to Philip and Alistair's office in time to see them arrive; she didn't want to miss either of them this morning.

Chapter Fifty-One

You never felt bad for going for a run, Chrissy knew. It might be hard mustering the motivation some mornings, but the feeling of accomplishment, and a beet-red face dripping with sweat on your return, made it all worthwhile. Chrissy stood panting on the pavement on Wilshire Boulevard.

Calories out meant calories in.

And vice versa.

Donuts!

Pulling out a handful of notes from her armband, she waited for someone who looked like they were about to head inside the donut store. A woman walked towards her and Chrissy politely excused herself.

"Hi. I'm a bit sweaty—would you mind getting a couple of donuts for me, please? Only I don't want to put others off." The young woman looked her up and down and grinned.

"I can see you've earned them. Sure. What flavours?" she asked.

"A huckleberry and a maple, thanks." She handed over the money and sat on the nearby steps to wait for her breakfast. She didn't have long to wait.

"Here you go," the woman said, and again Chrissy thanked her, taking the bag and reaching inside for the maple donut. The woman grinned at her again before walking away, and Chrissy wasn't sure if she was admiring her running efforts or thinking a sweat-soaked runner looked odd tucking into donuts for breakfast. It didn't matter either way. Her teeth sank into the first one and she groaned at the sticky goodness. Nobody made donuts like the Americans, and it was one of the first things she bought herself every time she was in town. She chewed each mouthful slowly, relishing each crumb. When the first one was all gone, she peered into the bag at the other one. It was meant for later, after her shower. Tradition. Patience was one thing Chrissy had in truckloads, so she set off back towards home, vowing to resist and wait until she was clean.

Plus, she had somewhere to be.

Her Uber driver waited out front. She slipped into the rear seat and they headed out into the rush hour traffic, destination Abbot Kinney and the offices of Banks & Crowley. Her second donut was burning a hole through the brown bag beside her, but her plan was to grab a coffee and sit watching the door from somewhere nearby, looking like any other worker having breakfast before heading into the office. She'd fit right in. The morning haze was hanging around, and it was warm both inside and outside the car. The driver's stereo was playing an Elvis song from way back. She hummed along with *A Little Less Conversation* and smiled at the irony of it.

I like my drivers silent.

Like this one.

Twenty minutes later, the car pulled up at her destination. Everything in LA was twenty minutes away, or so the saying went. Chrissy thanked the driver and stepped out onto the pavement. There were plenty of people about, and she stepped into a store doorway to gather her bearings and see what was what. Banks & Crowley's offices were almost opposite, but as yet there was no movement. Chrissy hoped she hadn't missed them.

A coffee shop a couple of doors down caught her attention; it had a long queue out the door. She joined it and kept an eye on the office door until the queue moved inside. A woman in the queue ahead of her caught her attention. She had stunning, long red wavy hair that beautifully complimented her tomato-coloured dress. As she collected her order and turned, her eyes met Chrissy's for a second and she smiled a little. Chrissy smiled back to be friendly, and watched as the woman crossed the street and opened up the front door of Banks & Crowley.

Well, what do you know?

How convenient.

Her turn to order came quickly. She then took her own coffee outside and found a place to sit and finish her breakfast. If the redhead had unlocked the office, she reasoned, neither of the men had arrived yet. Shading her eyes with her sunhat, she staked out the doorway with coffee and a donut, smiling as she realised she was behaving like a typical American cop.

Less than an hour later, the two men approached the building, takeaway coffee cups in their hands.

"And we're off," she said under her breath.

Her plan had been to 'accidentally' bump into one of them, preferably Philip Banks, while he bought his mid-morning coffee or lunch, depending on his routine, and strike up a lame conversation. Somewhere along the way she'd be forward and either suggest a beer or pretend to need a divorce lawyer and get time with him under false pretences. But the sun was getting too warm on her bench, and the thought of sitting there until something happened didn't thrill her. Plus, she needed to pee.

Change of plan.

Chrissy stayed for ten more minutes, disposed of her cup, then headed over to meet Philip Banks and Alistair Crowley in person.

Chapter Fifty-Two

Wednesday 12th August 1987

I'm planning to take her back to the river this weekend. I must escape the normalcy of this house, of my life. I simply desire to smell her, touch that soft spot on her neck, let her bend into me as I hold her tightly but gently. I'll take a soft blanket for us in case it's cool. We'll lie underneath it, with our skin touching, so that I might feel the warmth from her breasts as they press down onto my own naked chest from above. I'll gaze into those deep emerald eyes of hers as we move together silently, and witness the ecstasy as she finds her release. It, as always, will be beautiful. My darling Sylvia, my river Sylvia. . . Soon.

Chapter Fifty-Three

Philip and Alistair were in the kitchen, chatting about nothing in particular, man stuff, when Carmen put her head around the door. They ceased their laughing, and Carmen wrinkled her face up disapprovingly, like a grandmother might do, though in truth she wasn't offended. It happened all the time; it was man stuff.

Philip cleared his throat and turned his sensible face back on. "Sorry, Carmen. Men's—"

"Yeah, I know. Men's stuff. But listen up. I have a visitor in reception who'd like to buy some time with you—both if you're free, but either will do."

"Divorce?"

"Nope."

"We got to guess?" asked Alistair.

"She didn't want to say, actually. Just said she was happy to pay."

Both men looked at each other. Philip spoke first. "Jamieson up to something?"

Carmen looked blank, waiting.

"Let's find out, shall we? Carmen, show the lady into my office. We'll meet her in there. What's her name?" asked Alistair.

"Chrissy Livingstone. Not sure she's from LA, by her accent; it sounds a bit mixed up. But I'll show her through in a moment. You go and get settled." Her red head disappeared back out the door and both men slipped into Alistair's office, taking their seats at a small table rather than his desk.

There was enough time for Alistair to say, "It'll be nothing to do with him. Let's see what's on her mind," before the door opened and Carmen showed her in.

Philip did a double-take, his mouth open like a snake devouring a chicken. Chrissy sensed the unease, but if Carmen did, she didn't show it; she offered refreshments. Everyone declined, and she disappeared, closing the door discreetly behind her.

Chrissy sat down without waiting to be asked, and the air in the office shifted as she looked at each man in turn. Philip seemed nervous. And pale for the LA climate. Like his colour had drained away temporarily.

Alistair spoke first. "Hi, Alistair Crowley," he said. "And this is Philip Banks," he said, pointing with his chin and both men reached out to her to shake hands. There was a kind of clash as their three hands moved in at the same time, and one hand was left empty. *Awkward.* Chrissy wondered why Philip seemed so nervous; she didn't usually have that effect on people she hadn't met before. But his colour was definitely gradually returning, so she'd been right about that. Weird.

"Thanks for seeing me on short notice. I realise I don't have an appointment."

"How can we help?" Alistair asked, since Philip was still mute.

Chrissy rustled in her bag for a folder and slipped out the paper with the photographs of the boys' faces. She placed it on the table in front of them, then sat back to watch their reactions.

The little things.

The room stilled, but she heard two unmistakable intakes of breath. She kept quiet and waited. Alistair's jawline moved a fraction; the corners of his eyes twitched as he looked across at Philip, who still hadn't spoken and looked like he was going to vomit.

Chrissy said nothing. Neither did Philip.

First to speak loses.

What she wouldn't have done to see inside their heads at that precise moment.

Philip finally found his tongue. "What are we looking at here?"

Playing for time?

Acting dumb?

"Obviously these are you two," she said, pointing to two grinning teenagers. "And as you can see, I've written the other boys' names under each one. They're friends of yours, I believe?" She let the question hang.

First to speak loses.

"Who are you?" Philip asked.

You lose.

"Now, that's an odd question, don't you think?" Chrissy looked directly at Philip, and realisation finally dawned on her where she'd seen him before. She kept the discovery to herself and hoped he himself hadn't twigged.

"Not really. You know their names, so why ask us?"

"I'm trying to find out how they are connected, and not the school angle. There's more to it than that."

"What makes you so sure? Glendene was a long time ago. What year were these taken?"

Chrissy contemplated telling them the truth, but if she was going to find out... "1987." She watched and waited for telltale signs of recognition. The colour had drained once again on Philips face, and Alistair was now equally pale. She carried on. "What happened that year, gents? And why are half of these boys now dead, and within the last twelve months or so?"

The room stayed still and quiet until Alistair took control.

"I'd like you to leave now, if you don't mind," he said, and got abruptly to his feet. Philip stayed still, head bowed, and Chrissy took the opportunity. Was he weakening?

"Come on Philip," she said almost cajoling. "What's the big secret, what was it all those years ago?"

Alistair took a step forward and asked her again. "Okay, come on. I'm not sure what you want to achieve from this or who you are, but I've asked you to leave, so please. It's time to go."

Chrissy knew the moment had passed. Had she blown it? But one thing was for sure: there was a good deal more to all of this than she thought. Their reactions and now their request for her swift exit had her mind turning cartwheels to get to the truth. The moment was lost for now, though, so she reluctantly picked her bag up and headed for the door, muttering that she'd see herself out.

Once out on the street, she headed towards the coffee shop she'd been in earlier for a refill. And some time to run through what had just happened, and an important new piece of information: Philip Banks was the man she'd seen at her father's funeral.

Back in the offices of Banks & Crowley, Philip and Alistair were dumfounded.

"Who the hell was that, do you think?" Alistair asked, not really expecting an answer.

"I'll tell you exactly who that was."

"Oh?"

"That, my friend, was Chrissy Livingstone."

Alistair still looked blank. "Yes, she said as much. But who is Chrissy Livingstone?"

"Gerald Baker's daughter.

"Holy shit."

"Exactly."

Chapter Fifty-Four

Alistair was lost for words. He paced wildly up and down the small office space before finally speaking. It came out in a rush, like water gushing from a tap.

"How the hell did she find us, and why the hell is she digging?" He looked both angry and worried, his face strained.

"My question is, did she recognise me?" asked Philip. "Because if she did, she certainly didn't let on."

"I wondered why you looked like you'd seen a ghost." Alistair said. "And if I saw your reaction, I'm damn sure she did."

"Well, in that case, we're doomed. If she has recognised me and puts two and two together, she is going to want to know a great deal more."

Nobody spoke. The office was quiet while the cogs and wheels of both men's minds worked overtime, sifting through what had happened and what might happen next.

"Do you think Jamieson is behind this?"

"I've no idea, Philip, but it does seem like a huge coincidence. One minute we're going about our business as normal; next minute, Jamieson is sniffing around looking for trouble, and then this woman shows up. What are the chances, eh? And I don't like it one bit."

"Nah, I don't think they're connected. But I'd like to know why she is digging up the past, the events of 1987."

"What do you mean?" Alistair asked. "Of course they're connected. That's how this whole mess started."

"Well, only kind of. I mean, that was the catalyst, I suppose. But it's because of more recent events that I went to visit Baker, not because of what happened at school. It's just unfortunate, but now the two are connected, and quite honestly, I am not looking forward to the fallout. There will be some, you know."

Philip stood. "Well, I need some air. I need to think this through. As if I haven't got enough on my plate at the moment, now *she* turns up," he said, thrusting an arm out to the side as if she was still sitting there. He patted his trouser pockets for his wallet and said, "Do you want me to bring you anything back? I need a cold drink."

"I'll have whatever you're having. Just bring me the same; that will do."

Alistair sounded despondent to Philip's ears, but he had to look out for himself, and right at this moment he needed some space. His mouth was parched, and his head buzzed.

"I'll be back shortly," The door caught a draft and closed with a loud slam as he left. Out on the street, Philip stood for a moment and took a couple of deep breaths, filling his lungs with fuel fumes more than ocean breeze. It didn't really matter where he went; he just needed to take a walk. He turned left and set out, with nowhere in particular in mind. There were enough bars and cafés along the way to get a drink; he really didn't care which one. Perhaps he'd find the one with the cute waitress he'd seen a couple of times. Perhaps he couldn't care less.

She spotted him standing outside the office a few minutes later, no doubt wondering where to go. She'd seen it before, after she'd ruffled somebody's feathers. They always looked the same: stunned. Worried. Panicked, even. And Philip Banks was no different. Chrissy wasn't particularly hiding, though she wasn't advertising the fact that she was there, either, hat and shades on once more, watching. And Philip, in a world of his own, took no notice of her as he passed by.

When he was a few paces in front of her, she slipped money for her drink under the salt and pepper pots and headed out after him, keeping twenty or so paces behind. He carried on for half a mile, maybe, before turning into a café. She slowed her pace, stopping just short of where he'd entered. She debated whether to go in and try to talk to him further, but something told her to leave well enough alone, for now. So, she stayed outside and kept to the shadows as the sun climbed higher in the sky. In another hour or so it would be too hot to stay out, though, and she hoped he wouldn't be too long about whatever he was doing. Taking a seat on a nearby low wall, she took in the surroundings while she waited, thinking of her next move.

It was about fifteen minutes later when Philip left the café carrying what looked like a takeaway of fresh juice in his hand, straw sticking out the top. He appeared to be headed back to the office, and Chrissy was tempted to fall back in behind him, though it would serve no purpose. She let him pass, still in a world of his own, he hadn't seen her again. She watched him through her dark lenses. He looked defeated, his shoulders slumped forward as though the weight of the world was on them.

Suddenly she noticed that a man on the other side of the street, whom she'd observed earlier sitting and reading a newspaper, had now blended in with the crowd—and was walking behind Philip Banks, who seemed unaware of his new tail.

It appeared that somebody else had an interest in her Mr. Banks.

Chapter Fifty-Five

Chrissy kept her distance. She knew how to trail somebody too, and the man up ahead wouldn't be expecting anybody to be watching him. He was too busy watching his own target to watch his own back. She assumed Philip was headed back to the office, and she was curious as to what the man would do. Would he carry on somewhere, back to his car perhaps, or sit outside the office and wait? Either way, she was intrigued.

She didn't have to wait long to find out. As Philip entered the building, his interested party carried on a few paces past and slipped into a parked car. Chrissy tried to get a closer look as she approached the vehicle, but the glass was tinted all round. There was no way of seeing inside. No bother. She carried on past and pulled in just behind a rack of sunglasses that was conveniently displayed on the pavement, took out her phone and made a note of the registration details. It was a local plate, California tags. Somehow, she'd figure a way of finding out who the vehicle belonged to, though her old contacts these days were all in the UK, not in LA.

Pretending to browse, she watched the car drive away; the driver was obviously done for the day, whatever it was he was doing. Chrissy herself hadn't got anything else to achieve by hanging around, so she ordered her ride home. Her stomach was growling and in need of lunch, and she was suddenly overcome with fatigue. Knowing that somebody else had an interest in Philip Banks intrigued her but at the moment, she didn't have the tools to find out much more. Should she tell Philip? she wondered. Did he know?

By the time she got back to her own place, she was almost asleep. Jet lag was catching up with her, and the ride home, gently rocking her, had made her even drowsier. She gathered her book and reading glasses and lay on one of the soft outdoor loungers in the dappled shade. Within ten minutes she was sound asleep.

She woke with a start. Her sleep had been fitful, her head full of nonsensical images, odds and ends of dreams that made no sense, faces popping in and out—images of her father, of smiling boys. Her cleavage was damp with sweat, though it wasn't particularly hot where she was lying. She touched her forehead; it was equally damp, and her mouth was parched. What had woken her she had no idea, but she was suddenly alert, wide awake, as if a gun had gone off in her subconscious somewhere. Her heart raced in her chest, odd palpitations that gradually slowed down as she came to.

She swung her legs over the lounger and sitting up properly, tried to calm herself further and make sense of what had happened in her dream. She rubbed her temples with both hands as she sifted through the images that were still clear in her mind. One thought in particular disturbed her: What the hell had Philip Banks been doing at her father's funeral? She knew she had to confront him about this, and maybe should even tell him there was another person interested in his movements. What would he say to that?

She grabbed her phone to check the time; it was just coming up to 4 PM. She'd been asleep for a good deal longer than she'd intended to. "Shall I run, or shall I go get a shower?" she asked herself. She went into the kitchen and downed a glass of water, then paced up and down the room, pondering the best course of action.

Run or shower, run or shower, run or shower?

Running always helped her think, but she felt groggy. And she'd already run.

"Shower."

Thirty minutes later, she was back inside an Uber and headed back to Abbot Kinney and the offices of Banks & Crowley. She needed answers, and she wasn't going to be fobbed off this time. When her driver pulled up out front, she thanked him and headed straight inside, bypassing the redhead on the front desk, who tried her best to intercept her. Chrissy shrugged her off and was already halfway through the office door as a rather startled Philip Banks sat up straight at his desk, mouth open at the outburst. Alistair was nowhere to be seen.

"What were you doing at my father's funeral?" she blurted out. Any plans of subtlety had gone out the window as Chrissy threw the accusing question Philip's way. He stood up and stared straight at her. Chrissy could see he was wondering what to say next and pre-empted any bullshit. "And don't try and bullshit me. I know it was you. I just want to know why."

Philip tossed his pen down onto the blotter on his desk. His face seemed to have softened in the process.

"There's quite a simple explanation. I was there representing a client of ours. They couldn't get there themselves, and so I went instead."

"I wasn't born yesterday," Chrissy said. "Why on earth would a client want to send you and not go themselves? And who was this client?"

"I can't tell you that, but it's true. I was sent. And I'm sorry I didn't mention it earlier. But in truth, I didn't want to cause you any concern or suspicion because here you are asking questions from years back, and then it turns out I was at your father's funeral. It doesn't look good, does it?"

"You're damn right there."

"Look, take a seat. I'm not the enemy." Philip sat back down at his own desk to encourage her to sit also. He hated confrontation, and standing there having a heated debate seemed more aggressive than it needed to be. He held his hand out to the chair at the other side of his desk, and though Chrissy resisted for a long moment, she did eventually sit down. The air in the room shifted a little; the tension eased slightly. The act of sitting down took some of the wind out of her sails, and she relaxed a little.

"Look, there's something going on," she said. "I need to get to the bottom of what you and the other six boys have in common, and you need to tell me what's going on at this end."

"First of all, may I ask what your interest is in these boys? And second, what do you mean 'what's going on at this end'?"

"My interest in the boys is purely personal. I know they are somehow linked to my father; I just want to know how."

"And what about my second question?"

"I'm not the only person who's interested in you."

Philip's brow creased. "How so?"

Chrissy took a deep breath. "You were followed, just after I left this morning. I went to get a drink like you did, but on the way back to your office I noticed someone else. And they were most certainly following you. Care to tell me why?" Chrissy could see by the look on Philip's face that he'd had no clue; he looked concerned now. "You didn't know that, did you?" she carried on.

"No, I didn't. But I do now. I think it might be to do with a case that I'm working on."

Chrissy pondered that for a moment; since he was a divorce lawyer, maybe an unhappy spouse was behind it. Maybe it wasn't as sinister as she'd initially thought. Although Banks looked genuinely worried. However, the man following him wasn't her main concern, of course; she was more interested in finding out about the photos of the boys in her father's tin.

"Well, now you know, maybe you can call the dogs off yourself. I just thought you should be aware." She was keen to get to what she really wanted, and needed him to talk. She softened her voice slightly to reflect some concern, but pressed on. "Look, why don't you tell me about the boys, and how they are all connected? I know you and Alistair are part of the group, and you obviously know who the others are—or were, since three are no longer with us."

Philip seemed to flinch at the words 'no longer with us,' so Chrissy pressed on, knowing she was onto something. "Why don't you tell me what happened?"

"What makes you think something happened?"

"Because I'm not stupid. Something connects everyone together and I'm going to find out what."

"Let me suggest you leave well enough alone. It will serve no purpose. What happened back then was a stupid schoolboy prank, and will do no good to anybody if you revisit it now. I suggest you go back home and leave well enough alone," he said again.

"That's not going to happen, Mr. Banks, so what I'm going to do is give you some time to think back, because I'm here for a few days. And maybe you can see your way to filling in some of the gaps that I have, for my own sanity, I suppose. I know my father was involved somehow, and he's dead now, and nothing will bring him back. But I have an inquisitive mind, and I won't rest until I find out the full story. And mark my words, I will." Chrissy stood as she said the last sentence and repeated it for good measure: "Mark my words, I will."

Philip stayed quiet as Chrissy left the office and headed back out into the sunshine. Would he tell her more when he'd had time to think on it? She hoped so.

Chapter Fifty-Six

Friday August 14th, 1987

"Can I have a word?" Sylvia Marsh asked. She was standing half in and half out of his office, tentative.

"Hello, Sylvia. Come on in. What can I do for you?" the head-master, Frederick Browning, said, beckoning her through the half-open door. Sylvia strolled over the thick wool rug that dominated the room, its dark colourways dulling the whole room. His office was like something from an old movie—all rugs and dark wood. It smelled of sandalwood and musk.

"It's a bit embarrassing, to be honest, but I do feel that I need to tell somebody because things are getting out of hand," she said, approaching his desk.

"Oh?"

"Yes. Oh, you could say that."

The headmaster pointed to a seat in front of his desk and Sylvia took the hint, making herself as comfortable as she could under the circumstances. She fidgeted, and her hands were sweaty. She looked as nervous as a kitten.

"What is it, Sylvia? You look worried sick."

"Things have gotten out of hand. I don't know what to do."

"What sorts of things?"

Sylvia took a deep breath and debated exactly how much to tell the headmaster, how much detail she needed to go into. It was all rather personal, extremely private; it was about herself, but if she didn't say something... She took a deep breath and ploughed into it.

"I'm being blackmailed," she said simply. She let it sink in for a moment before carrying on. "I'm being blackmailed by some of the students. I think I know what I've done, what they've seen, and they're using it for their own gain."

"Who are these students, Sylvia?"

"I'll get to that in a moment. My question is what to do about it. They're blackmailing me—for me to give them better grades. Their last year is coming up."

"And you're their year head," he finished. "May I ask what they've seen?"

"It's very delicate. I'm a wee bit embarrassed. Like I said, it's extremely personal."

"I can't help you if I don't know all the facts."

Sylvia had no choice to tell him, clearly, though she didn't see what difference it would make—apart from embarrassing her even more. "They saw me and a friend of mine down by the river."

"A friend of yours?" he enquired. Sylvia looked at him with appealing eyes. Need she spell it out to the man?

"Ah, I see," he said, catching on to what she was trying to avoid actually saying. He looked almost disapproving, though she wasn't sure why. She was a single woman, after all. Not that her personal life was his business; she was merely explaining her predicament.

"What have they said so far, and how?"

"I've had a couple of notes, and today I received another one. They've not signed their names, but I think I know who's behind it."

"How so?"

"The looks I've been getting. Seeing those same boys with other boys, deep in conversation. There's a handful of them. Maybe more."

"How do you know they've seen you?" he asked.

"The notes said 'we've seen you,' not 'I've seen you.' With him. And boys seldom go down to the river on their own. They're always with their mates." Tears started to well up in her eyes, threatening to tumble at any moment, and she paused to compose herself before going on. "I'm pretty sure one of the boys is Alistair Crowley. I've seen him and a couple of his mates down there before, when I've been reading. On my own. I know he goes there. And the handwriting on the note looks like his."

The headmaster rested his chin on his clenched fist and set his elbow on the desk in front of him. He chewed his top lip a while, and Sylvia focused on it, waiting.

"How has it been left currently?" he asked thoughtfully.

"The last note said they'd let me know what I need to do in a couple of days. And if I don't do it, my friend's family will find out. About me." She dipped her chin as she said the last words, her face flushing with embarrassment. The tears streamed down her face uncontrolled now, and she wiped at them with her wrist.

Frederick Browning reached into his drawer, pulled out a box of tissues and offered them to her. She blew her nose quietly and dabbed her eyes dry. More tears sprang free. She dabbed again.

"I see." He sounded like the headmaster he was as he said it. Two words, not a sentence. *I. See.* She waited for his opinion and hopefully a solution. It was a long moment before he spoke again.

"Well, you can't hand out greater marks than have been earned, now, can you? That wouldn't be fair. And what you do in your personal life is of no interest to the school. The reputation of this establishment is entirely my concern, and I will not have anything taint it."

Sylvia couldn't believe her ears. She looked up at the man in front of her, dumbfounded. She knew where this was going: his precious school was more important than her being caught in an uncompromising position. She gathered herself for the final blow of his selfish words.

"I'm afraid there's nothing I can do, Miss Marsh."

The formal use of her name was not lost on Sylvia. This was turning out like a bad performance review.

He went on, "Without proof of who it is, there is nothing I can do. I can't haul the whole school in here and interrogate them one by one. Nor will I allow you to increase the letter-writers' grades, even if you or I could confirm who they are."

"But if I don't do what they want, they'll destroy me and ... and my friend. Please, Mr. Browning: I need to find out who they are and make the adjustment, and then this whole sorry business can be over and done with." It was almost a scream.

The headmaster delivered a withering look that felt more like a slap across her tear-stained face. "You are not understanding me, Miss Marsh. Whoever is responsible, I will not sanction their marks to be increased. And even if I did, they could still carry out their threat. And then where would we both be?"

Sylvia couldn't believe his callousness. She stood and ran from the headmaster's office, sobs catching in her throat as she fled. The door slammed closed behind her and she carried on to the ladies' toilets in the next block, where she sobbed until she could sob no more.

It hadn't been the outcome she'd hoped for.

Chapter Fifty-Seven

Saturday 15th August, 1987

Gerald had a standing Saturday morning appointment, though it wasn't where he told his family it was. Saturday mornings were his time with Sylvia, a stolen couple of hours where they spent their time in one another's arms and talked about their future together. He was supposed to be at the office catching up on paperwork, but of course that never happened. They only ever managed a scant few hours per week together, him trying to squeeze her into his busy schedule without their secret ever being found out.

Most times, they would meet at their spot down by the river. Sylvia would bring a flask of coffee and they would share it, sitting in the sunshine and chatting. When the weather was inclement, they met in a car park nearby and drank the coffee in her car. It was safer that way. If anyone ever recognised his registration plate, they would assume that perhaps Gerald Baker was out walking on his own in the rain somewhere. But two people sitting in Sylvia's vehicle wouldn't raise any eyebrows, since Sylvia was a single woman. It seemed the most sensible thing to do.

240   LINDA COLES

But this day, thankfully, the sun was shining, though the breeze was cool. Gerald walked towards their meeting place, pulling his light jacket a little tighter to his chest. He could see Sylvia in the distance, already there, her jacket wrapped around her shoulders. The tartan rug was already laid out and she was sipping coffee from the flask. She must've heard him behind her, for she turned, smiled and waved lightly as her lover approached. Checking there was nobody around, Gerald sat down beside her and leaned into her neck, giving her a light peck on the cheek and running his hand down her bare arm.

"Mmmm, you smell so good. I'll never get tired of your perfume," he said lovingly. Then, once again checking there was nobody walking their dog nearby or ambling down by the river, he turned to her fully and kissed her urgently on the lips.

"Be careful, Gerry—someone might see us," she said, and, reluctantly, pulled away from him slightly.

"I've been thinking about doing that to you all morning, my love. I can't get enough of you. And I have already checked: there isn't anybody about." He leaned in again and pressed his lips to hers, gently caressing them with his own, lovingly though with more urgency. He gently laid her backwards onto the rug, and only then did he slow his kisses, staring down deeply into her eyes as she gazed back up at him.

She groaned lightly at the pleasure of it all. "I want to be in your arms forever, but I know I can't be," she said.

Gerald looked at her questioningly. "Whatever is the matter, Sylvia? What's happened?" It was a moment before Sylvia spoke again; she lay there quietly on the rug with Gerald leaning over her, birds tweeting in the trees nearby and the river flowing not far away. It was the most romantic spot in the world. Gerald sensed her listening to the river and waited for her to include him in what was on her mind. Finally, raising herself she looked straight at him. Her eyes were already welling up with tears.

"I've got something to tell you, Gerry, and I don't know what to do."

"Then tell me what it is, my love, and we will work it out together." He waited patiently for her to begin. He could see by her pained expression that it was something serious and immediately feared the worst. When she began to speak, he was relieved that it wasn't what he thought it might be; nonetheless, he was astounded.

"I'm being blackmailed. They know about us and are threatening me."

And so, Sylvia poured out everything that had gone on—the anonymous notes, the threats to expose them both if she didn't do what they wanted, and her visit to the headmaster, Fredrick Browning. Her tears spilled down her cheeks now, and Gerald put his arm lovingly around her shoulder.

"I think that bit hurts the most," she said. "The fact that he won't support me, even though my private life is nothing to do with the school. I wasn't prepared for that reaction. I'm on my own with it. I don't see any other way out of this, Gerry. We can't risk our love being found out; you'll be ruined."

Their eyes locked while each searched for an answer on the other's face. Gerald, for his part, knew he could never leave Sylvia; he was besotted with her, and wanted their relationship never to end. Indeed, he wanted to pursue it further. They'd talked long and hard about how they could be together, how he would leave his wife when the children grew up. But now, it looked as though his chance at happiness might well disintegrate. As tears continued to fall down Sylvia's face, Gerald took her in his arms and stroked the back of her head lovingly as she sobbed into his shoulder; he felt as though his heart had broken into pieces.

For the rest of the morning, they'd talked things through, trying to figure out how Sylvia could escape the blackmail, and how they could prevent their affair becoming public knowledge. It wasn't how they'd chosen to spend their time together, but it was all they had.

As their time came to an end and Gerald kissed Sylvia goodbye, he vowed to come up with a plan to put an end to her worry. He had to find a way around this: he wasn't about to let a group of spotty teenagers ruin his relationship with the woman he cared so much for.

And if the school wasn't going to support her, then Gerald Baker would.

He'd find a way.

Chapter Fifty-Eight

Saturday August 15th, 1987

I can't allow Sylvia to fight this alone. It's not fair. She is worried sick, I can see; she doesn't want this to come out—our affair, our love for one another. And for that, I love her even more. I'll figure something out—I have to—and that means finding out who these boys are.

I'm not ready to leave Sandra yet; things are not in place as they should be for my new life. I need to wait a while. I need to pick the right moment if ever there will be one. I worry for my girls. But today, seeing Sylvia so upset, I realise I may need to rethink things. My heart is breaking too. I have to fix this.

Our lovemaking this morning was tender. Lying by the river with the softness of her skin underneath me is all I desire—for our time like that to never end. She is perfection in every way.

Tomorrow, I will learn more and set up a plan. I can't stand seeing Sylvia so distressed. She doesn't deserve it. But our love for one another is real, and it will never die. And the sooner we can be together, the better it will be. But not like this. I have to make a plan. I have to put it right.

I can't live without Sylvia. I won't live without Sylvia.

Chapter Fifty-Nine

Sunday 16th August 1987

You were as I'd imagined in my thoughts and dreams, Sylvia. Every part of you was perfect: every movement, every thought you shared, every . . . everything. You cried out loud; you were as ferocious as the river I've named after you and as exquisite. We didn't need the blanket—the sunshine warmed our bare skin, though I hope not too harshly, my love. I never wanted to leave that spot, never without you, but I had to. I had to come back here, to this house, to my life. To my children. They, and you, my love, are the beings that keep my spirits high. How I hope we can share the future together.

We will ride the coming storm. Fret not, my love. Forget the school: you have me.

Until I see you again, soon, Sylvia my river.

Chapter Sixty

Monday 17th August, 1987

Sylvia Marsh was sitting at her desk in the empty classroom, her last lesson for the day finished. Piled high on the left side of her desk was her own homework: marking her students' assignments. She hoped they weren't too dull. English literature didn't suit every student, and while some excelled at writing their thoughts about what they were currently reading, others found the task impossible. And she knew exactly who those students were before she'd even looked at the homework they'd turned in. Not everyone enjoyed reading, and she knew she shouldn't judge people by her own interests. She could never understand, though, why reading fiction didn't excite some people; it was escapism. Reading a story was something very personal, a form of art that you alone took part in: nobody helped you or guided you or gave their opinions until you'd finished a book and formed your own. It wasn't like going to the movies; movies were something to be shared with friends or a room full of strangers, or both. No, reading was something far more personal, far more beautiful.

She gathered the assignments up and slipped them into her bag, then opened her drawer to grab a couple of extra pens. As soon as she opened the drawer she froze. An envelope sat on top of the tray that held her pens and pencils.

The others before it at had all looked exactly the same. However, this was the first that had been delivered directly inside her drawer, in her personal space, and that in itself made it feel even more wretched. Tentatively, she reached her hand out as though it might bite, then hurriedly slipped it into her bag along with the assignments for later.

During the short journey back to her home, the envelope felt like it was burning a hole through the cloth of her handbag. But at the same time, she wanted to fling it out of the window, get it out of her car, as if the act itself would help get the nightmare out of her life for good.

She pulled up outside her small cottage, turned off the engine and stayed seated inside the car; the sun warmed the interior in the cooling afternoon. She sat a while longer, gathering her courage. Finally, she pulled out the envelope and stared at it; it was like an unwelcome Christmas present. She wanted to rip into it and find its contents, but the same time wanted to destroy it. But if she didn't open it, she'd never know what it contained for sure, so she slid her finger into the small opening and ripped along the top edge.

The message inside had been handwritten once again. She was conscious something had fallen into her lap, but was busy concentrating on the note. It described in great detail what the writer had seen only a couple of days ago down by the river. But this time there was a photograph—she reached down and retrieved it from her lap. It was a cheap Polaroid taken from a distance, but it was obvious who was in the picture and what they were doing. She gave an agonised cry and then clamped her hand over her mouth, tears streaming down her face.

Chapter Sixty-One

Monday 17th August, 1987

Gerald had thought of little else but Sylvia. She was on his mind a great deal anyway, of course, but now she was so distressed, he could focus on nothing else. He picked at his evening meal with his fork, conscious that his wife was babbling on about nothing in particular. He wasn't paying her the slightest notice. Suddenly he became aware that something had changed in the room: dismayed, he realised she had raised her voice, and he looked up from his plate to see her glaring down at him like he was a naughty schoolboy himself.

Maybe if he was a schoolboy, he could do something about the culprits that were causing Sylvia so much distress. He'd be in the perfect position.

But as a grown adult he didn't have that luxury.

"I'm sorry, dear," he said. "I was miles away."

"I can see that," Sandra said caustically. Her eyes seemed to drill into his face; her stiff, lacquered hair made her seem even more severe than usual.

Sandra Baxter was not the woman he'd married all those years ago. She'd hardened somewhere along the way, though he couldn't be sure when it was. She'd been a good mother to their two girls; she'd kept the family together when Gerald was busy at work. About that, he had no complaints. But her softness had gone; something had hardened her soul, and she had become a bitter, ageing woman. He tried hard not to compare her to the woman he was so in love with, a woman who was filling his mind every waking moment.

"What did you say, dear?"

"I asked if there was a problem with your meal. Only you haven't touched it."

"I don't feel very hungry, that's all. I'm sorry. I'm terribly tired. Perhaps I'll go and have a lie down. I hope I'm not coming down with something." He pushed his chair back noisily from the table, and his wife glared at him once again. This time he chose to ignore her; he really couldn't care less, he realised sadly. He paid her no attention as he left the dining room and headed for his den, where he locked the door behind him.

In front of the large bay window was a leather chaise longue, a place where Gerald often lay to think. And to dream. And where he invariably filled out his diary. Finding the small key on his keyring, he opened the old wooden cupboard and pulled out the relevant notebook. On a small oak table nearby, he kept a decanter of whiskey and a couple of crystal tumblers. He poured a couple of fingers into a glass and took it and his diary back to his spot in the bay window. He took a refreshing mouthful of the golden liquid and let its welcoming warmth burn the insides of his throat. Refreshed and fortified, he began to write his thoughts and feelings from the day before it ended.

Monday 17th August 1987

I'm scared. So very scared. My world will tumble without you in it, Sylvia, though my world is tumbling around me anyhow. I've had a note, you see, a note telling me they know about us, about our river—your river,

Sylvia. They watched us on that soft blanket. They saw us together, enjoying one another's bodies, and now they want to be silenced with money. How crude. Is that what our love has come down to? Vulgar money for their silence? Our love was destined to grow like the sweet peas, to bloom strong and tall, dazzling the world with its beauty. But now it will be stunted, stunted by silence. Could I be strong and leave my children for my river, Sylvia? Let the rogues tell the world and not care? That man is not me; I am the weak one. That's why I love being in your arms. I am undoubtedly the weak one.

And so, I shall pay. To save us both. This can't be the end for us. I'm weak.

By the time he had finished his tumbler of whiskey, his diary entry for the day was done. He stood and walked back to the cupboard, replaced the notebook and relocked the door. He'd been keeping a diary for as long as he could remember, and he'd never shared its contents with anybody, not even Sandra. He doubted he ever would. And certainly not the journals from the last year, since he'd met Sylvia.

Usually after he'd done his diary entry, he'd go back through to the lounge and watch a little television with Sandra, but tonight he just couldn't face that. He chose instead to stay where he was, daydreaming about his Sylvia. Later, when his wife had gone to bed, he'd slip upstairs and climb into the matrimonial bed, though its joy and appeal had long since vanished.

He smiled as he thought about his plan. He hoped the headmaster would be obliging. If he had any sense, he would be.

Chapter Sixty-Two

Tuesday 18th August, 1987

There was no way Gerald was going to do nothing. He'd managed to persuade Sylvia to tell him who she thought was behind it, and with that information fresh in his mind he was now headed to Inkpen, to Glendene School. Even without an appointment to see the headmaster, he felt sure he'd gain access. After all, he was an old boy himself, had attended the school many years ago and had contributed to various fundraising projects handsomely since then. And if the headmaster needed reminding of who funded the 'Baker Boys' lacrosse trophy each year, he'd gladly remind him.

As he pulled into the visitors' parking space out front, he said a prayer that the headmaster would see sense and come around to Gerald's way of thinking.

He straightened his tie and climbed the steps of the old stone building. Its grandeur seemed to have increased with age, and Gerald took a moment to turn and take in the immaculate grounds before entering the front hall. The oak panelling was impressive, as were the paintings of ex-pupils from generations ago who had once attended the school and gone on to achieve greatness in their field; most were sportsmen and politicians. It was quieter than normal now; while boarders and summer school attendants had stayed on, many of Glendene's pupils were back home for the summer holidays.

An older woman, her grey hair pinned into a tight chignon, hurried over to greet him; she must have heard his car draw up.

"What a pleasant surprise. How may I help you this morning, Mr. Baker?"

"Good morning, Darlene. I must say, you look younger every time I see you."

Spots of crimson glowed in her cheeks, and she bowed her head slightly, a little embarrassed, though clearly enjoying the compliment. Gerald had always dished out the compliments where they were due.

"I need a moment with Mr. Browning, actually," he went on. Could you tell him I'm here, please?" His smile looked authentic enough, he was sure, but it wasn't delivered from his heart.

"Oh," she said uneasily. "I'm not to disturb him this morning, I'm afraid. I gather you don't have an appointment booked?"

"I don't, no. But I do only need a few moments. Please, can you tell him I'm here?" His smile this time carried something more than simple politeness, and Darlene picked up on it; her own smile faded abruptly. She scurried through a doorway and headed towards Mr. Browning's office.

Gerald spent the next few moments slowly pacing the entrance-way, hands clasped behind his back like a drill sergeant. In short order, a door opened, and Gerald smiled inwardly. Donations served their purpose at times like these. A male voice called out to him and he turned.

"Gerald! Great to see you. Please, come on through," the head-master said. He held out a hand and Gerald shook it, then followed him into his office. Darlene brought up the rear. "Can I offer you some tea perhaps?" Browning enquired.

"Please."

The headmaster nodded to Darlene, who left to fetch their refreshments, and then resumed his seat at his great old desk, motioning Gerald into a chair facing it. The desk was probably as old as the building itself, with many headmasters having used it over the years, both for paperwork and the caning of boys' backsides.

Gerald looked directly at Mr. Browning and stated his business.

"I'll get straight to the point, if I may. I come with a delicate matter," he began. "I believe some of the boys are blackmailing a good friend of mine. She spoke to you about it recently—Friday, I believe." His smile had vanished now. "I'd like to speak to the boys concerned."

The headmaster stayed quiet, and Gerald assumed he was deciding what to say. Browning's mouth twitched slightly, not with a smile, but more an expression of recognition.

"Ah. I see. You must be the friend she mentioned to me. Yes, I can see how this would be embarrassing for you, if it all came out." Browning smiled coldly now as he added his dig. "And for your family."

Gerald kept quiet, letting the man have his salacious fun at his expense.

"But I really can't let you have their names," Browning went on smoothly. "Because I don't actually know who they are." He sat back fully in his chair now, looking satisfied, like he was winning.

"Come now, Frederick," Gerald said. "Alistair Crowley is one of them, so it shouldn't be hard to find out who the others are. Of course, I could always speak to Alistair myself, or to his father. Though I don't like to mix business with pleasure if I can help it."

"Is that a veiled threat, Gerald? Because if it is, it's not welcome and will get you nowhere."

Gerald leaned forward in his chair and focused his stare directly at the headmaster. "Not veiled at all. And neither is what I'm about to say. Let me be clear. I want those names, today. And if I don't get them, you can forget my support next year. Nothing veiled there,

Frederick. I hope that's clear enough for you." He sat back again to wait for his opponent's next move.

Finally, the headmaster spoke again. "She must be worth it, is all I can say." He took a couple of deep breaths, steepling his fingers at his chin as he stared at the wall opposite.

Gerald waited, hoping he'd come through. He wasn't disappointed.

"I'll see what I can do," Browning said at length. "I'll get Crowley in here after lunch and see what he's got to say about it. That's all I can offer." He got to his feet; the meeting was over.

Gerald followed suit and added, "I'll look forward to your news, then. I'm sure next year's lacrosse team will be grateful for our arrangement; I hate disappointing people. And I'm sure I don't need to tell you: not a word of my visit to Sylvia."

They headed out to the front entrance together, the tension in the air between them as taut as a drum skin.

He'd got what he come for, Gerald thought with satisfaction as he started his car. By the end of the day, he'd have all of the names, and the stupid schoolboy prank would be over.

Their secret would be safe.

Chapter Sixty-Three

He drove back to his office deep in thought. He knew Alistair Crowley's father, all right, though he didn't much like the man; he was big and arrogant with a lazy drawl from somewhere in the US deep south; an utterly crass individual. But Gerald would have leaned on him if he'd had to.

He hoped Sylvia hadn't seen him drive up or enter the school building, and he hoped the nosey secretary didn't mention anything to her either—though he doubted the old lady knew of their relationship. Frederick Browning, however, could be a different matter: he'd experienced the man's spiteful side before, so if anyone was going to be the proverbial fly in the ointment, it could be him.

Gerald was back in his office and behind his own desk within the hour. He'd give Browning until 4 PM, and then he'd be on the telephone.

Frederick Browning was annoyed, He'd been threatened, and he didn't like bullies, for starters, and Gerald Baker could be domineering. He idly wondered what Sylvia saw in him—apart from his wealth maybe, though he didn't think she was that shallow.

A light knock at the door interrupted his thinking. Darlene entered, with Alistair Crowley close behind.

"Ah, Mr. Crowley," he said, with a tight smile. "Sit."

Darlene left the room, closing the door behind her and leaving the two of them alone. Browning sat down again behind his desk, the young man sitting opposite him. Browning couldn't help but notice that the boy looked a little nervous, and so he should.

"It's come to my attention that you and your merry little gang have been spying, down by the river." He let his words sink in and watched the young man's Adam's apple bob a little. Yes, he was nervous.

"Sir."

"Were you hoping I wouldn't find out? Because I know everything there is to know about what goes on in these grounds. So that means I know about your blackmailing scam, too."

Alistair glowered at his shoes, no doubt knowing he was now in a heap of trouble.

"Look at me when I'm talking to you!" Browning thundered, and Alistair jumped in his seat. He forced himself to make eye contact.

"That's better. Now stop being a mouse and tell me who else is involved. Because I will find out, and it will be much worse for you if I go the long way around. Through your father, for instance." Browning secretly hoped the boy would talk so he didn't have to call his father. "I'll give you two minutes to choose."

The headmaster made a show of looking at his watch. As the first minute passed in silence, he glanced at the boy in front of him and said, "Forty-five seconds. Thirty. Fifteen." Then, "Time's up Mr. Crowley."

Alistair looked fearful about what might happen next but was obviously willing to take his chances.

"Now that is unfortunate," the headmaster said as he stood. The boy didn't move. Browning picked up his telephone and started to dial a number from a file laid out in front of him.

"Okay, okay!" Alistair shouted.

The headmaster replaced the handset and sitting back down, waited.

"What will happen to us if I tell you?"

"It's more what will happen if you don't. Are you prepared to take that chance? Your families pay handsomely to send you here for your education, and I know how much you want to be a lawyer. Your grades could suffer because of something like this."

Alistair knew when he was beaten; he looked deflated now, like a discarded party balloon.

"You see, it doesn't feel nice being blackmailed, does it? Grades can go up as well as down, though your hope was clearly for an increase rather than a decrease. So, tell me, who else is involved?"

Alistair had no choice now. Slowly, he recited the names of the other six boys who had dreamed up the scam with him. They'd all been down by the river mucking about, he said miserably, and had seen Sylvia meet with a man on several occasions. One of the boys thought he recognised him as a local businessman with a wife and family, and the plan had come to life.

"We wouldn't have gone through with it. It was a bit of fun, really. We thought we could get better marks, that's all," Alistair whined; he wasn't as tough as he liked to think he was.

"Well, it's backfired on you now. I'll need to decide your punishment, but for now, I suggest you don't say anything to anybody about this— especially not Miss Marsh. You've upset her enough. Until I decide what I'll do, leave it be. Is that understood?"

"Yes, sir."

"Dismissed."

Alistair couldn't get out of the room quick enough; he scrambled to his feet, wrenched open the study door and disappeared down the hall with a clatter of shoes. Browning, his heart sinking, looked again at the list of seven names. All the boys were exceptional students and doing well with their studies, so he was at a loss as to why they wanted better grades out of the prank. Straight A's in every subject was unheard of; perhaps they wanted to be the first ones to achieve it. And now he had to decide their fate, because that damned Gerald Baker was involved.

"Why the hell didn't Sylvia choose someone a little less prominent?" he moaned as he picked the telephone back up and dialled. Gerald Baker's secretary put his call through, and Browning gave the names of the seven boys over.

It didn't feel good.

But his side of the bargain was now complete.

Chapter Sixty-Four

Wednesday 19th August 1987, 12.35 PM

Michael Ryan needed petrol for his car. He waited for a motorcy-clist to leave the filling station before refuelling his silver Astra, and then pulled out a rifle and fired two shots at the female cashier inside. Thankfully, he missed, and the cashier was unhurt. Ryan then drove off towards the town of Hungerford. The motorcyclist who had been there only moments ago, however, sped to a nearby village and reported that what looked like an armed robbery had taken place and the culprit had driven off.

At around 12.45 PM, Michael Ryan was seen at his home at South View loading his car with guns, presumably ready to take off, but his car wouldn't start. Neighbours reported seeing him looking agitated, moving in and out of his house before finally going back inside and shooting the family dog. He then doused the house with petrol and set it alight. On his way out, he grabbed his guns from the boot of his car and shot two of his neighbours dead before taking off on foot towards the town's common.

On that terrifying journey, he shot and killed men and women randomly, including his mother, whom he shot once in her abdomen and twice in her back, before heading to Hungerford town centre where he carried on his random killing spree.

It was early afternoon when Michael Ryan broke into a community college where he had been a pupil at some years before and barricaded himself in. Luckily, the school was closed for the summer holidays. Police attempted negotiations to coax him out, but nothing worked.

During these negotiations, Ryan said, "Hungerford must be a bit of a mess. I wish I had stayed in bed."

At 18.52, Ryan shot himself fatally in the head with a Beretta pistol. He shot himself in the right temple; the bullet went straight through and out the other temple, and then lodged in a noticeboard across the classroom. When the pathologist entered that room afterwards, the pistol was pointing straight at him, though Ryan was already dead. The room, said the pathologist, smelled of sweat, chalk and blood.

Ryan never gave a reason for his killing spree. Sixteen people, including a police officer, had lost their lives, plus Ryan himself. Another fifteen people had been shot, though not fatally. It was Hungerford's darkest day.

And one that kept the emergency services and authorities busy for some time.

Chapter Sixty-Five

Wednesday 19th August, 1987.

It was so peaceful down by the river, mid-morning on a bright August day. The water flowed like it had nowhere to go in a hurry, carrying ducks lazily downstream. Drooping branches overhung the water's edge, providing generous shady spots to sit. Sylvia threw out her blanket, *their* blanket, and sat peacefully for a while watching the water. It was mesmerising. She stared out to the other side; a young family with a dog ambled past, perhaps enjoying some time away from their daily routine.

There would be no school for Sylvia today. She'd called in sick with a migraine, though it wasn't something she could ever recall doing in all of her working life. It wasn't who she was; she told the truth to the bitter end, no matter the consequences.

Sylvia had made her mind up. Since the last letter she'd received, along with the grainy Polaroid photo, she'd made her decision on how to end it all. The pressure had been building for a couple of weeks, and even though she'd taken her concerns to the headmaster, he'd made it clear it wasn't his problem. Sharing her troubles with Gerald hadn't made her feel much better, either, though he had been a good deal more supportive and sympathetic. But the truth was, she couldn't go on like this, hiding her love away like a dirty secret, and she couldn't risk Gerald's family knowing and the shame that would come down on her, the other woman. He'd promised he'd leave his wife when the time was right, and she believed him. But that wasn't yet; she knew that.

Tears rolled silently down her cheeks as she took the flask from her bag and poured herself a cup of coffee. She began by sipping, then, caught in a wave of despair, downed the contents in one. She filled the cup again hurriedly and finished that off, too. It tasted unremarkable.

She told the truth to the bitter end, no matter the consequences.

In the shade of a burly tree, Sylvia Marsh lay back on her blanket and waited for sleep to come.

It was to be her last.

The body of Sylvia Marsh was not found until the following morning, after Hungerford had been forced into lockdown while the killer had been at large. Everyone had been told to stay indoors. She was found by same dog walker she herself had watched from the opposite riverbank the previous day as she'd drunk her coffee. Or rather, the dog found her. She'd looked so peaceful, family said.

Sylvia Marsh been taken to the nearest mortuary, where she lay waiting her turn with the many gunshot victims. Including Michael Ryan himself.

It was chaos that day.

Chapter Sixty-Six

When Frederick Browning received the news at school that one of his staff, Sylvia Marsh, had been found dead, he'd assumed, naturally, that she'd been caught up in the previous day's dreadful events. But when the police officer told him that that had not, in fact, been the case—that she had been found by the river with no evidence of a gunshot wound, and that suicide was suspected—he instinctively knew what had driven her to her death.

Blackmail.

He also wondered if Gerald knew. After all, why would the police think to inform him? With no other next of kin, the school had been all the family Sylvia had had.

And they'd let her down.

He'd just shown the officer out and was still standing, stunned, in the entranceway when Darlene came up behind him, startling him.

"Heavens!" he exclaimed, whirling to face her. "You made me jump."

"Sorry Mr. Browning. So sorry. Only, I wondered if everything is all right. Was it to do with yesterday's events?" She meant the police officer's visit, of course.

The headmaster wondered for a moment what he should tell her. She'd find out soon enough, the entire school would, but he needed a bit of time to think before he told everyone. He evaded her question entirely and asked her to bring a pot of tea to his study. She looked at him quizzically, but had left it there and gone off to make his tea while Browning made his way back to his desk to think.

A moment or two later, she knocked, entered and left the tea tray with him, deciding not to revisit her earlier question.

Once alone, Frederick Browning ran through his options. He picked up a biscuit and nibbled on it; it was something to do with his fingers as his brain worked through what had happened.

Sylvia was dead. Had the students, *his* students, been the cause of her distress to such an extent that she'd taken her own life? A schoolboy prank gone much too far? Surely, he reasoned, if her actions had been the result of her relationship with Gerald Baker, he'd have seen something more of it when the man himself had visited just two mornings ago. He picked up another biscuit and chewed mindlessly. If this came out, the school would carry the shame forever and he'd likely lose his job over it. He couldn't allow that to happen.

"Damn those boys! Why hadn't they all gone home for the holidays, like their friends?" he moaned. Few boys went home in reality, he knew; their parents chose to send them to boarding school for a reason.

His thoughts turned anxiously to Gerald now: he knew about the blackmail, and he had the power to create havoc for him.

"But does he have proof?" Browning asked himself out loud. "Because it doesn't sound like she left a note. The officer had said 'possible suicide,' which meant it wasn't a certainty." He poured tea and sipped at it, washing biscuit crumbs from his mouth. He picked up another and chewed, his cup still in the other hand, eyes focused somewhere in the distance, thinking.

"The boys will keep quiet," he said decisively. "They have to. I can make sure that happens. I'll talk to them soon." As often happened, his oak-panelled walls were his only sounding board. When he was satisfied with his plan, he called Darlene to send the boys through. They'd be at lunch anyway, and no one would be any the wiser.

Fifteen minutes later, seven uneasy-looking boys were waiting to see their headmaster. Darlene regarded them curiously. Usually the headmaster informed her of what these sorts of meetings were about, but today was different. She'd followed her instructions, of course, and refrained from asking. Perhaps it had something to do with the policeman's visit?

At last, the headmaster opened his study door and called them through. Sitting back at his desk, with the seven boys lined up in front of him, he took a moment to study each boy's face before he spoke. Did they know why he'd called them in? Did he even have the right boys? He certainly hoped so; there was only one crack at this to get it right.

When he was satisfied that they'd withered under his gaze for long enough, he spoke. "So, whose idea was it to blackmail her?"

Seven heads simultaneously dropped an inch or two. He had the right boys, all right.

"I'll ask again. Whose idea was it?"

Nothing. He admired their solidarity. "Let me put it this way. You're all caught up in this equally. If you are the instigator, you're in no more trouble than the others, but out of idle curiosity, I want to know who it was." He looked directly at Alistair, and asked, "Why, Mr. Crowley? What was your motivation?"

More silence.

"I gather you all wanted better grades out of your plan, am I correct?"

Seven heads stayed bowed; a couple nodded ever so slightly.

Alistair found his tongue. "What will happen to us, sir?"

At least he'd raised his head and looked directly at his accuser when he spoke, Browning noted. A confident individual today.

Smart in general. Yet he'd got mixed up in something stupid that had now turned deadly.

"It depends. I've given this a lot of thought. You don't know the half of it yet, but you will do soon enough. And that troubles me. The fallout from your stupidity reaches much farther than you anticipated, I'm sure. So, here's the deal."

Seven heads dared to turn to their neighbours, each boy anxiously wondering what their headmaster was going to do. The signals were confusing, no doubt.

"You'll get your grades."

Seven startled faces shot rapid looks at their friends, as if to say, 'Come again?'

"But on one condition. You never instigated this plot, never spent a moment thinking about it, never sent any anonymous letters, nothing. Do I make myself clear?"

Seven voices said, "Yes sir," in unison.

"I don't care who asks, or how hard they try: it was nothing to do with you or anyone else at this school. Got it? It never happened. It was a rumour."

"Yes, sir."

"Now, before you all disappear, I have some other news for you. And this, boys, is your punishment. No doubt it will stay with you for the rest of your miserable lives."

The boys flicked questioning looks at one another.

Finally, Alistair dared to speak. "But I thought—"

The headmaster stood, knocking his chair backwards as he barked the words out. "Sylvia Marsh is dead. She killed herself. And it's on you!" There wasn't another sound in the room until he finally thundered, "Dismissed!"

Seven stricken boys filed out of the room, each deep in thought. They'd killed Sylvia Marsh.

She was dead.

And it was their fault.

And they were to keep quiet.

Chapter Sixty-Seven

The news on everyone's lips was about the previous day's carnage. Everyone had their own story, their own version of what had happened, victims they knew. There was so much gossip, fact and extended truth in the air it was hard to know what to believe and what to ignore. The press had swooped in, everyone from the local papers to national TV, and they did their job like vultures on road kill. Headlines screamed the news around the world, and England's first mass shooting became the topic of conversation across many languages. The town of Hungerford had just become famous for all the wrong reasons.

At Gerald's office, his small team gathered in the lunch room and chatted in hushed tones about their own experiences. Many of them had been in the office, at work. Some had stepped out on an errand or for lunch, and luckily none of them had been caught in the crossfire, or taken a direct hit, as the gunman had fired away indiscriminately. For this, they were thankful. Gerald let them have their time; it was important they were allowed to express their feelings, as he had done himself with Sandra, his wife, the previous night. They'd stayed up talking, something they rarely did any more, until late in the evening. It was a kind of therapy.

But Sylvia was on his mind now. He wanted to speak to her, to make sure she was all right and not too upset by the shootings. But she'd be at work now, and even though it was the summer holidays, there were still boarding pupils to look after, summer education and sporting programmes to oversee. Sylvia would have been safe, he suspected, confined to the school as she was during working hours. But that didn't stop him wanting desperately to reach out to her, to hold her and soothe her. There was only Gerald to love her and protect her like no one else would, and he knew she would need him today.

He drained his coffee mug, rinsed it at the sink and left the other staff members to rehash the events of the last twenty-four hours. He'd call the school and see if he could be put through. It was about lunchtime anyway; she should be free to talk.

Back at his desk, he made the call and spoke to the office secretary, who told him Sylvia hadn't been in to work since she'd left on Tuesday evening. She'd called in sick with a migraine and was staying indoors. Gerald frowned uneasily; that was most unlike her. Before he rang off, the secretary had asked him to give Sylvia her regards if he did speak to her, to wish her a speedy recovery; migraines could be quite debilitating. Gerald assured her he would and hung up. He glanced at his watch. There wasn't time to get over to her cottage and be back before his next appointment, but the urgency inside of him pulled hard. He pressed the intercom button and waited for his own secretary to answer.

"Can you reschedule my afternoon appointment for me, please, or see if Trevor can take it? I have to go out unexpectedly."

She said she'd handle it, and Gerald grabbed his car keys and set out to his car. He knew he'd never get any more work done today; there was too much disruption, and the thought of Sylvia being ill and all alone at home wasn't conducive either.

The car was stifling inside; the midday sun was directly overhead. He wound both front windows down to let the meagre breeze in. It'd cool down when he got moving. His steering wheel was almost too hot to hold as he pulled his door to and set off, through the town centre and on to Sylvia's cottage a couple of villages away. He wondered if he should stop and pick something up for her— some flowers, maybe, or a tin of soup—but decided against it. If she was hungry, he was sure he could make her something to eat with what she had in already.

He ploughed on. The car was cool, now, as he approached the boundary of Kintbury, and he turned into her street and pulled up outside her cottage. He sat for a moment, looking up at the front windows. All the curtains were open.

"Strange," he said out loud. "Maybe she's feeling better."

He got out and headed up the front path, half expecting to see her opening the front door, but she didn't. He glanced across at the driveway and noticed her car wasn't there either. It didn't add up. The school secretary had said she'd not been in, yet it didn't look like she was home either. He knocked on the front door anyway. And waited. And knocked again. Nothing. He formed a shield with both hands and used it to look through the lounge window, but even through the net curtains, he could see nobody was home.

A voice called out to him and he turned to see where it was coming from.

"Are you looking for someone?" an elderly man called. He was peering over the hedge between his place and Sylvia's.

"I'm looking for Sylvia. But it looks like I've missed her," Gerald said, smiling.

"Haven't seen her today," the old man said. "In fact, now I think of it, last I saw her was yesterday morning. Yes, that's it. Looked like she was off for a picnic with someone—carrying a blanket and basket, she was."

"Really?" Gerald asked. It didn't sound like she had a migraine, then, if the old man was correct. Those usually required a dark room and a lie down. A picnic in the sunshine was the exact opposite. "Are you sure? Maybe that was Saturday morning?"

"No, I'm sure, all right. Did it Saturday, too. Yesterday, I called out good morning to her, but she mustn't have heard me. Carried on by without a word. Distracted over something. I remember thinking it wasn't like her. Definitely yesterday morning."

"Thanks, then," Gerald said, and went back to his car. He was stumped. The old man was adamant he'd seen her yesterday, but he was also right about something else.

It wasn't like Sylvia at all.

Now he needed to find her even more.

Chapter Sixty-Eight

Gerald was dumbfounded, then horrified. Until it hit him: perhaps she'd been a victim of the shooting. His blood ran cold in his veins. *Could she have been murdered?* He stamped on the accelerator. There was only one place she could be if she'd somehow got caught up in the rampage: the hospital. She had no next of kin, so if she'd been injured, heaven forbid, she and the hospital staff would have had no way of letting him know.

"Yes, that's it!" he said triumphantly. "I'm on my way, my love." He was almost smiling with relief now. Injured, he could cope with.

At the hospital, he parked in the visitor's area and raced inside to the reception area.

"Hello," he said breathlessly to the young woman at Information. "Sylvia Marsh—what ward is she on, please?"

"One moment, and I'll take a look for you," the woman said. "When was she admitted?"

"Yesterday, I think."

The woman typed Sylvia's name into her computer but came up blank. She looked gravely up at Gerald and gently asked, "Was she a victim of the shooting?"

"Well, that's it. I'm really not sure, but she's missing. You don't think. . ." He trailed off, unable to ask the next obvious question. He'd been so sure she'd be here, sitting up in bed with an injured leg or something fixable. Now it appeared she wasn't.

The woman picked her phone up and made a call. Gerald heard her ask about Sylvia Marsh—was she on their list? She lowered her voice and asked, "The list of the known deceased?" After a pause, she looked up, shook her head at Gerald and smiled a little. Sylvia's name wasn't on that list. "Do you know if she's actually in this hospital?" she asked him. "She may have been sent on to another."

"Thanks. I really don't know where she is. I'll try them. I'll phone them," he said, dazed. He'd felt so sure. He slowly walked away from the woman and was headed back to his car when another thought hit him.

She'd had a blanket, a picnic basket. But they hadn't arranged to meet. . .

"Oh god, no!" he exclaimed out loud and turned on his heels back towards the woman he'd been talking to. She was now busy talking to another man and Gerald stood behind him, willing him to finish what he needed so he could ask her another question. He moved from one foot to the other, in an agony of frustration, and when the man finally moved on, he dashed forward and blurted out his request.

"Maybe she wasn't a shooting victim. Was anyone else brought in recently, a woman, shoulder-length brown hair, thirty-five, pretty? I expect she had her purse with her, all her things. Please, can you ask again?" He sounded like the desperate man he was, his voice frantic now, his eyes pleading.

The clerk obligingly made the call and asked the question. Her face told him all he needed to know as she looked back at him. An anguished cry burst from Gerald's chest before she'd even hung up, and he clenched his fists across his eyes. The woman stood and rounded her desk. He didn't feel her put her hand on his shoulder to try and comfort him. She waited patiently, as she had done with all the others over the last twenty-four hours, and then she asked him softly, "Are you next of kin for Sylvia Marsh?"

"Kind of," he said. "She doesn't have any family. I'm a close friend," he said, his voice hoarse with tears.

"Please, take a seat, and I'll get somebody to come and see you," she said, pointing to a chair not far away.

Gerald sat down to wait.

Chapter Sixty-Nine

Thursday 20th August 1987

I don't know what to do with myself. My love has gone. Forever. I'd hoped she was a walking injured, sitting up in a hospital bed waiting for me to find her. I'd hoped that's why I couldn't find her. But it wasn't to be. Taken, gone forever. The hospital mentioned suicide, but surely not. She—we—had so much to live for. I'd have put a stop to the blackmail; the headmaster would have seen sense. And we would have been together, like I'd promised her. But not now. She's gone. I don't think I will ever be happy again. There's nothing left for me. I may as well join her.

Chapter Seventy

Even at 7 AM, it was hot as hell. Chrissy had idled on the patio long enough, sipping coffee and eating toast putting off the inevitable, trying to justify not going for a run this morning staying here for another mug of caffeine. The jet lag seemed to be lingering longer than it normally did, but then perhaps she hadn't noticed it so much on other journeys over. This time, she had a purpose to attend to, whereas every other time, she'd lounged about, relaxing and drinking in her 'me time' with no agenda ahead, nowhere to be, no one to monitor. There wasn't much of that on this trip.

"Come on, lazy bones, get your arse into gear," she said to herself, standing and taking her mug into the kitchen. "Work to be done." She slipped out of her shorty pyjamas and into her running kit, pulled her pink cap down to keep the low morning glare out, and she was almost ready.

"Do I fancy music?" she asked herself.

Apparently, she did, because she found herself flicking through playlists to find something to suit her mood. She stopped at Gin Wigmore and hit play. Her earphones filled with the woman's gravelly voice, and she headed out onto the pavement and quickly got into her stride. Chrissy hated listening in order; everything had to be on shuffle. She found comfort in the unexpected at times, and since a playlist order was not a matter of life or death, this was a simple one to allow. And a little serendipity could amuse.

The first song out was 'Black sheep.' Chrissy smiled; she'd always been the black sheep of the family, even in her childhood. Julie was the good girl. Chrissy sang along with the first couple of lines as she set off towards the boardwalk at a steady jog. She passed two homeless men lying in the shade of a couple of nearby trees, their worldly belongings by their side in shopping trolleys. There didn't appear to be much more than a tarp and a few odd clothes, and she wondered about their stories. How had they got to be sleeping rough? Bad luck or chosen lifestyle? She'd never know.

By the time she'd reached the boardwalk, she was glistening with sweat. She turned to look across at the ocean on her right, its silvery light flickering against the distant haze that was slowly lifting. She'd take a dip on the way back for sure. A running group went by, three abreast and ten people deep, keeping in step with each other drill style. Each wore an orange running vest; they were all part of the same club. Their speed was a few beats faster than her own, and they passed through quickly. She was tempted to join on the end, but resisted. Right now, she didn't have the extra energy she'd have to muster to keep up.

That's when she'd remembered the man in the green cap from yesterday, trying to keep up with another group. Why had he popped into her mind? He'd stood out to her for some reason; maybe it had been the green cap. Or maybe it was just her overactive, jet-lagged mind. Still, Chrissy wondered if he was out this morning; most runners were regulars, and as she neared Venice Beach, she found herself watching out for him. There were plenty of faded blue and grey caps about, but no green today.

She carried on all the way to the muscle gym then pulled over to catch her breath a little and pulled her earphones off. She was about halfway, with just the return journey to complete. She stood for a moment to watch the men working out, the gulls crying overhead. It was going to be a scorcher today and the dip in the sea at the end of her workout would be extremely welcome. She bent for a drink at the water fountain there, splashing some over her face and a handful down the back of her neck. It wasn't ice cold but it was better than nothing. As she bent for another long drink, she was conscious of someone waiting behind her; she wiped her chin with the back of her hand and then stood up straight and turned to leave.

A male voice said, 'Thank you.' Without turning to look, she instinctively knew who it was. Voice recognition had been part of her training, and her sense of hearing was well tuned in even now. Should she stop and say hello? Or carry on back to that swim she was looking forward to?

Serendipity.

She turned slowly to say hello to Philip Banks, who stood waiting in his green cap. She watched his face change, looking like he wished he'd kept his mouth shut. They stood looking at each other for a couple of seconds, then Chrissy spoke.

"Good morning." She smiled brightly, removing her shades so he could see her eyes. It always made communication easier. Eyes gave a lot away about a person, about a situation. About what was to happen next. Boxers, lovers and animals thought so, anyway.

"Ah. Good morning to you, too. I see you didn't take my advice and go back home?"

"No, and no need to look caught out—I'm not going to harass you. I'm only out for my run."

Philip relaxed his shoulders a little; the woman in front of him was indeed astute.

"That's better," she commented knowingly, and Philip risked a tight smile. "You're obviously heading out. Maybe I can run back with you? If I can keep up, that is?" More smiles; she was teasing him. The man was too uptight.

"Do I have a choice?"

"Not really," she said, still all smiles, and they set off towards the pier at a slow jog. Another running group in drill-step style paced by, much longer than the first one. They wore fluorescent pink tops. There must have been forty people. When they'd passed by, Philip asked the first question.

"If I tell you, will you stop pestering and digging up the past?"

"Well, that kind of depends on what it is, don't you think?"

They ran alongside each other in silence as Philip decided what he was or wasn't going to share. Chrissy waited patiently, keeping pace easily. They'd run nearly a mile before he spoke again.

"Let's pull over."

Chrissy followed his lead and they made their way across the grassy dunes to a tree. The shade was welcome and she wiped her face on the front of her shirt. That swim would have to wait a while.

"I'll tell you about some of it, okay? That's the best I'll do."

"Okay."

They were sitting on the grass. Philip stared out to the distance, somewhere across the ocean in front of them, then began. He told her of blackmailing a schoolteacher and how it had all come out after the woman was found dead. She'd committed suicide. The headmaster had sworn them all to secrecy, concerned for the school's reputation. It had been a terrible time for all the boys. They'd carried the guilt for many years.

"I don't get what that had to do with my father, though."

"The woman we were blackmailing was called Miss Marsh." He watched her for signs of recognition, but Chrissy looked at him blankly. "She was having an affair with your father." He let that sink in before adding, "We didn't know who he was at the time."

Dad was having an affair?

It was Chrissy's turn to look caught out. After a moment, she collected herself and said, "And knowing my father, he'd want to know who was responsible. Hence the photos of the culprits," she said, nodding her head almost to herself.

Philip cringed at the word 'culprits.' "So, you can see why it wouldn't achieve anything to drag it all up again. Your mother doesn't need to know, I'm sure."

Chrissy watched a gull trying to eat part of a sandwich without attracting its buddies. It failed. Seconds later, it was surrounded by around twenty more of them.

"And your visit to his funeral?" she said at length.

"Purely for a client, on behalf of someone else." Philip turned his gaze from the sea back to Chrissy and smiled at her. "It's the truth."

Chrissy stayed thoughtful for a moment. "Okay. Thanks for telling me. Mystery solved." She stood up to leave. "I'll see you around," she called as she set off back to the dip she'd promised herself.

Philip remained under the tree, watching her head off. Thinking.

He hoped what he'd told her would be enough.

He wasn't going to tell her the rest.

Chapter Seventy-One

As she headed back down the boardwalk, her mind was spinning. She wasn't stupid. She knew there was still a lot more to the story and Philip wasn't for spilling the rest of it. He'd started by telling her he wouldn't go into all the story, only some of it.

"I'll tell you about some of it, okay? That's the best I'll do."

But who could she ask? If this Sylvia Marsh had committed suicide, that was a dead end.

Oh, unfortunate choice of words, Chrissy!

Her mind went darting back to the three missing diaries. It seemed like those might be the key to all of this. Could her father have them hidden somewhere else for even safer keeping? At his office, maybe? Where would she hide something so damning?

"A safe, I'd bet!" she said out loud and pumped a fist in the air.

She was almost at the end of her run. When she was about level with the steps that led back up to the streets, she slowed and caught her breath, then headed to the water's edge. Sweat poured out of her as she quickly removed her shoes, tucking her phone into one of them. The beach itself was quiet here; everyone was still pounding the concrete boardwalk. The tepid water felt soothing on her feet as she sloshed forward up to her knees. Bracing herself for the coolness to come, she dove forward and swam out further into the sea. The current wasn't strong, and she swam easily out to a place where she could no longer feel the sand beneath her feet if she stood, but not far enough to be completely out of her depth. She submerged herself completely, then burst back through the surface and shook her head like a wet dog, hair flicking droplets back into the sea. It was a few degrees cooler where she trod water. She lay back and let the salty water move through her hair, separating the blond strands like pale seaweed in an ocean rockpool. It felt therapeutic. It reminded her of her other home, of Adam and the bath she'd taken just after her father's death. Had that only been a week or two ago?

"So, what to do next? What's the next move?" she asked herself. Floating languidly, with the sun drying her salty face, she turned her attention to Alistair. Perhaps it was worth a conversation with him, too, maybe another accidental meeting? There were still plenty of questions she'd like answers to, not least why some of the seven had since ended up dead, at their own hands. Surely a woman's suicide thirty years ago hadn't solely been the reason? No, something had changed; something had reared its head and set a boulder rolling down a hillside somewhere. And she wondered if her father had somehow pushed that boulder.

Three of the seven were deceased: Cody Taylor, Stuart Townsend and Sam Moore had all died a year or so ago. That only left the two here in town—Philip and Alistair—two plus more she knew little about. One, Robert Newsome, was a doctor; the other, Steve Marks, she'd no clue.

The diaries.

Of course!

But not the missing three: the ones from a couple of years ago.

She swam back towards the shore, her realisation propelling her forward like a steam boat. She sloshed back up onto the pebbles, retrieved her phone, rammed her wet feet into her shoes and set off back towards her home.

. . .

By the time she'd arrived, she'd formed the resemblance of a plan. But could she pull it off? First, she needed to find out if the gardener had already put a match to the bag of diaries. Second, if he hadn't, she had to somehow get her hands on the two or three she wanted—while she was halfway around the world. She knew she couldn't ask her mother; she was already too suspicious as it was, and Chrissy wasn't about to explain what her father had been up to —either back then or possibly more recently.

What about Julie? She quickly discarded the idea. Julie wasn't reliable, and hurting her family was not Chrissy's intention. Adam? But how could he possibly get into the garden shed undetected? And both Julie and Adam would ask awkward questions. The obvious answer was that neither of them could help. There was only one other person she could think of who wouldn't raise any suspicions and could gain access to the shed: the gardener himself.

But how could she get hold of him? She didn't even have his name. She discarded that idea too.

What to do... What to do?

I'll think of something.

Do that.

And on the one-person, two-sided conversation went as Chrissy headed inside the shower cubicle and washed sweat, seawater and sand down the drain. By the time she was clean and fragrant again, she was ravenous. In the kitchen she made a plate of scrambled eggs and a fresh pot of coffee and made herself comfortable out on the patio in the shade. Her phone chirped: a text from Julie.

"Nothing urgent. Mum's not too good. Doctor has been, says she needs rest. Looks like a virus of some sort. Love you. Jx"

She'd thought her mother had looked tired when she'd seen her last, but she'd put it down to the stress of her husband's death and the funeral. It was never going to be a cheery time for anyone. She compiled a text back:

"Sending my love. Drop her a kiss from me. Keep me posted. Cx"

That done, she returned to her eggs. And the problem of

getting into that damn garden shed. Her mother was on bed rest. Could that be an opportunity to exploit?

You'll come up with something.

Will I?

You always do.

Chapter Seventy-Two

With the matter of the diaries still to take care of somehow, she moved on to what she could do while she was still in the vicinity of Philip Banks and Alistair Crowley. Surely the last couple of years' worth of reading would show what this whole saga was about, how her father was connected, because it couldn't only be about the death of his lover. Not with three of the boys, now men, dead in recent months. There was a catalyst for sure; it was a matter of finding what it was.

She turned her attention to Alistair again. She hadn't noticed a ring on either his wedding finger or Philip's, though that didn't mean that either of them wasn't in a settled relationship. For some reason, though, she particularly doubted Alistair was. So, if he was single, he'd have a social life. But where exactly did he live? A quick look in the telephone directory revealed nothing, so he obviously had an unlisted number.

So, paying him a surprise visit at home, wherever that might be, was out of the question. No, she'd have to waylay him at his office again.

Right, then. So that's settled.

Just beware of the redhead.

. . .

Clearing her throat, Chrissy dialled Banks & Crowley once more. When Carmen answered, Chrissy enquired, in her best Irish accent, whether Mr. Crowley was available. She was told he'd be back around 4.30 PM. Would she like to leave a message? Chrissy declined and hung up. Now she had a time to aim for, at least. Time to get ready for another episode of *Loitering in LA*, she thought wryly; she should have been an actress. She'd have fitted right in. Maybe in another life.

At 4 PM, she headed upstairs to change and make herself look a little more presentable. If she was going to turn his head and persuade him to have a cold beer with her, she had to look a bit snappier than she did right now in her shorts and T-shirt.

Twenty minutes later, dressed in a linen shift dress and heeled sandals Julie would have been proud of, she was opening the rear door of yet another Uber, destination Abbot Kinney, her target Alistair Crowley. She hoped he was feeling charitable.

From her vantage point a couple of doorways from the office, Chrissy spotted her quarry. She ran her fingers through her smart blond hair and stepped out of her hiding place into a well-timed collision.

"Oh, I'm so sorry!" she exclaimed, avoiding Alistair Crowley's eyes and reaching down to pick up her shades. She steadied herself upright and made a show of being flustered, apologies gushing from her mouth like a hosepipe. When she'd finally righted herself and 'realised' who was standing in front of her, she took in the look on his face. He didn't look impressed, nor convinced of their encounter.

"Hello again," she said smiling sweetly. "Sorry about that. I'm such a klutz at times."

"It's fine," he said coolly. "As long as you're okay. No harm done here." He brushed the front of his shirt as if something had been spilled on it. Reflex action, maybe.

"Listen, I feel awful. You must think I was lying in wait for you or something," she said, giggling. The look on his face said, 'You were.' Damn—she was losing him. He turned to walk away. "Can I get you a cold beer?" she piped up, trying not to sound desperate. "You look like you could do with one and it's not far off five PM."

"Thanks, but no thanks. I've got work to do." He turned away again, but she called him back.

"Come on, Alistair. It's as hot as hell. Let me buy you a beer—a quick one, eh? Fifteen minutes, tops. What harm can it do?" She noticed his shoulders relax a little. Either a cold beer sounded good, or he was losing the will to be bolshy. He turned back to her slowly and caught her eyes, searching for something.

First to speak loses.

"A quick one. That's it," he conceded.

She'd won.

"Great! You choose—you're the local." She slipped her arm through his uninvited. A seemingly sweet gesture, but it also meant he couldn't escape easily. He glanced down at her arm, but, gentleman that he was, he refrained from saying anything.

The bar he chose was only a short distance further on and they slipped inside into the coolness, away from the hot sun. Chrissy noticed a young waitress wink at him as she made her way over.

"What can I get you, hun? Nice to see you again." She looked Chrissy quickly up and down.

A regular, eh? She ordered them both beers and the waitress sauntered off. Chrissy noticed Alistair watching the woman's rear end, which was clad in tight black shorts. Legs went on up to her ears, almost.

No wedding ring, and no relationship.

"She's cute. You should ask her out—she clearly likes you," she said teasingly, trying to get the man to lighten up. If she was ever going to get to her point, he needed to relax a little. A glimmer of a smile creased his lips. "That's better!" she encouraged him, and they both laughed lightly together. Ice broken.

"Look, I'm sorry I turfed you out the office," he said, almost sheepishly. "It was rude of me. But you threw me off balance."

"Apology accepted," she said graciously, bowing her head and smiling.

"Now, why don't you ask me what you want to know? I'm not foolish enough to think this encounter was anything but accidental."

Chrissy opened her mouth to protest, but he raised his eyebrows and she converted it to a smile instead. He wasn't stupid.

"In that case, here goes," she said conceding. "I'm sure you know by now who I am, right?"

"I do."

"So, how are you connected to my father?"

Alistair took a deep breath while he considered his reply. "Let's say this. A couple of us invested in one of his schemes. We didn't know it was your father's company then, and the scheme fell over. A lot of money was lost. And that's it."

"That's it?"

"Yep."

The waitress returned with two bottles of beer and Alistair took a long drink from his; froth lay horizontally inside the bottle like a moving landscape of creamy white as he gulped.

"Who else invested with you? Did Philip?"

"Yes. And a couple of others."

Chrissy was quickly catching on. "And they all lost money too. I can see why you perhaps didn't want me in your office."

"Correct. Bad taste and all that, though we realise you're not your father. Did you work for him?"

Chrissy suppressed a grin. "Far from it. And thanks for filling me in." More sombrely, she added, "I'm sorry for the trouble he caused you." She took a sip of beer, then asked, "And the three deceased friends? Had they invested?"

It was a while before Alistair spoke, and Chrissy gave him the space to think for a while. If her father had inadvertently been responsible for their deaths, the least she could do was show some respect for his pain. Finally, he drew a deep breath and replied. "Yes, they did. And a good deal more than Philip and I. It's all still rather raw." Alistair's voice grew husky. He cleared his throat and stared at the table top.

Chrissy gave him a moment, again. Then, her voice softer now, she asked, "So, Philip's presence at my father's funeral—that was nothing to do with a client wanting representation there, was it?" It wasn't really a question.

Alistair turned to her, tears welling in his eyes.

"No!" he shouted, startling her. Heads turned their way. He lowered his voice and leaned closer to her. "It was to make sure the old bastard was finally dead!"

Chapter Seventy-Three

Chrissy sat back, heartsick. No wonder he'd wanted her out of the office: she was a living, breathing reminder of a man who had caused them almost unimaginable grief, shame, and heartache.

As she watched Alistair collect himself, something else clicked ominously in her head. Julie had asked the question not long after her father's death. And she had to ask him now, no matter how grief-stricken he still was. God, this day was just not ever going to get any easier, was it?

"My father died of a heart attack," she said, plunging in. "Tell me neither of you had anything to do with that? Since Philip was in the country at the time?"

"We're not murderers, you know!" His face had gone deathly pale now.

"Look, I have to ask. It just seems like such a coincidence. A heart attack is easy enough to create and go undetected. Particularly if a doctor is involved. And you do have a friend who's a doctor."

"And how would you know that? Have you 'brought on' a heart attack?" he spat, doing air quotes with his fingers. His eyes were filled with fire now, and people were starting to stare at them again.

She half expected the waitress to return and ask them to quieten down.

"TV, I guess," she said trying to return their conversation to a more congenial level. "Like I said, I had to ask. I'm sorry. Forget it."

"The answer is no. Your father was already gone when Philip got there. Yes, he went to have it out with him, but like I say, he was too late. I told Philip to come home, but he didn't. Not right away. He hung around for the funeral, just to make sure he went in the ground."

"He was cremated," Chrissy said in a tiny voice.

"What?"

"My father was cremated, not buried."

"Whatever."

It was time for her to leave him be. She got to her feet.

"Look, thanks for filling me in. I appreciate it, really I do. And for what it's worth, again, I'm really sorry about your friends. It must have been a hard decision, a desperate decision, to take their own lives. I'm truly sorry."

Alistair stayed where he was, not looking up from the beer bottle he was twiddling in his hands, as she left money for their drinks and headed for the door. She stood outside the bar for a few moments in the glare of the early evening sunshine, utterly exhausted. She now knew the truth about her father's connection with Philip and Alistair and the others, though she didn't like it.

Choosing to walk a while, she slipped into a nearby shoe store and purchased a cheap pair of flats to get her home; her strappy heels were definitely not up for the task. She took her time and headed down towards the waterfront and Venice Beach, all the time turning over what she'd learned. Even if there were the funds left in her father's business, it wouldn't bring the three dead friends back. There really wasn't anything she could do for the men, but at least now she understood.

Or did she?

She stopped dead in the middle of the pavement. People passed her by on both sides as she stood staring at the concrete under her feet.

"But why those individuals, Dad? That wasn't bad luck, was it?"

"Hey, lady!" someone moaned loudly as they almost bumped into her. She took the hint and stepped aside.

There were seven faces in the tin in all. Five that she knew of had lost money; three of those were dead. What were the chances the remaining two had also lost money in her father's scheme? Pretty good, she thought unhappily. And if they had all been roped into his scam, had that been deliberate on his part? Had he, in fact, targeted the seven, holding them responsible for his long-ago lover's suicide? If he had, in fact, set out to teach them a lesson, then why wait so long to get his revenge?

Once again, there was only one way of finding out for sure.

The diaries.

They kept popping up.

She hurriedly sent a text to Adam before it got any later; it was the only solution she could think of right now. Desperate times and all that. She'd suffer the inquisition from him later.

She also wondered how her mum was doing.

Perhaps she should fly back home, she thought with a sigh. Her work here was likely done anyway.

Chapter Seventy-Four

Chrissy stopped off at a restaurant for dinner, then, once she was back at her house, sent a text to Julie. It was the early hours back in the UK, so she wasn't expecting a reply and was surprised when Julie responded quickly.

"She's not so good, actually. I'm stopping overnight with her. Don't worry, though. Didn't want her alone. Jx"

"Oh no. Really? No better, then."

"No better. But no need to worry either. Jx"

"Glad you're there. Kisses from me. Cx"

"By the way, did I see Adam in the shed????"

Damn!

Think quickly, Chrissy.

"Yes, you may have. He mentioned something about something." It sounded lame but she hoped Julie would leave well enough alone. If it wasn't celebrity or fashion related, she generally showed little interest.

"Ok. Speak soon. Enjoy the rest of your conference. Jx"

Chrissy smiled. Bullet dodged.

Something about something?

Really, Chrissy.

I know, I'll try harder.

She'd almost forgotten she was supposed to be at a conference. *"Back soon. Cx"*

But should she fly back home? If her mother was unwell and Julie was staying over, it was more than a bad cold. The woman had looked even frailer than normal last time she'd seen her, except when she'd gone berserk over Julie and her finding the diaries. A gorilla would have had less strength than their petite, elderly mother that day.

Well, at least she knew the answer to the other text she'd sent. Adam had indeed been over and gained access to the shed. Had he got what she'd asked for, though? Looking at her watch, she realised it would be at least another three hours before he woke up and replied. She'd have to wait. In the meantime, she fixed herself an iced tea and went back out to the patio.

The streets around her were alive with conversation, the chatter of neighbours on their way out for the evening; a car horn blared in the distance. Laughter rang out from a group of girls not far away, and suddenly she missed home. And Adam and the boys. It hadn't been the same kind of visit she'd come to enjoy, and since she'd set off only a couple of days ago, she'd thought of not much else besides the box of photos, the diaries and her father. She hadn't realised how much she missed him.

Perhaps it is *time to head home, Chrissy.*

Are you sure?

As sure as I can be.

Then get your stuff packed and change your flight.

Righto.

She found her laptop and logged on, then changed her flight to the following morning. There was no point struggling to get the next one home later that evening. The boys would be chuffed at her early arrival home, as would Adam, and she could finalise this whole mess and put an end to it from the comfort of her home. She was sure Philip and Alistair would be thrilled at her departure too. All she'd managed to do there was open old, deep wounds.

Her thoughts suddenly circled back to the man she'd seen following Philip. Was he in trouble from another angle? He'd dismissed the man as a client; maybe it had been.

Not now, Chrissy. Not your concern.

I know; you're right.

Let them handle it.

With her bags ready for the morning, she slipped into her pyjamas and cranked up the TV for a movie. She'd only just got settled when her phone pinged; it was Adam. She looked at the clock; it was far too early for him, but no one else had that ringtone allocated to them.

The message was simple: *"I have them. How are you?"*

"You're an early bird. Not sleeping?"

"Up for a pee. Missing you."

"Sign of getting older. I'm heading home early. Set off in the a.m."

"How come? Conference?"

"Mum's not well, and I'm not doing much here."

(You mean you've done all you can here, don't you, Chrissy?)

"Well, that's good news. Miss you, babe. What time? Meet you?"

"I leave first thing. I'll get a driver. Stay with the boys. Home before you know it."

Chrissy was desperate to know about the diaries, but there was little point asking Adam; he wouldn't know what was important or not if he looked inside them. And she didn't fancy his questions right now either. She smiled again at her sister's ignorant bliss at seeing Adam in the shed and not thinking it strange. It would have been to anyone else.

"Travel safely, then. Love you. Ax"

"Love you back. Cx"

Tossing the phone onto the sofa she felt happy with her decision to leave and get home, her real home, and finally get to the bottom of what had been going on before her father died. The death of a teacher many years ago was certainly not the reason three of those boys were now also dead.

In the morning, she'd be on her way back, to cooler climes, for sure; it would be nice to see all her boys. Whether it had been her father's death or something else entirely, she'd missed everyone a good deal more on this trip than usual. Perhaps it was also time that a chapter in her life closed. She'd never been one for all the deceit that had gone with the job, but she'd been doing it for so long it had become second nature. Even when she'd the chance to stop, she had willingly carried on. Her place in Santa Monica, her cottage in France— perhaps she should take up pottery or golf or something else for time out.

Time to sell up and come clean, Chrissy Livingstone.
Sure about that?
Not at all.
Didn't think so.
She slept like a log that night, the first time in a long time.

Chapter Seventy-Five

Saturday 20th September 2014

Business arrived at Gerald Baker's doors in all kinds of ways, though mainly through referrals. If people wanted a level of security when they invested, word of mouth from a satisfied client was about as good as it got. And it was easy business for Gerald and his team. It was a referral from such a client that took him to one of the larger homes in Surrey, in Rickmansworth, and the home of Cody Taylor, a successful businessman in infrastructure. Taylor had developed acute business skills that complemented his engineering knowledge and built one of the biggest roading companies in the UK. It would be fair to say he'd made it in life and had spare cash to look after. That was where Gerald was to come in: providing sound financial advice and making sure Taylor's excess cash was well looked after.

Gerald pulled up outside the front door of the man's home and took in the view across the rolling countryside while he slipped into his jacket. The sun made most places pleasant, but the stark contrast between the bright green of the surrounding pasture and the clear blue of the summer sky was breathtaking, and Gerald took a moment to drink it in. It sure was *Black Beauty* country, he mused.

"Beautiful, isn't it?" a male voice behind him said. Gerald turned to see a man in his early forties, looking more like a country gent than a roading engineer. But then it was Saturday morning. He had blond wavy hair, something quite uncommon on men. His green and brown tweed suited him.

"Stunning. All too often we miss what's around us, we're so busy bustling along. It's good to take a moment every now and then, don't you think?"

"I do indeed. Gerald Baker, I'm assuming?" The man had an easy smile and Gerald realised he hadn't introduced himself.

"Oh, how rude of me! Yes, Gerald Baker." He put his hand out and the two shook.

"Cody Taylor. Come on inside. Tea or coffee, perhaps?"

"Thanks. Tea would be lovely." Gerald followed the man inside; the coolness of the interior was a welcome contrast to the warmth of the morning sunshine. A woman appeared as if from nowhere and the man, Cody, ordered tea for them both. They headed into the lounge towards the back of the house which was decked out in pale shades of beige and sage green. A huge vase full of white lilies and garden greenery sat on a grand piano near the bright bay window that looked out onto a perfectly striped lawn. It was a truly beautiful room, and one, Gerald assumed, created with a woman's touch. Maybe the woman he'd ordered tea from? He waited for Cody Taylor to sit before doing the same, and a moment later a tray with tea and biscuits arrived, the china cups and pot matching the room in which they were to take it. *Homes & Gardens* magazine came to mind.

"I'll cut straight to the point, if I may, Gerald. I know your work, so I don't need impressing there, and I have money to invest. Chunks at regular intervals. Likely to be a couple of hundred thou each time, say, several times per year. I'm fairly open when it comes to where to put it, but I do like to get the best return I can. And that means don't bother with the bank or the really 'safe' funds."

He added speech marks around the word 'safe' to emphasise he knew nothing in finance was ever safe. "So, let's talk about what's on offer, shall we?"

And that's what the two men did over the course of an hour or two and another pot of tea. It was a rather cordial and easy meeting for Gerald; he wished all his prospective clients could be so laid back. As their business drew to a close, Gerald stood and made his way to the window, passing the beautiful grand piano. Instinctively, his fingertips touched the lid and lingered for a second or two longer than most people's would. The wood was cool and as soft as silk.

"You play?"

"Used to, but no longer. You?"

"No. It was my wife's. Sadly, she passed, so it doesn't get played anymore. A shame, really; I loved listening to her play." Gerald sensed the man's solemnness and also felt he was now intruding a little, so he changed the subject by picking up a framed photo of a group of boys that was adjacent to the vase of flowers. It looked like a camp somewhere, and the sunlight had faded it a little, but Gerald could tell by the clothing the boys wore that it was some time ago. Seven faces looked back at him, all smiles. In the centre was a blond young man, obviously Cody Taylor. Gerald studied it for a moment.

"Ah, so long ago," Cody said. "Summer camp one year. That's me," he said, pointing to the blond boy. "You never appreciate your childhood at the time, do you? We had the best times back then; not a care in the world, eh?"

"No, I know what you mean. Every day was summer, wasn't it?"

"Sure was."

Gerald was still studying the photo; something inside him shifted, and the blood in his veins ran a little cooler. He'd seen those young faces before.

A long time ago.

The boys in the picture had killed Sylvia. He was looking at Sylvia's murderers.

Realisation dawned on him who he was looking at, and now whose house he was standing in, who he was chatting with, drinking tea with. He needed to leave, to get some air, but he was frozen to the spot, his feet glued to the carpet, incapable of carrying him forward. All those years ago, an event he'd successfully filed away at the back of his mind, so that he could get on with his life, such as it was. Such as his life with Sandra was. His two girls had been his saviours and carried him through those dark times. And now, in the lounge of one of those responsible for all the anguish, he found himself stifling a cry.

"Are you all right?" asked Cody. "Only you look like you're about to faint."

Forcing the blood inside of him to run warm again, Gerald smiled briefly and said he wasn't feeling too good. Needed some air, he said; he'd be okay. Almost staggering to the door, he mumbled his goodbyes, found his way back to his car and got inside. He thanked Cody Taylor again, told him he'd be in touch. He accelerated away a little faster than he would have normally.

When he was a couple of miles further down the lane, he pulled in at a layby, turned the engine off and sobbed into his hands. How he'd managed to keep control and get himself out of that house he'd never know.

"Sylvia, oh, Sylvia!" he moaned, as his tears fell in torrents, and he wept until all the pain and anguish he'd bottled up for so long had finally drained away.

It was replaced with a calm that surprised him.

That was the moment Gerald Baker vowed to do something about his loss. About losing his Sylvia. Now those boys were grown men, he'd make them pay. Their debt was long overdue.

Chapter Seventy-Six

He'd then driven straight to the river. To their spot, where they'd used to sit on her blanket. Where they'd found her body on that day when all hell had let loose.

For so many people.

There was no coffee today, no little flask, no stolen kisses. The grass was dry as Gerald sat by the water and watched its gentle flow, the occasional leaf and twig gliding past. He'd rarely been back to their spot, unable to cope with the emotion that churned inside of him as he remembered the loss he carried after all those years.

He'd always known the boys' names, of course; the headmaster had handed them over to him. But he'd done nothing more about it at the time, and done his best to forget how they'd driven Sylvia to kill herself. He hadn't wanted to spend his energy on the lives of those he detested; getting himself to function each day had been hard work enough. But the events of the morning had dragged it back and pushed it with fury to the front of his mind. Like someone keeping their foot on an accelerator in his head. Maybe it was fate, maybe it was timing; maybe it was neither. But he now had the strength and opportunity to teach them all a lesson.

He lay back in the shade and let his mind dance off to wherever it wanted to go as he relaxed and pondered what shape his retribution would take. He then drove home, poured a whiskey and went straight to his den to write a diary note of what had happened.

And what he'd do about it.

A financial scam designed for seven select individuals. And one that would bring their worlds tumbling down—like they had his. It was beautiful in its simplicity.

Chapter Seventy-Seven

She was dog tired.

Again.

Chrissy's body clock had only just tuned in to LA time, and now she was forcing it into another time zone. But it felt good to be home. It was almost 7 PM when she staggered in through the front door, her bags dragging behind her. A grinning Adam wrapped his arms around her and squeezed her tight, planting a firm kiss on her lips. Their two boys chorused their hellos and gave her quick pecks on her cheek. Teenage boys found it hard to show their true emotions, she knew, but there was no point in chiding them about it. When they had children of their own, they'd realise what she'd meant when their own teenagers replicated them.

"Hi boys," she called to their retreating backs. With the boys out of sight, Adam pressed his lips to Chrissy's again, lingering this time.

"I've missed you. And I'm glad you're home earlier than expected."

"So am I. And so have I, not necessarily in that order," she said smiling and leaning forward for another kiss. "I need a drink."

"I'll bring your bags through. Wine?"

"Tea, I think. And a shower." She could hear him straining slightly with her bags, odd grunts and groans as he tried to get them both together. Smiling fondly, she turned and took the smaller one from him.

"Toiletries," she said by way of explanation. "Quick shower and I'll be right back down." Then she was gone, leaving Adam to follow with the larger one and deposit it in their bedroom. Ten minutes later, she was back downstairs, with wet hair and wearing her bathrobe, ready for an early night. A mug of tea and a slice of toast awaited her. And she couldn't help noticing the three diaries that sat next to it. She willed herself not to pick them up yet, conscious of Adam deserving her full attention.

"Drink your tea first," he said, smiling.

"You know me too well, Mr. Livingstone."

"What did you want them for anyway? I had to rummage around in the dark for ages. Why the secrecy?"

"I'm not sure yet. But as soon as I find out, I'll let you know, eh?" She took a mouthful of toast and chewed, watching his face. "Have you read them?"

"Might have," he said somewhat sheepishly. "A bit boring, so I gave up. Except one of them."

She stopped chewing, her eyes bulging at him. "Really?"

"I'm guessing that's the one you're interested in? The one where he conjures up a plan?"

Holy shit!

"Tell me."

"Tell me why first, then I'll tell you."

"Adam!"

"Yes, Chrissy?"

She paused for a moment, deciding what and how much to say. If he'd read them anyway, he could know most of it already.

"Dad was up to something, wasn't he? There were the letters around the time of his funeral, and some other stuff. I think he might have been up to no good." She took another bite and waited for Adam to fill in some blanks.

Whoever speaks first loses.

"You guessed right, I'm afraid. Yes, there was a scam. He talks about it openly. From what I could glean, though, it was for a certain group of people, not general consumption. Like he did what he did on purpose. Tried to ruin them financially."

"Are the people's names mentioned?"

"Yes, though I can't remember them. All male."

"Do the names Cody Taylor, Stuart Townsend and Sam Moore sound familiar?"

Adam looked at her quizzically, head slightly to one side, like a Labrador trying to understand a human conversation.

"Yes, they do. How did you know?"

"I'll tell you later. Promise. What was the scam?" She was desperate to know the details now, rapidly slotting jigsaw pieces together in her head. The picture was beginning to look bleaker than *Wuthering Heights*.

"An investment scheme, designed to crash at some point and lose the participants a good deal of money. Which it did. He'd noted their investments, significant amounts I might add, and their losses. Again, significant."

"Did they each invest and lose a lot?"

"A couple of those who invested lost smaller amounts, but it would still have been painful. Not like the others, though. Are you going to tell me the rest of the tale now?"

How could she not?

"There's still bits I'm trying to understand, but here's what I know." She prepared to spell the story out so far, but in broad terms. "Dad had a lover some years ago."

"You're kidding ..."

"No, I'm not. There's more. Some schoolboys saw them together one day and decided to blackmail the woman. She was a teacher at their school. I guess she couldn't cope and committed suicide. The boys were found out and blamed, but nothing ever happened."

"Then Gerald found them," Adam said. "He wrote about meeting the blond one and conjuring up the plan."

"That part I didn't know about; you'll have to fill me in."

So, he did. By the time Adam had recited what he'd read, Chrissy sat open mouthed. "I wondered what the catalyst had been," she said, almost to herself.

"So, you know about the suicides?"

"Yes, of three of them. I'm guessing because of their losses and the shame of it, am I right?"

"Yes, though Gerald would never have known that part for sure. Just that they were dead."

They both sat in silence as they digested what her father had done, what he'd been responsible for. No wonder Philip Banks had been so vehement about him.

To make sure the old bastard was dead!

Her father had been responsible for the suicides of his three friends. All because of a stupid schoolboy blackmailing prank. It was unreal, too hard to contemplate.

"Who sent those letters, then, do you think?" Chrissy asked.

"My guess would be one of the other two remaining, or both."

Steve Marks and Dr. Robert Newsome.

"And there's one more thing," Adam added. "Someone else has read the diaries."

"Oh? How do you know?" Chrissy felt a chill run down her spine. How could he know that?

"Because of the notations in the margins. A different handwriting. And what they say."

"Really? What? Who was it?"

"I'd say your mother, if I'm not mistaken. She's known. All along."

Chrissy remembered back to that day when they were planning her father's funeral and her mother's terse remark: "Not after what he's done."

She'd thought it had to do with the 'Thief' note. Obviously not.

Chapter Seventy-Eight

As bone tired as she was, Chrissy hardly slept a wink all night. After Adam had told her about the diary's content, and what her father had deliberately done to ruin the boys, now grown men, she couldn't get over the fact her mother had known about the scam all along. And nobody had been any the wiser. She'd slipped out of bed again and gone downstairs to her chair in the kitchen, where she'd curled up with yet another mug of chamomile tea.

So, she thought. That's why her mother had been so bitter at the end, about what he'd done: she'd been angry about Sylvia, not the money.

She checked the clock on the cooker. Three AM in Surrey meant early evening in LA, so there'd be nobody in the office. Then she remembered Banks & Crowley website, which listed the men's mobile numbers! She dialled Philip first; she'd upset him the least. If he hung up on her, she'd call Alistair and hope they weren't together in a bar somewhere.

The call connected quickly. "Philip Banks."

"It's Chrissy Livingstone—don't hang up!" she shouted, a bit too loudly for the sleeping house she was in. She screwed her face up, wincing, and listened for both footsteps upstairs and Philip hanging up. Neither happened.

"What do you want?' He was cool. Maybe even cold. Not even a hint of tepid.

"I wanted to say sorry, actually. For what my father put you all through, mainly. I'd no idea." There was silence on the line. He was somewhere quiet, home maybe; the sound of his breathing all she could hear.

"Thank you," he said eventually. "But you don't need to apologise; it was his doing, not yours."

"But three of your friends died from his doing! I don't know what else to say or what I can do to put it right."

"There is nothing to put it right; they've gone now. But at least no one else will die because of it."

"Because he's dead, you mean?"

"Yes. Because he's dead too." A spark flashed in Chrissy's brain and something else dropped into place.

"You came over to see him, to kill him, didn't you? Because three of your friends had committed suicide. It was nothing to do with a client at all, was it? But you didn't manage it." She was conscious of her voice rising again, but this was important.

"No, I didn't kill him," he said wearily. "By the time I'd got to talk to him he was already dead. You have to believe me on that."

"How can I be so sure?"

"Because I'm not a killer, simple as that. And Alistair told me of your conversation about all of this, so why ring and speak to me now?"

"Because I didn't know my father had set it all up on purpose, to get you all back. I thought it had been bad luck. That's why I wondered if maybe you'd had a hand in his demise. Like I'd said to Alistair, easy enough to do. Particularly if you've another close friend who's a doctor with the required knowledge." She left the subtle accusation to hang in the air.

Whoever speaks first loses.

Nobody did. Philip Banks had hung up.

Chrissy stared at the phone; the screen was blank.

"One of the others, by chance?" It was Adam. He'd been stood in the doorway listening. Chrissy nearly jumped out of her skin in the semi-darkness.

"Hell's bells, Adam!" He flicked the light on and they both squinted in its brightness.

"And what did he say when you asked him if he'd done it?" He was filling the kettle as he talked and flicked the switch on to boil.

"He said no, of course. And I believe him. But I had to ask. He was here, at Dad's funeral, for goodness' sake."

Adam turned to her and said, "To make sure he'd gone, eh?"

"Yes, something like that."

He knelt down in front of her chair and wrapped his arms around her legs, looking up into her eyes. "Look. It's a shitty thing to find out about your dad, but it's all over and done with now. It wasn't your fault. He chose and found his revenge. That's it. Done. And you should try and forget it all ever happened and remember your dad as the decent man you knew and loved. Let the past stay in the past."

She knew he was right, but still. It hurt her, too.

"And there's no point telling Julie and upsetting her. Or saying anything else to your mother. Let it be now."

Chrissy stayed silent for a moment. "Okay. But I'm going to see how Mum is tomorrow."

"Absolutely."

She sighed heavily. "Love you, Adam Livingstone."

"Then turn the kettle off and let's go back to bed."

Chapter Seventy-Nine

It was mid-morning when she got to her mother's house. Letting herself in, she called out that it was Chrissy and headed straight upstairs to her mother's bedroom. Sandra Baker was sitting up in bed, looking both pale and frail. The remains of her breakfast tray were still at the side of her bed from Julie's earlier visit. Chrissy bent in to kiss her mother on the cheek and perched on the edge of the bed. It sagged a little as she took her mother's thin hand in her own.

"Hello, Mum. How are you doing?" she asked, giving her half a smile, half a concerned look.

"I'm on the mend. I think the worst is over. A virus, I expect, and, well, with the funeral and everything ..." Her words trailed off like she'd run out of steam already.

"Can I get you some more tea?"

"Yes. That would be lovely."

Chrissy stood and collected the breakfast tray to take downstairs.

"How was your trip?" her mother asked faintly.

"I cut it short. I'd seen enough and you aren't well, so I came home last night. A bit of a flying visit, but you're more important."

Her mother seemed to like that and smiled her appreciation, catching Chrissy's eye for a moment.

"I'll be right back up."

A few minutes later and Chrissy delivered a fresh pot of tea and a plate of biscuits.

"Keep your strength up," Chrissy said, as if the Custard Creams were going to have the same effect on the old woman as spinach did on Popeye.

"Lovely."

Chrissy sat back down on the side of the bed and poured her mother a cup.

"Could I trouble you to pass me something from the bedside cabinet on your father's side, please?"

"Of course," said Chrissy, standing and making her way round the bed. She knelt down to undo the cupboard. "What do you need?" She opened the little door and peered inside, and then froze.

Holy shit!

They were there. At the back. All three of them.

The missing diaries.

The room filled with silence so loud that Chrissy wanted to put her hands over her ears. She stayed frozen in place, staring at them.

"Pass them up, would you?" Her mother's voice was barely audible.

Chrissy reached out to them, her finger tips caressing the spines before her hand pulled all three forward. She showed them the light of day and stood to look at her mother, questioning.

"Julie told me Adam had visited. And you'd made that excuse to get inside the shed looking for something you'd left." She was almost breathless with the effort. "You're not stupid. And neither am I."

"No. I'm a little disappointed, yes, but not stupid."

Her mother patted the place where Chrissy had been sitting

only a moment ago. Chrissy watched her mother's face as she passed her the diaries.

"It's all in there," she said, pointing. "All the sordid details of his adulterous affair. I nearly vomited at his words. He was desperately in love with her, you know."

Chrissy was silent, thunderstruck. Her mother had known of the affair all along and kept it to herself all these years. Should she feel sorry for her? She waited for her to catch her breath and go on.

"But I couldn't have him leave me, leave us," her mother said. "It wasn't right. What would we have done? What would people have said?"

"So, what happened?"

"I went to see her that morning."

"That morning?"

"When that gunman went berserk. I went to her cottage. I told her he'd never leave me for her. Never leave us all. Never."

Chrissy stayed motionless, listening, watching her mother's face. The woman—the boys' teacher, her father's lover—must have been hysterical at the news. And desperate.

"She killed herself, Mother."

"I know. I'm not proud. I couldn't let it carry on, though."

"Do you know what you've done? Really done?"

"I stopped their affair, stopped them loving each other!" Her mother's strength had suddenly returned.

"No! You killed her. But you also killed three other people! And Dad's getting the blame for it, even now. How could you?" Chrissy stood and paced around the bed, flicking looks back at the woman she thought she knew so well, as she again tried to make sense of events she had thought were settled. "And that probably killed Dad too!" she screamed.

The colour drained from her mother's face.

"Yes!" Chrissy went on, unable to stop herself. "There were seven boys that were blackmailing Dad's lover. Dad has always thought *they* were responsible for her death. But it was you behind Sylvia Marsh's death all along! Dad set their punishment in motion without realising the truth. Three of them died because of it. The others vowed their own revenge; one came to see Dad. Then he had his heart attack." She glared furiously at her mother. "I can't believe it. Sylvia Marsh and three others are dead, entirely because of you!"

"Don't mention that woman's name in my house,' Sandra Baker spat, her voice low and level.

"Is that all you can say? Did you hear me? Four people plus Dad are all gone because of what you said to her. Do you not care? Even about Dad?

"Our marriage had died long ago," she said, as cold as a gravestone. "And I didn't want *her* to have him. Not anybody."

Chrissy stood silent and dumbfounded, trying to understand her mother's twisted logic. Had the woman ever loved Gerald Baker at all? Had it always been about the lifestyle he'd provided for her all these years? Could the woman in front of her be so spiteful and show no remorse at all? Not even for her own husband, the father of her children?

Clearly, she can't.

Best leave her to it, then.

Best had.

Without another word, Chrissy Livingstone left the house, with her mother calling behind her. Where she would go, she'd no idea but she couldn't stay inside another minute. Her car was out front. She climbed numbly behind the wheel, put the key in the ignition and pulled away from the house she'd grown up in—and vowed never to return.

Chapter Eighty

Two months later

"Feel that wonderful sunshine on your skin, Adam. Isn't it glorious?"

"Mmm. Tell me about it."

Chrissy raised herself off her sun lounger and leaned over to Adam, casting a shadow over his torso. She planted a light kiss on his shoulder.

"What was that for, and why are you diverting the sun's rays off my body, Madame?" He still hadn't opened his eyes.

"For being you, for being a rock when I need it most."

"That's what lovers do, isn't it?" Adam sat up and looked at Chrissy, lifting his sunglasses off his eyes as he did so. She followed suit. A gentle breeze picked up a few wispy pieces of her blonde hair and blew them across her eyes, and she instinctively pushed them away. The late afternoon sun in the south of France, was the ideal temperature to enjoy without becoming too hot. Thomas and Harry were lounging in the shallows of the pool a few feet away, sipping coke from a can each.

"You could have been a shit about it all. And I don't mean Mum and what she's done. Though that was right up there in the 'worst family secret ever' stakes, if ever a game were to be invented. She'd take top prize for that one."

"Indeed. And I know what you're talking about. But look, here's what I think. You had your other life when we first met. Yes, you could have told me when it finished, but you chose not to, and you had your reasons. But I knew, because you'd changed. For the better, I might add. You're far less stressed now, more present. I figured it would come out one day, and as long as you weren't running guns or doing something dumb with your time..." He was smiling, his eyes dancing.

"HR contractor is a far cry from running guns, but I get the connection."

"So, when we've finished here at your little French getaway, will you show me the rest of your portfolio?" He was teasing her, and Chrissy was lapping it up.

"I might not, actually," she said coyly. "A girl needs her space, you know. Might save it just for me. Or. . ."

"Or what?"

"Or it could be the start of my LA office."

"You're going to expand HR into LA?" he teased her.

"Nope. But I enjoyed getting to the bottom of what happened —you know, with Dad and the boys in the tin. It brought back some of the excitement of days of old, but without so much of the danger. And I've been mulling it over."

"I sense a biggie coming."

"How would you feel if I became a private investigator?"

Adam raised both arms, hands together, and traced the letters of an imaginary sign in the air above him. "'Chrissy Livingstone, P.I.'" he said with a smile. "A female Magnum, eh? And a lot better looking, I should add." He leaned across for a kiss.

"I think that just sealed the deal, then."

"Indeed, I think it did," he said as he lay back down on his sun lounger and closed his eyes again.

Chrissy did likewise, resuming her position on her own lounger.

She was glad everything was now out in the open. No more lies, no more feeling bad about away time.

Their patio fell silent again; the boys paddled quietly in the pool as the sun slipped down in the sky.

Two minutes passed.

Adam chuckled lightly.

"I'm married to a private investigator," he said, giggling. Chrissy reached over and flicked him hard with a powerful middle finger.

"Ouch!" he cried, as her phone buzzed with an incoming text. Picking it up, she gasped out loud at the contents. And the sender.

Adam watched as her brow furrowed and a smile began to spread across her face. "What is it?" he asked her.

"It looks like I've got my first case. The two divorce lawyers in LA, Alistair and Philip? They need a hand getting some movie mogul off their backs."

Adam sat up on his lounger to face her. "That's great news! Looks like you're off the starting block already," he said, grinning. "Can you finish your holiday, or have you got to rush off?"

"I'll call them later and find out a bit more. But for now, Mr. Livingstone. . ." she said teasingly, turning her body towards him and making his eyes drop to her cleavage.

Adam cleared his throat at the sound of footsteps Chrissy obviously hadn't heard. Two dripping wet boys approached them, hair stuck to their heads, their bodies lightly tanned from the French sunshine. They were the very picture of happy and healthy.

"What's for dinner, Mum?" Thomas asked. "We're half starved."

Chrissy exchanged a grin with Adam. "Well, I know of some things that will never change," she said.

~

Want to continue on to the next book in the series? Click here to start reading.

Also by Linda Coles

The DC Jack Rutherford and DS Amanda Lacey Series:

Hot to Kill

When a local landscaper vanishes, Madeline Simpson knows she was the last person to see him alive – because she killed him.

With a serial sex offender on the loose, Detectives DC Jack Rutherford and DS Amanda Lacey already have their hands full. It's only when another death occurs that a link between the two cases comes to light, and Madeline finds herself the focus of their investigation.

While attempting to keep her deadly secret, Madeline stumbles upon clues that point to the true identity of the sex offender. She's closing in when tragedy strikes, and the death toll increases.

But DS Amanda Lacey has no idea how close she is to the killer as her work and personal lives collide.

How long will she have to wait to find out the full truth?

If you like interesting characters, imaginative story lines, and British crime drama, then you'll love this captivating story.

The Hunted

The hunt is on...

They kill wild animals for sport. She's about to return the favour.

A spate of distressing big-game hunter posts are clogging up her newsfeed. As hunters brag about the exotic animals they've murdered and the followers they've gained along the way, a passionate veterinarian can no longer sit back and do nothing.

To stop the killings, she creates her own endangered list of hunters. By stalking their online profiles and infiltrating their inner circles, she vows to take them out one-by-one.

How far will she go to add the guilty to her own trophy collection?

Dark Service

The dark web can satisfy any perversion, but two detectives might just pull the plug...

Taylor never felt the blade pressed to her scalp. She wakes frightened and alone in an unfamiliar hotel room with a near shaved head and a warning... tell no one.

As detectives Amanda Lacey and Jack Rutherford investigate, they venture deep into the fetish-fueled underbelly of the dark web. The traumatized woman is only the latest victim in a decade-long string of disturbing—and intensely personal—thefts.

To take down a perverted black market, they'll go undercover. But just when justice seems within reach, an unexpected event sends their sting operation spiraling out of control. Their only chance at catching the culprits lies with a local reporter... and a sex scandal that could ruin them all.

One Last Hit

The greatest danger may come from inside his own home.

Detective Duncan Riley has always worked hard to maintain order on the streets of Manchester. But when a series of incidents at home cause him to worry about his wife's behaviour, he finds himself pulled in too many directions at once.

After a colleague Amanda Lacey asks for his help with a local drug epidemic, he never expected the case would infiltrate his own family...And a situation that spirals out of control...

Hey You, Pretty Face

An abandoned infant. Three girls stolen in the night. Can one overworked detective find the connection to save them all?

London, 1999. Short-staffed during a holiday week, Detective Jack Rutherford can't afford to spend time on the couch with his beloved wife. With a skeleton staff, he's forced to handle a deserted infant and a trio of missing girls almost single-handedly. Despite the overload, Jack has a sneaking suspicion that the baby and the abductions are somehow connected...

As he fights to reunite the girls with their families, the clues point to a dark secret that sends chills down his spine. With evidence revealing a detestable crime ring, can Jack catch the criminals before the girls go missing forever?

Scream Blue Murder

Two cold cases are about to turn red hot...

Detective Jack Rutherford's instincts have only sharpened with age. So when a violent road fatality reminds him of a near-identical crime from 15 years earlier, he digs up the past to investigate both. But with one case already closed, he fears the wrong man still festers behind bars while the real killer roams free...

For Detective Amanda Lacey, family always comes first. But when she unearths a skeleton in her father-in-law's garden, she has to balance her heart with her desire for justice. And with darkness lurking just beneath the surface, DS Lacey must push her feelings to one side to discover the chilling truth.

As the sins of the past haunt both detectives, will solving the crimes have consequences that echo for the rest of their lives?

Butcher Baker Banker

A cold Croydon winter's night and pensioner Nelly Raven lies dead and naked on the floor of her living room. The scene bears all the hallmarks of a burglary gone wrong.

It's just the beginning.

Ron Butcher rose to the top of London's gangland by "fixing things". But are his extensive crooked connections of use when death knocks at his own family's door?

Baker Kit Morris will do anything to keep his family business alive. Desperate for cash, he hatches a risky plan that lands him in trouble. As he struggles to stay out of prison, he forges an unlikely friendship with an aging local thug.

And then there's the Banker, Lee Meady, a man with personal problems of his own.

Just how does it all fit together?

As DC Jack Rutherford and DS Amanda Lacey uncover the facts surrounding the case, the harrowing truth of the killer's identity leaves Jack wondering where the human race went so badly wrong.

The Chrissy Livingstone series:

Tin Men

She thought she knew her father. But what she doesn't know could fill a mortuary...

Ex-MI5 agent Chrissy Livingstone grieves over her dad's sudden death. While she cleans out his old things, she discovers something she can't explain: seven photos of schoolboys with the year 1987 stamped on the back. Unable to turn off her desire for the truth, she hunts down the boys in the photos only to find out that three of the seven have committed suicide...

Tracing the clues from Surrey to Santa Monica, Chrissy unearths disturbing ties between her father's work as a financier and the victims. As each new connection raises more sinister questions about her family, she fears she should've left the secrets buried with the dead.

Will Chrissy put the past to rest, or will the sins of the father destroy her?

Walk Like You

When a major railway accident turns into a bizarre case of a missing body, will this PI's hunt for the truth take her way off track?

London. Private investigator Chrissy Livingstone's dirty work has taken her down a different path to her family. But when her upper-class sister begs her to locate a friend missing after a horrific train crash, she feels duty-bound to assist. Though when the two dig deeper, all the evidence seems to lead to one mysterious conclusion: the woman doesn't want to be found.

Still with no idea why the woman was on the train, and an unidentified body uncannily resembling the missing person lying unclaimed in the mortuary, the sisters follow a trail of cryptic clues through France. The mystery deepens when they learn someone else is searching, and their motive could be murder...

Can Chrissy find the woman before she meets a terrible fate?

The Silent Ones

An abandoned child. A missing couple. A village full of secrets.

When a couple holidaying in the small Irish village of Doolan disappear one night, leaving their child behind, Chrissy Livingstone has no choice but to involve herself in the mystery surrounding their disappearance.

As the toddler is taken into care, it soon becomes apparent that in the close-knit village the couple are not the only ones with secrets to keep.

With the help of her sister, Julie, Chrissy races to uncover what is really happening. Could discovering the truth put more lives at risk?

A suspenseful story that will keep you guessing until the end.

Also by Linda Coles

Jack Rutherford and Amanda Lacey Series:

Hot to Kill

The Hunted

Dark Service

One Last Hit

Hey You, Pretty Face

Scream Blue Murder

Butcher Baker Banker

The Chrissy Livingstone Series:

Tin Men

Walk Like You

The Silent Ones

About the Author

Hi, I'm Linda Coles. Thanks for choosing this book, I really hope you enjoyed it and collect the following ones in the series. Great characters make a great read and I hope I've managed to create that for you.

Originally from the UK, I now live and work in beautiful New Zealand along with my hubby, 2 cats and 6 goats. My office sits by the edge of my vegetable garden, and apart from reading and writing, I get to run by the beach for pleasure.

If you find a moment, please do write an honest online review of my work, they really do make such a difference to those choosing what book to buy next.

If you'd like to keep in touch via my newsletter, use this link to leave your details:

http://eepurl.com/gwfVqL

Enjoy! And tell your friends.

Thanks, Linda

Keep in touch:
www.lindacoles.com
linda@lindacoles.com

Follow me on BookBub

Made in the USA
Middletown, DE
07 March 2021